CHOSEN DAUGHTERS

JESSICA CARRASQUILLO

Songbird Books LLC

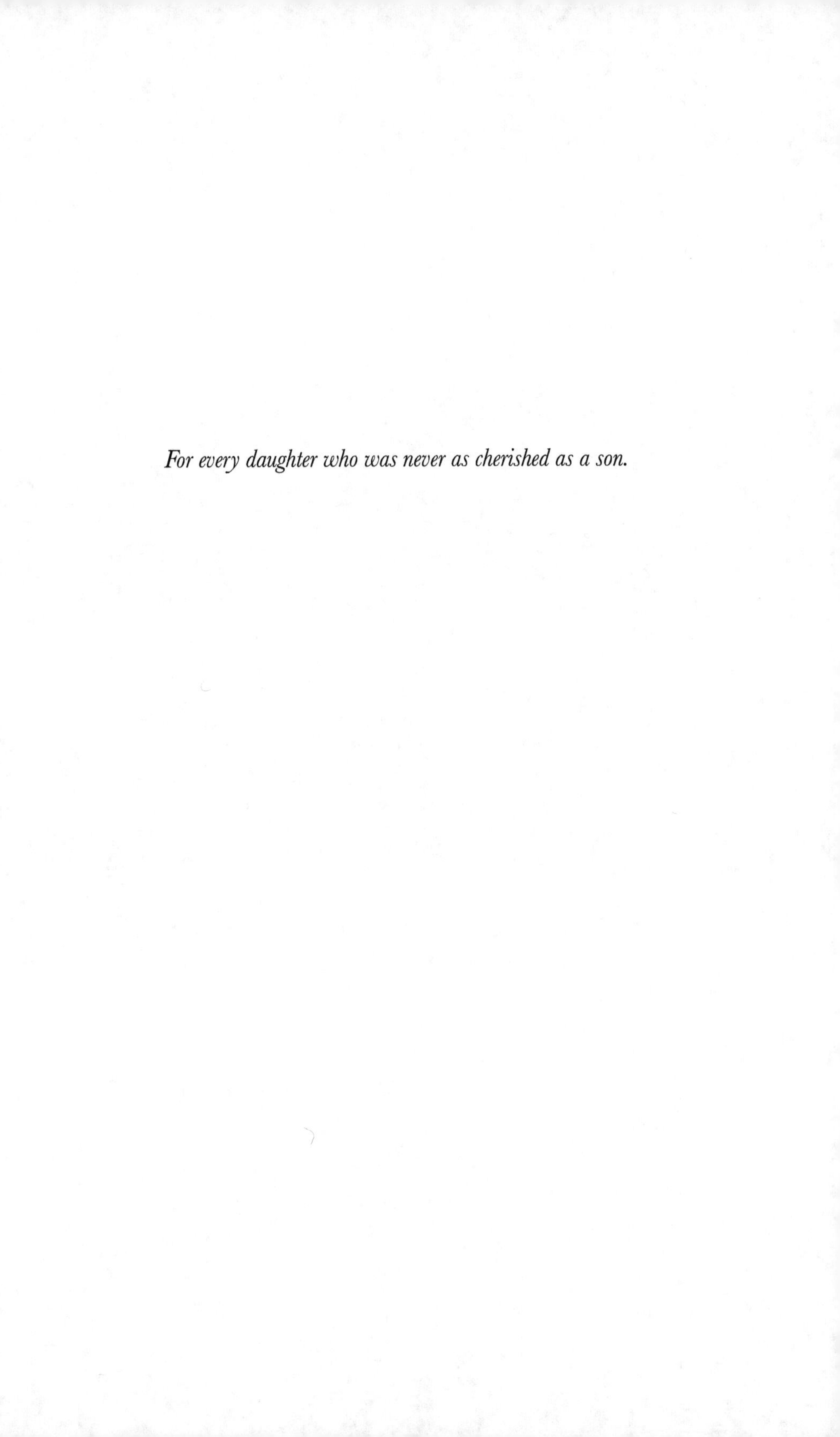

For every daughter who was never as cherished as a son.

The Church

THE NINTH ORDER OF ANGELS, guardians of humanity in service to God, will descend upon sinners like stars falling from the sky. Their wings will obscure the sun, casting the immoral world into final darkness. Blessed are the obedient, for they will be saved. But those who reject faith, who commit vile acts—together with murderers who slay outside of divine judgment, the sexually perverse, sorcerers, idol-worshipers, liars and every soul that dares question His Order—shall be stripped of His mercy. Their flesh will be made ash. Their voices will be silenced. Their sins will be washed away in fire and blood.

Prologue

THE MEN ROSE IN UNISON, *fanning out to block every exit with eerie precision, as if rehearsed. At the altar, the Prophet John Russell Thorne summoned a man forward. "Kneel," he ordered. Then, with a single gunshot, ended his life.*

On that Easter Sunday, Ulysses sat in the front pew with his little sister, Calliope, close enough to feel the man's blood spatter warm against his cheek. By that summer, Thorne and Calliope were gone, and his family's ties to the Church of the Ninth Order were severed and buried.

The smell of gunpowder and blood had stayed with him long after that morning. Even now, twenty years later, the memory lingered. That's why he'd been stunned when Sofie begged him to return there.

"It's not the place you remember," she'd insisted in her southern drawl. "My dad's working hard to fix it. It's better now."

They'd been lying in their bedroom, his laptop perched on his knees. His Border Collie-Poodle mix, Domino, nestled between them as Ulysses typed up notes from his therapy sessions, work that usually calmed him.

"We can make good memories this time."

The suggestion he uproot his life when he and Sofie had only just gotten back together was absurd enough on its own. Asking him to do it so he could return to the Order was so outlandish he didn't hesitate to reject it. "You're not serious."

But when he turned to her, the pleading in her glassy eyes stopped him cold. She meant it.

Sometimes, Ulysses knew, people unconsciously recreated their trauma to control it, to rewrite the ending. But there were safer ways to heal that didn't involve abandoning their lives in Tampa—his job at Palms Waterside Recovery, his apartment, the fragile stability he'd scraped together after their last breakup.

"I think you're forgetting how twisted it was. It's not like their rules have changed. No technology, no pre-marital sex," he said with emphasis.

Sofie didn't answer immediately. She tucked her legs beneath her, smoothing her hands over the blanket. "He's my dad. I need to fix things with him."

Her father, Lang Randall, had stayed behind when their families fled the Order. He divorced Sofie's mother, filled the power vacuum left by Thorne's disappearance, doubled down, and rebuilt the Order in the rural town of Whispering Hope.

"Do you know what he said about you? He said he was proud to see you staying sober."

Ulysses's fingers stilled on the keyboard. "He said that?"

Growing up, Ulysses was always compared to the Randall children—how their accomplishments stacked up, or in Ulysses's case, how his failures did. His drinking began not long after Calliope disappeared, and he spiraled into chaos: repeated suspensions, expulsion, and fights. By all accounts, Ulysses was a fuckup.

Even after rehab and building a career as a mental health counselor, his past was a stain he couldn't scrub out. Sofie had kept their relationship secret from her father, afraid of how Lang would react.

That secret unraveled when *Mysteries of the Southern Gothic*, the true crime podcast, reopened the investigation into Calliope's disappearance. The show's hosts, Rosario and Shawnee, dredged it all up again—his failures, his grief. Hearing the worst moments of his life replayed for strangers had left Ulysses raw and untethered.

Worse, he'd let Rosario into his heart and she'd used him. Played with his emotions and broke his heart.

As rumors about Calliope's whereabouts swirled, Ulysses fell to new lows. Drunk on rage and whiskey, he'd stormed back to the Order, shotgun in hand, firing into the night sky and demanding answers. He'd expected Lang to kill him then, or at least throw him out. Instead, Lang took him in, let him sober up for the night, and set him straight over breakfast.

Ulysses had to admit, if a forgiving man like that was running things, maybe the Order really had changed. After all Ulysses had been through, it was Sofie who helped him get his head on straight. Maybe he owed her this.

"You really believe it's different now?"

She wiped her cheek. "I do, and I need this, Uly. *Please.*"

For a long moment, he said nothing, the memories and doubts swirling in his mind. He thought of the alternative—saying no and possibly losing Sofie for good.

"This really means a lot to you, doesn't it?"

"It does," she whispered.

After hours of debate, they agreed to a trial period: three months.

For Ulysses's boss, Dr. Okafor, the timing was less than ideal. He had been planning to expand the Palms Waterside brand of rehabilitation centers, and losing one of his dedicated counselors would be a setback. Even so, Ulysses knew Dr. Okafor's warning wasn't made out of self-interest. It was clear he was genuinely concerned for Ulysses's safety, having heard all the horror stories of the past.

Dr. Okafor had rocked his head pensively after Ulysses submitted his leave request, his elbow resting on the desk, hand against his cheek, a posture Ulysses recognized as the doctor preparing to level with him. His lilting Nigerian accent softened the words.

"You know this will always be your home. But tell me, are you sure about this? Have you truly considered the risks? You have made real progress. Impressive progress. But four months is not four years. You, more than most, know recovery is not a thing to gamble with."

Dr. Okafor's sincere worry gave Ulysses pause. But he'd already made up his mind. His sobriety and Sofie were his two highest priorities, and the Order's compound was strictly dry. He couldn't relapse if he wanted to.

"I know. But it's for Sofie. She needs this."

Ulysses took a leave of absence from Palms Waterside Recovery, broke his lease, and put all his big furniture into storage to move into a trailer on the compound's remote acres. Because they were unmarried, Sofie moved into the Main House with her father and the other church leaders. Ulysses hadn't worked up the nerve to ask Lang for her hand. It didn't feel right. This was about her healing. He didn't want their relationship to be a distraction.

Then, one late summer morning in Whispering Hope, just a day shy of one month under the Order's eye, Ulysses was awakened by Domino's frantic barking and an urgent knock on his trailer door. He leapt from his bed. Peeking through the window, he found Lang waiting outside. He'd only cracked the door an inch before Lang shoved past him in a hurry.

Half awake and clad only in boxers, Ulysses stumbled aside as Lang stormed to the bed, yanking the blankets to the floor as if expecting to find Sofie sinfully curled beneath them. Lang's rage had been barely contained, scorching through every nook of the quarters before Ulysses snapped, "What's going on?"

"Where is she?"

"Who?" Once the question left his mouth, he realized what had happened. It wasn't the first time he'd found himself here. "Sofie."

She was gone.

Later, after a search of the Main House, Lang's wife approached Ulysses, her gloomy visage shadowed with worry, and handed him a folded piece of notebook paper she'd found in the kitchen with a hastily scrawled message.

Tell Uly I'm sorry.

His pulse thundered in his ears as he turned on Lang. "How did this happen? No one saw her leave?"

Lang's jaw was tight, his demeanor composed, a stark contrast to the man who'd ripped through his trailer that morning. He lifted his chin, bereft of emotion. "She's made her choice. All we can do now is pray for her."

Ulysses scoffed at the idea that prayer was the best they could do. "I'm going after her." He clutched his keys in his pocket, but Lang stepped in front of the door, his broad frame blocking the exit, stern yet poised.

"No, you're not."

Ulysses stiffened. "Excuse me?"

Lang exhaled slow and measured, as if he had expected this reaction. "I know you're hurt, son. But do you really think chasing her down is going to change anything? That girl's been running her whole life." His voice was calm, almost pitying. "This isn't the first time she's left you. Have some self-respect."

The hit was precise, searing, like a knife between the ribs, cutting straight to the ugly truth he'd tried to bury: Sofie always leaves. She runs from one thing to the next, and whenever she needs a place to rest in between her bursts of chaos he finds a warm place for her in his arms.

Ulysses's fists clenched at his sides, ready to swing, but Lang's hand clamped down on his shoulder first. He zeroed in face to face, eye to eye.

"Let her go."

Ulysses hated how Lang could reach into him, how he could rifle through his dark places and pluck out a doubt then smooth it out like an errant lock of hair. It turned his defenses to dust.

His grip stayed firm, steady. Ulysses stood there, breath ragged, fists trembling at his sides. The fight had already left him. He was dazed, too beat up to realize he'd already lost. He'd let out a slow breath. Unclenched his hands.

Lang clapped him on the shoulder, a fatherly gesture, warm and patronizing at once. "Now come on. You'll think clearer once you've had a decent breakfast."

Chapter One

THE SIRENS in his head never stop singing. The songs try to lure him to his end, but up on the scaffolding early on a Sunday morning, brush in hand, the world around him fades to silence. The methodical rhythm of brush strokes is the only thing that keeps him steady.

Before he knows it, the congregation trickles into the chapel. Parishioners scrunch their faces at the half-painted angel wing on the ceiling. The dark-stained pews gleam with fragrant citrus oil and creak as men in suits and women in prairie dresses settle into their seats. Ulysses descends the ladder, then shoves his hands in his pockets as he waits for them all to pass.

Lang had suggested the mural. Not directly. The Order's leader never demanded. But once Ulysses was abandoned and had no reason to stay, Lang found him in his trailer. He made conversation, let the silence stretch. Then, in that mild yet insidious way of planting ideas, he said, "The chapel ceiling could use your touch."

No one was forcing Ulysses to stay. He could go back to Tampa and start over any time. Again. But he couldn't picture pulling up to that seedy extended-stay motel, the one with the lime-green walls and the tiny stove where he'd last spiraled to rock bottom. Not without drowning his sorrows in Jack Daniel's.

Maybe he needed to stay. Just long enough to wrestle his emotions and protect one hundred seventy-two days of sobriety.

Deacon Zeke strides in, every bit the southern gentleman—slicked-back hair and carefully groomed mustache—flashing Ulysses a half-smile. "Well, if it isn't Michelangelo," he says, swatting Ulysses's bicep before shuffling on.

Ulysses takes his seat between Erma, Lang's dowdy wife, and Mary, her fair-skinned daughter. Erma pats his shoulder, a polite but firm touch. Mary stares ahead, lost in thought. But when Ulysses sits, she snaps from her haze, her lips tugging into a subtle smirk.

"Father will be glad to see you dressed up," she murmurs, raising an eyebrow at his paint-streaked T-shirt and shorts.

He nudges her ribs lightly with his elbow. "I left my prairie tuxedo in the trailer."

Sunlight filters through the chapel's eastward-facing lancet windows, catching Father Lang in a divine glow as he rises to the altar. The small congregation—no more than fifty souls—stills, drawn in as if caught beneath a spell.

"Just this morning, as I walked the grounds, I was struck by the quiet beauty around us, the sunlight spilling over our humble acres," Lang starts, his resonant voice alive in the modest chapel's acoustics. "Gifts that too many in the secular world overlook. Out there, people wake up and reach for their devices before they even rise from their beds. They look to screens instead of the sunrise, asking, 'What can the world do for me?' The broken wait to be fixed. But here, a broken man can be a builder."

The congregants rock and nod their heads, some humming in agreement. Lang's volume rises, eyes sweeping over the congregation until he finds Ulysses. The look pins Ulysses in place.

"Where the immoral world sees ruin, the Lord sees a foundation. Out there, you're weighed down by sinful burdens. Here, you set them down and pick up a purpose. The tools to rebuild what the world tried to break in you."

The moment stretches too long, and Ulysses's quickening pulse forces him to look away, focusing instead on rubbing off a bit of paint clinging to his wrist. But breaking eye contact doesn't keep Lang's words from finding their mark. It's as if he knows exactly what wounds Ulysses has been licking, and he's offering just the right medicine to make staying here with the Order feel like a cure.

The church bell's toll fades into the afternoon, and one by one, the congregants file out into the harsh sunlight. Ulysses follows, squinting against the brightness, the sudden warmth a jarring contrast to the heavy repose inside the chapel. It's autumn in Florida; the day is cool, and the resinous musk of fallen pine needles rides on the breeze. Lang is already holding court near the church doors, and his deep laugh carries over the cacophony of the congregation.

Two armed guards flank him, rifles slung over their shoulders on fraying leather straps. Dressed in faded camo pants tucked into scuffed boots, a holstered pistol sits snug at each man's hip. No uniforms. No badges.

Their presence is a reminder: out here, the Order takes care of its own, cradle to grave. One way or another. The law stops at the gate.

Under the thin shade of a southern oak draped in Spanish moss, Erma, Mary, and Ulysses sit around a picnic table with plates of potato salad and buttery rolls made from scratch. Nearby tables are crowded with families or clustered with teenagers slouched and exchanging stoic, muted looks, bereft of the joyous rambunctiousness that makes being a kid special. He'd almost forgotten how thoroughly the Order sucked the joy of youth like marrow from a bone.

Mary sits beside him, and he can't help but notice how much she looks like his sister, Calliope. The way Calliope might have looked had she grown up. Mary's large, blue eyes catch the light—Thorne's eyes.

It's strange how eyes belonging to a man so evil could stir such affection in Ulysses. Thorne had fathered more illegitimate children than anyone cared to count, including Mary and Calliope. But not

Ulysses. Of that, he was sure. Thorne had made it clear enough: Ulysses was fatherless.

The resemblance between Mary and Calliope is striking. Mary is fair and petite, though her slight frame hides a surprising toughness. He'd once watched her calmly stitch up her own hand, injured on a barbed wire fence while freeing a frightened goat. She hadn't even flinched.

"Ulysses," Erma says, "the mural looks to be coming along nicely."

"Thank you, ma'am."

"How much longer before you finish?" Mary asks.

"You in a hurry to get rid of me?" he fires back with a playful wink.

Erma scoffs. "Do you really plan on leaving us?"

He'd been avoiding the topic, worried Erma and Lang would keep offering him more excuses to stay that he'd have to awkwardly decline. Glancing back at the church doors, he notices Lang watching them. Not glaring, but observing. Ulysses shifts on the bench, unease settling in his gut as he sets down his fork. Instead of answering her question, he pivots to something answer-adjacent. "Got a decent amount of work ahead of me. You'll have me around for a while still."

"Good." Erma pats his arm affectionately. If someone standing nearby were to capture them in that moment, they might confuse this group of people for a family.

Maybe Ulysses needed that too, if only to make this experience mean something. A payoff in exchange for this suffering. All of Sofie's broken promises had left him with pieces he didn't know how to fit back together, jagged edges and hollow spaces. He wondered if it wasn't in him to understand women, or if they saw what was broken in him. Either way, he knew better now than to look for someone to fill those empty spaces.

Chapter Two

"I'M PREGNANT."

Even hidden in the pantry, Kia's whisper barely rises above the rhythm of chopping, bubbling water, and clinking utensils from the kitchen.

Ez staggers back, her hand flying to her mouth as a gasp slips out. Thoughts crash into each other, a chaotic rush in her mind.

Pregnant? How?

Well, she *knows how*. But still. Kia's unmarried.

Kia gives her own breasts a squeeze, as if she's telling Ez how she knows. Scanning Kia's face for any hint of fear, there's nothing but a tight-lipped grin.

Why doesn't she seem worried? Unmarried women who get pregnant are usually ostracized, unless…

"Was it one of the Elders?" Ez asks.

"Where is Kia? Where is Esme?" Erma clucks from across the kitchen.

Shit. Ez would give anything to be out from under Erma's constant surveillance.

Kia tucks a loose curl behind her ear and rushes off. "I was looking for a clean rag, ma'am."

Lingering in the pantry for a moment longer, Ez lets the news settle over her.

Pregnant.

The girls sent here by their families, known as the Chosen Daughters, live in the large plantation-style mansion called the Main House. Father told them it was so the Elders could '*protect their chastity*,' but Kia's will be the third pregnancy in the decade Ez has lived here, so the old men seem to be doing a pretty lousy job of it.

The thought makes her dizzy. Not just the pattern but… has she really been a Chosen Daughter for ten whole years?

They should be called the Forgotten Daughters—a dozen or so young women Father claimed were 'chosen' by God to remain here. But that's bullshit. There's nothing holy about their captivity. They'd aged out of the Order's program. Their families had forgotten them. No one was coming to save them.

But at least the pregnant ones always ended up as Elder's wives. If one of them got Kia pregnant, she was probably excited to be moving up in the world.

"Hey, Ez," Mary says, hammering a cleaver into a chicken spine with frightening precision. "I heard Deacon Zeke asked Father for permission to marry you."

Still steadying herself from the bomb Kia just dropped, Ez hesitates over a pile of potatoes. The image of Zeke—a widower in his late fifties—makes her curl her lip in disgust. She remembers how he'd whipped out his penis after inviting her to "take a break" with him in the gazebo. She'd just wanted to get off her feet for a moment. Instead, the second she saw that ugly pink thing poking out of his trousers, she shrieked and ran back inside so fast she might've set a record.

"Glory to God," she says flatly.

"Glory, glory," Kia echoes, pressing a hand to her chest like she's about to catch the Spirit. Then, with a dramatic inhale and a clearing of her throat, she belts out an off-key wedding hymn. "*Oh per-fect loooove…*"

Ez's laughter bursts free before she can stop it. Kia holds back a smile, stirring a large iron pot, the rising steam carrying the aroma of fresh rosemary and sage. The air outside has finally cooled, but in the kitchen, with the brick hearth, wood-burning stove, and all the bodies milling around, it's still sweltering.

A blunt thwack cracks Ez on the back of the head. She stiffens, trying not to drop the potato as pain throbs through her skull.

Erma stands over her, a wooden serving spoon clutched in her fist. Her weapon of choice.

"The Lord hears laughter made in mockery," Erma says.

"Sorry, ma'am," Ez mutters. "I was just overcome with joy."

Once Erma turns away, Kia offers Ez a tight, half-smile, half-grimace in apology.

"Zeke is a good man," Erma says. "He's well respected and can provide for you. The decision has already been made."

Ez's stomach sinks. "What?"

She knew he'd been courting her, but she assumed there would be more steps before cutting across the lawn to marriage.

"You should be flattered. Of all the girls in the Main House, he picked you."

It's like being the healthiest cow brought to slaughter. She can't celebrate facing a lifetime—at least *his* lifetime—with a man she doesn't love. The thought of him makes her skin crawl, and acid creeps up the back of her throat.

"I am, ma'am," Ez says, bundling up discarded potato skins in a rag. "I'm highly favored."

The autumn sun has nearly set by the time the women serve dinner. Six o'clock. The same every night. Tonight, at least, for the first time of the season, it's dark as midnight and flames from torches color the congregation with a warm glow while they break bread. Elders, other church leaders, and their wives sit at the large table under a pole barn, with Father Lang at the head. The families of the flock, kids from the Youth Quarters, and the unbetrothed Chosen Daughters set up tables of their own under the shelter to enjoy a shared meal they prepared.

Beside Father are his stepdaughter, Mary, his wife, Erma, and his daughter, Sofie's...well, she's not sure what he is. They might have been engaged, but she'd fled in the middle of the night weeks ago. The idea that Father's own flesh and blood could be so incompatible with their way of life was kind of a scandal. But the man she left behind, Ulysses, seems to have been adopted by Father like a son.

Ulysses talks to Mary across the table, gesturing toward his plate with a fork, unknowingly drawing Ez's attention to the inked images that wind up his arms, disappear beneath his shirt sleeves, then reappear on his neck. He wears his long, thick hair in a bundle on his head, his neatly groomed short beard shifting as he smiles. She's not close enough to hear what he's saying, but he seems pleased. Probably complimenting Mary on the food, she assumes.

Something about him is fascinating. He's so…unique. Most of the men here are content to spend their days with the manual labor of a homestead or fishing and hunting, but Ulysses seems to prefer spending his days hidden away painting a mural in the chapel. Now, being in the chapel reminds Ez of the museums her mother used to take her to when she was little. Seeing Ulysses makes her remember that feeling of curiosity, back when the world still felt infinite.

Maybe it was the artist in him that fascinated her. Before she came here, Ez had almost gone to a school for the arts—dance, painting, music. It doesn't matter now, of course. Dancing isn't allowed. She's pretty good at sketching angels and playing piano to accompany the church choir, but her fingers don't remember the progressions the way they used to.

"My girl," Zeke says, breaking her from her drifting thoughts.

Ez stiffens as Zeke settles in beside her, his knee nudging hers under the table. He smells faintly of sweat and stale tobacco, and she forces herself to keep her eyes on her plate, counting her peas. Her hands itch to be anywhere else, even peeling more potatoes or scouring a pot.

Zeke leans in close, his voice low and gravely. "You're looking lovely tonight, Esme." He sweeps his fingers across his salt and pepper mustache. His long hair is combed back and curls at his ears.

She keeps her face blank, barely managing a nod. "Thank you, sir."

Gripping her knee, he gives it a small unwelcome squeeze. Resisting the instinct to recoil has become tiresome. More often than she'd like, she finds herself debating whether marrying a deacon, having status in the Main House, is really a bad thing. No more brittle fingernails. No more chapped skin. Even if she could somehow ignore her physical revulsion toward Zeke—not because of his age or looks (he'd be handsome if he weren't so creepy)—the thought of settling here, of resigning herself to never leaving, is too depressing to fathom.

She looks back at Ulysses. He doesn't belong here either. It's obvious from every movement, his every gesture; he's living proof of a world outside this place. Maybe that's why she can't seem to look away.

Chapter Three

THE WEATHERED CHAPEL door creaks open below the scaffold where Ulysses focuses on the sable tip of his brush. "Beautiful work, Ulysses." Lang's voice carries in the cathedral-like acoustics. "Our Lord's house is blessed by your hand."

Ulysses pauses, brush mid-air.

Lang's footsteps echo, stopping at the ladder beneath Ulysses. "I was hoping to ask a favor of you."

With a sigh, Ulysses sets down the palette streaked with colors. "What's up?" he asks, descending the rungs.

"I'd like it if you could help with a little counseling, perhaps."

Counseling? He's not sure he wants to know what the Order's idea of 'counseling' even entails. "How do you mean?"

A guard stands by the open door, sweeping the horizon with militant scrutiny as the faint lowing of cattle and bleating of goats from nearby pens wafts into the chapel. As Lang approaches, Ulysses can smell the slight tang of cigarette smoke that clings to his flannel work shirt. It's a far cry from the white-and-gold vestments he wears during Sunday sermons, but it fits the self-sufficient world out here. "A young woman could use some guidance."

"A woman here wants me to counsel her?"

Lang's mouth tightens, just barely. "Well, not directly. But there are concerns. Zeke has taken an interest in one of the Chosen Daughters, but in all her time here, she doesn't seem inclined toward men."

Ulysses snorts before he can help himself. From the way Zeke strutted around in polished shoes and satin vests, he'd figured the man thought highly of himself. "So Zeke thinks she's a lesbian because she's not interested in him?" he asks, crossing his paint-streaked arms over the word *Nirvana* printed on his T-shirt—an affront to the Order's ban on secular music that Lang seems to ignore.

Lang's stare sharpens, losing all pretense of warmth. "It's not a joke, Ulysses. If her inclinations are perverse, it's a threat to the Order's values. She needs guidance to find the proper path. Erma tells me she's rather willful. I think you'd put her at ease."

Ulysses wipes his hands on a rag, letting Lang's request settle in. It's none of Ulysses's business if she's gay, and it wouldn't bother him if she was, but he knows how this place works. "Did you ever stop to think maybe she's just not interested in Zeke?" he says finally. "She's an adult. If she hasn't asked for counseling, then maybe she doesn't need it."

The tendons in Lang's neck stand out for a moment as he lifts his chin, his composure strained by patience he rarely had to exercise. "Zeke wants to pursue a Godly union, and he's concerned about her moral fitness. We're simply asking for you to help clarify matters."

Ulysses lets out a slow breath, resisting the urge to roll his eyes. He'd been chipping at Lang's patience, but it's clear he's not going to stop until Ulysses agrees. Lang's presence can sometimes shrink Ulysses back to thirteen again—small, obedient. But he forces himself to stand taller. His ethical duty is too important to let that version of himself take over now. "If she confides in me, that's between me and her. I'm not reporting back to you or Zeke. That's not how counseling works."

Lang clasps his hands behind his back and rocks on his heels, directing a pensive look toward the stained-glass windows. After a beat, he turns back to Ulysses with a soft grin that's almost cheerful. "Of course, son. Zeke just wants to know that we've tried. That's all I'm asking."

It's just the two of them in the chapel, bathed in soft natural light and scattered oil lamps. There's a pause, and Lang rests a heavy hand on Ulysses's shoulder, snuffing out any remaining objections before they can be raised.

Ulysses exhales. There's no harm in talking to her, he supposes. "Alright."

"Good. I'll send her over this afternoon." Lang's smile returns, cold and satisfied. "You're doing the Lord's work, Ulysses."

As Lang leaves, Ulysses turns back to the half-painted angel and scrubs a hand over his face. The idea of counseling someone on who they should love leaves a sour taste in his mouth. But maybe this woman, whoever she is, needs someone to talk to.

If she's been living here long enough, she probably does.

For the rest of the morning, Ulysses contemplates hypothetical scenarios. She'll come in, he'll have to explain the purpose of their meeting, and then what? Ask her why on earth she wouldn't be falling head over heels for grandpa Zeke? He chuckles to himself. This place is so fucking weird.

HE'S SO immersed in his work, the groan of the chapel door startles him. It echoes through the space before thinning into silence.

"Excuse me," a woman's voice says. "Father said you wanted to speak to me, sir?"

Ulysses stumbles down the scaffolding, dusting off his hands as he glances at her. She stands framed in the doorway, the soft light behind her giving her an almost ethereal glow.

He's seen her before. Hard to miss, really, even with how she tends to keep her head down during meals and Sunday service. But this might be the first time he's heard her speak.

Her dark hair falls in soft waves around her shoulders, framing a face from a Baroque painting—olive complexion, thick lashes, and deep, dark eyes like polished onyx. She's striking. He clears his throat and extends an awkward hand.

"I don't think we've officially met before," he says. "I'm Ulysses."

She hesitates for a moment, then moves closer to take his hand. "God's grace to you, sir," she says, avoiding his eyes.

Keeping to himself, he'd forgotten how scripted everyone is here, especially the women, and he almost winces at the formality. "You don't have to say any of that kinda stuff or call me sir. Just Ulysses is fine. Uly, actually, if you want."

"Okay," she says, managing a small, polite smile. "I'm Esme."

"Ez-may?" He'd never heard the name before.

"Exactly. Everyone calls me Ez. You wanted to see me?"

"Well, sort of," he says with a strained chuckle. "Um, I'm a counselor. Or I was. Before I came here. I worked with teens and young adults mostly. With substance abuse."

She blinks at him as if the words have no meaning.

He tries to clarify. "Drug and alcohol addiction."

Her brow furrows slightly, eyes widening. "Does Father think I'm on drugs?"

"No, no, not at all," he stammers, his words tripping over themselves. "Would you like to sit?" He gestures to a pew, and she nods, moving over and sitting beside him. She smooths her skirt and her gaze falls to her hands in her lap, her fingers twisting together while the rest of her stays stiff, as if bracing herself for the worst.

As they sit, a delicate fragrance drifts from her—citrus and something sweeter, jasmine maybe, or gardenia.

"I actually don't know that you need counseling," he begins. "But if I can just be totally transparent here, I was asked to speak with you. Apparently you're being, um, courted, I guess, by Deacon Zeke?"

She flinches at his name. Just barely, but he catches it. She nods, though her gaze stays fixed on her knees. "Yes, sir."

There it is again: *sir.* The word rises between them like armor she wears without even thinking. "You don't seem too thrilled about it."

She jolts upright, her eyes flashing to his for a single, desperate moment before dropping again, pressing her hands together in apology. "But I am thrilled, sir. I'm very favored in His glory. Deacon Zeke is a good man. He's a respected member of the—"

"Hey," Ulysses says, holding up his hands palms out. He offers her a reassuring smile. "Look, you don't need to convince me. Trust me, I'm not going to report you. Actually, I think most young women in your position wouldn't be excited about having an arranged marriage, especially with someone you probably don't have much in common with."

Her lips press together. She doesn't speak, but her shoulders lose some of their rigid tension. For a moment, the twisting in her hands slows.

"If you were to choose a partner," he asks, almost without thinking, "would it be someone like Deacon Zeke?"

"I—I'm not sure." Her voice is small, careful.

Watching her, the thorn of Lang's request bites deeper into Ulysses's side. Heat prickles up his neck and he glances away with a quick cough into his fist. "Sorry. You don't have to answer that. It's none of my business."

"Okay." She toys with a stray thread of her skirt, probably praying for him to get to the point.

What is he doing? He exhales, leaning forward, elbows on his knees. This is absurd. Never in his time with the Order had anyone been forced to marry, at least not that he can remember. This woman clearly is uncomfortable with the idea, but she seems too frightened to say no. Maybe she doesn't even realize saying no is an option.

"Look, if you don't want to be with Zeke, who says you have to?"

She turns to him, her pretty eyes holding steady on his for the first time. There's a flicker of something there. Relief? Or maybe disbelief.

"What?"

"Yeah. I mean, sure, Lang gave his blessing or whatever, but it's your choice. Isn't it?"

She blinks, a small, tentative smile tugging at the corner of her mouth. "You're new here, aren't you?"

He laughs under his breath. "I'm really not. I grew up here." He catches himself. "Well, not *here*. But with the Order. Many years ago. It was worse then, actually. Under the Prophet Thorne." The mention of the name is almost a question to catch a hint of recognition.

"Mary's father," she says, a note of gloom in her voice that suggests she knows Thorne is a name synonymous with fear, one rarely spoken aloud.

"Yeah. Anyway, my mother was a member then, and trust me, she always did exactly what she wanted to do. If you don't want this, just say the word. I'll talk to Lang."

"You will?" she asks, like she's testing whether he's serious.

"Sure."

She sighs, her body sinking and the tension in her shoulders easing as if she'd just set down a boulder she'd been hauling a long distance. She looks down at her hands, almost as if gathering the courage to say it. "I really don't want to marry him."

"I didn't think so."

"And not just 'cause he's older. He's creepy," she says, an almost conspiratorial gleam in her eye as she leans in. "He watches the girls," she says, widening her eyes for emphasis. "Like, *watches* us. When we're out in the garden or hanging up laundry. You feel him staring at you all the time."

There's a resigned tone in her words that touches a nerve, like she's already decided there's nothing anyone can do about it. He leans back, careful to keep his tone casual. "That sounds uncomfortable."

Her head tilts just slightly at his words. For a moment, she seems to weigh what he's said, her posture loosening just enough to suggest she's no longer bracing herself.

"Thank you," she says. "For understanding."

"No problem."

She nods, glancing down again, tracing absent circles on her gauzy skirt. There's a hint of hesitation, like she's weighing whether to say something more.

"I almost didn't end up here, you know," she says. "I was supposed to go to an arts high school. It feels like a lifetime ago now, but I loved it. Art, I mean." Looking toward the incomplete mural on the ceiling, she goes on. "I still keep a notebook and sketch sometimes, whenever I have time."

Ulysses raises an eyebrow, genuinely surprised. "You draw?"

She flushes, her lips curving into a small, shy smile. "It's nothing special."

He looks at her with newfound curiosity. There was something disarming about her. "I'd love to see your work sometime," he says, surprising even himself.

The position of her head shifts slightly, exposing the delicate curve of her neck, and she blinks, as if the idea that someone might want to look at her work hadn't occurred to her. "You would?"

"Of course. I mean, if you want to show me."

She observes him for a second longer. "Maybe," she says through an awkward giggle. She turns her focus to the mural. "They're nothing like this. You're so talented."

The compliment hits unexpectedly, paired with the soft, almost dreamy look she gives him. It stirs something in him, a faint tingle that works its way up from his core rendering him witless. He shouldn't be surprised, he's been abstinent for months. By choice, sure. But that doesn't make the ache of longing any quieter.

Noticing the tattoos on his forearms, she lingers there. "These are nice too."

He glances down at inked images of shattered Grecian busts like he's seeing them through her eyes for the first time. "Thanks."

For a moment, he wonders if she'll ask about them. But she doesn't, and he doesn't offer, though the space between them seems to shift, no longer awkward but something comfortable.

"I should get back," she says, rising slowly. "Lots to do before dinner."

Watching her walk away, he lingers for half a second longer than he should, following the graceful sway of her skirt, tracing the delicate taper of her waist, and the soft curve of her hip. She pauses at the doorway, one hand resting on the frame as she glances back, her lips curving again into a soft smile. "Thank you, Uly."

Her words linger in the empty chapel long after she has exited, leaving Ulysses wondering if he'd just made a promise he couldn't keep.

<h1 style="text-align:center">Chapter Four</h1>

EZ CAN'T STOP SMILING.

The sky seems brighter, grass greener. Her lungs swell with air, the freshest she's breathed in years, as she makes her way back to the Main House. Gliding into the kitchen, she finds the other Daughters around the work counter. Their chopping makes a repetitive beat. Kia's eyes flick up from a half-peeled carrot, landing on Ez.

"Someone's in a good mood," Kia says, a smirk tugging at her lips.

Ez shrugs, picking up a potato from the pile on the counter. She starts peeling, feeling the familiar rhythm of the work, her hands steady, lighter than they've been in weeks. Her heart is pounding, her mind spinning, but she keeps her secret close, holding it tight.

Mary glances over. "What happened, did Zeke die?"

Ez is careful to keep her voice casual. "Just having a good day, that's all."

Shooting her a knowing look, Kia lets her smirk widen. "A good day, huh?" There's a flicker of something mischievous in the way she lifts an eyebrow, but Ez doesn't take the bait. She knows better than to share her newfound hope. Not here. Not yet. Saying her wishes aloud is a good way to make sure they never come true.

Once the meal is prepared, the girls move to set the long dinner table outside. Ez slips away amid the bustle of Chosen Daughters moving in and out of the kitchen, her heart pounding as she hurries up the creaky staircase to the girls' quarters, a section of bedrooms branching off the main hall where the Chosen Daughters bunk together.

She's got five minutes, maybe less, but it's just enough time. She ducks into her shared bedroom, closing the door quietly behind her, and kneels by the edge of the bed. Her fingers reach under the thin mattress until they find the worn leather edge of her sketchbook. She pulls it out, feeling its familiar cracked texture.

Tucking it close to her side, she sneaks back downstairs, hoping her absence went unnoticed. Just as she's about to reach the dining area, she spots Erma coming from the opposite direction, her sharp eyes sweeping over Ez.

"What's that?" Erma asks, nodding toward the book under Ez's arm.

Ez forces a smile, keeping her tone light. "Deacon Zeke asked me to bring him his notes. For scripture study."

Erma's eyes narrow, but she seems satisfied. As soon as she turns away, Ez hurries over to her place at the long table and tucks the sketchbook behind her, keeping it hidden between the seat and her back. She settles in, smoothing her dress, trying to appear calm and composed even while her heart is racing.

Across the table, Ulysses takes his seat at the far end. She can't help but admire him. He's different. It's not just his long hair and tattoos but because he spoke to her like she mattered.

He looks up, his eyes meeting hers across the table. They're a striking shade of green that's clear and vibrant. His mouth curves in a small, private smile, and he shoots her a subtle wink. A fire crawls up her neck as she quickly looks away, hoping no one noticed her reaction.

When the meal is over and evening socializing winds down, the others begin to clear the table. Ez quietly retrieves the portfolio, clutching it close as she slips away toward the chapel. She's not entirely sure she'll find Ulysses there, but she hopes. Her heart flutters with a mix of excitement and nerves as she enters and spots him near the front, adjusting the scaffolding.

He looks up at the sound of her footsteps, his deep concentration shifts into a warm smile. "Hey, Ez. Everything alright?"

"Yes," she says, a little breathless. She takes a step closer, clutching the portfolio to her breast. "I, um, I brought something."

He raises an eyebrow, intrigued, and gestures toward the book in her hands. "Oh yeah? What's this?"

Without a word, she hands it over, feeling like she's put all her hopes and dreams into a basket and handed it to him to rifle through. As Ulysses's fingers brush the cover's edge, a sharp current zips through her—as if he's touched her directly, in a way that shouldn't feel so intimate but does. Heat floods her veins, quick and searing.

His eyes widen slightly as he flips to the first page, taking in the sketches, then continues. He pauses on one page, a pencil drawing of a rose with delicate petals, its stem twisted around a cross.

"These are beautiful," he says, his expression softening, as if genuinely impressed. He runs a thumb along the page's edge, then glances down at her with a quiet warmth, taking her in thoughtfully. Like he's seeing her. Like he wants her to *feel* seen. "You must really like flowers and angels."

Ez's cheeks pulse with heat. "It's all I'm allowed to draw." A hint of frustration slips into her voice. "Anything else would be against the rules." She shrugs, attempting a small smile. "So I try to make them interesting, even if it's the same stuff over and over."

He nods in acknowledgment as he continues through the pages. "You make them more than interesting. They're amazing, Ez. But it's a shame. You shouldn't have to hide your talent, or be limited like this."

Her heart swells at his words, a mixture of gratitude and longing she can barely keep contained. In a place where everything is confined, Ulysses seems to carry an air of freedom, a reminder of possibilities beyond the Order's rigid standards.

"What's it like?" she asks in a near whisper. "Outside of here."

He pauses, taking a moment to think as he shuts the book and leans against the wall. "Different, obviously. Everything moves a lot faster."

For Ez, the outside world now just a vague memory. A dream. She runs her fingers along the edge of her sketchbook, images surfacing in little flashes. "I remember going to the grocery store with my mom," she says, almost like she's speaking to herself. "She'd always let me pick out a candy bar at the checkout. I don't know why I loved that so much. Oh, and the belt that moves and scoots your stuff up to the register." She glances up at him. "Do they still have all that? The same candy and magazines and stuff?"

"Yeah," he says, nodding. "Most of the candy's probably the same. Well, except now you can check yourself out."

"Like no cash register?"

"Self-checkout station."

"Who takes your money?"

"The machine."

"Huh," she says, trying to picture it. She searches her past, trying to confirm the fragments that are still there. "You know what I miss? Ice cream."

"Mm. What flavor?"

"Chocolate. And I used to really love long trips in the car. Looking out the window and watching everything go past." She pauses. "Long stretches of road with places to stop, like gas stations and restaurants."

"It's all still there," he says.

The thought of it floods her with the feeling that she's still connected to it, even just a little. "I'd love to drive a car. Just to see what's out there, not because I have to go anywhere." She hesitates, then adds, "I used to think I'd see so many places."

"You still can, Ez."

There's something about the way he says her name that grips her heart and makes fireworks explode in her head. Maybe it's because he believes there's a chance she'll leave this place someday. She's just about to tell him how she's always wanted to see the

Pacific Ocean when they're interrupted by the sound of the creaking door. She instinctively tucks the portfolio under her arm.

"Esme," Brother Whitlock says, his attention flitting between Ez and Ulysses from the threshold of the chapel. "What are you doing in the chapel at this hour?"

She freezes, her mouth opens but no sound comes out.

"I asked her here," Ulysses says. "I wanted her opinion on the mural progress."

"Ah," he says. "My apologies for interrupting."

"You weren't interrupting, sir. I'm just on my way back now," she says.

Ulysses gives her a soft smile, one that makes warmth spread through her, and for a moment, she wonders if he feels it too, this gravitational pull. As she turns to leave, she sneaks one last glance at him before scurrying out and returning to the Main House.

Slipping into her small, dimly lit room, Ez closes the door as quietly as she can. The room is plain—bare walls and two narrow beds pressed up against the wall across from each other—and she shares with Kia, who stirs slightly at the sound. Ez slides the portfolio carefully under her mattress and changes quickly, folding her clothes neatly and setting them aside before climbing into bed. The worn springs creak beneath her as she settles under the thin blanket.

Across the room, Kia peeks out from beneath the covers wearing her bonnet. "Where were you?"

Ez hesitates, a small smile tugging at her lips. "Just running an errand," she whispers back, hoping to keep her excitement from showing.

Kia hums a drowsy response and turns over, already drifting back to sleep. Soon, her soft snores fill the quiet. Ez lies wide awake, staring up at the darkened ceiling. Her heart beats steadily, a warm pulse that seems to echo with every thought as she replays their conversation. Every glance, every quiet moment between them, the way his eyes grew gentler when he looked at her, how they crinkled slightly in the corners.

It reminds her that he's older. That he talks like he knows things —so smart, so confident.

And her? She talked about ice cream. Candy bars.

God. He must think I'm a child.

She clutches her blanket, listening closely to Kia's breathing as she glides her hand underneath, the memory of how close he'd sat to her making her cheeks warm. The room is dead calm, and in between Kia's sputtering, she can hear every squeak of the bed when she moves her hand even slightly.

Her pulse quickens at the memory of his handsome smile, his steady, gentle attention that felt like it saw straight through her. She visualizes him unbuttoning his shirt to give her a better look at the inked artwork covering his chest, before letting his hair down for her to touch.

Her fingers pretend, they become Ulysses as she conjures his striking features cast in the soft glow of the chapel's lanterns. Closing her eyes, she lets herself imagine how lovely the weight of his body would feel on hers, how the scruff of his short beard might brush her cheek as he kisses down her neck, until the friction makes her muscles jerk and the mattress coils beneath her screech. The sound makes Kia's snoring pause in a moment of disrupted sleep.

Ez lies motionless, barely daring to breathe, her heart still pounding as her thoughts slow, settling. She turns onto her side, listening to Kia's snores resume, relief washing over her as the room sinks back into its familiar, stifling stillness.

Her mind drifts back to Ulysses. There was an intensity to him, something she hadn't seen in anyone else, something safe and kind. She closes her eyes, wondering what it might be like if he could see her the way she's begun to see him.

Chapter Five

THE GIRL MOVES QUICKLY, slipping through the doorway like she can't escape fast enough. Ulysses barely gets a glimpse of her—gauzy linen dress, curls escaping a messy bun, hands twitching over her bodice. As she steps into the hall, her wide eyes meet his for half a second before she drops her gaze and curtsies in a hurried motion. She doesn't wait for acknowledgment before scurrying past.

Behind her, the door groans open wider. Lang steps out, his tall frame filling the doorway.

"Ulysses." With a wave of his hand, he gestures him inside.

The two guards stationed outside remain rigid, emotionless as Ulysses steps past them and into Lang's study. The door clicks shut behind him. The room is dim, thick with the scent of cigars and old paper.

Lang moves to his desk, exhaling as he sinks into his chair. "The girls like to involve me in their silly squabbles." He waves a dismissive hand. "What brings you here?"

A clock on the wall ticks steadily, each second punctuating the heartbeat thudding in Ulysses's ears.

"It's about Ez." He keeps his voice even. "I talked to her like you asked. She's not comfortable with this arrangement with Zeke."

Lang's expression remains stony, but his eyes narrow.

"And you think that changes her obligations here?"

"I think she deserves a choice. Zeke's old enough to be her father." The gravity in the room seems to shift as Lang studies him for a beat longer.

Ulysses knows he's pushing his luck by even bringing this up, but he made Ez a promise. It's not like he hadn't noticed how women behave around here, but he'd always thought they had a choice.

"Ez has responsibilities to fulfill. Just because she's having doubts doesn't mean we cast that aside."

Ulysses drags a hand over his face, biting back the urge to snap. "So that's it? You're going to force her to marry some creep?"

Lang's voice drops as he stalks from behind his desk to face Ulysses. "Careful." He leans in close, eyes darkened under his brow. It's remarkable how fast his expression can turn from warm to menacing. "Zeke is a respected—"

"Member of the community. I heard. Lang, you should have seen the relief on her face when I told her she didn't have to marry him."

"Well, I'm sorry you've made promises you can't keep, son. Ez was sent to us because her father couldn't manage her. We've made an arrangement, and that arrangement will be honored."

"What kind of an arrangement?"

Lang's mouth tightens, his demeanor growing impatient. "The Order has invested years of effort into her, and we've made arrangements accordingly. Promises have been made. If you want to start questioning the Order's decisions, Ulysses, perhaps you should consider your own role here first."

"What's that supposed to mean?"

"It means you've been back among us for months, yet you continue to hover at the edges, reluctant to take on any real responsibility. You want to play the observer? Fine. But don't expect that to grant you a vote in the Order's decisions."

Ulysses takes a half step back. It's not that Lang was wrong— just that he didn't expect him to lob it at him like this. The people here believe in the Order. They believe in angels and apocalypse, in the promise that rejecting the secular world and obeying whatever newly ordained prophet takes power will somehow bring them closer to God. He used to believe it too. Once. Not anymore.

But there are still things here worth holding on to: the simple way of life, the connection to nature, the sense of service to a community. If only it didn't come wrapped in so much control.

"I still object to many of your policies."

"Then do something about it." Lang's posture is calm, but there's a steeliness beneath it. "Men with conviction lead, they don't sit on the sidelines and criticize. That's what you're doing by hiding in the chapel all day. I'm sorry, but if you want a say in matters like Ez's future, you have to earn it."

He'd thought he could just ride out the darkened skies here, take shelter from the storm inside him. That he could be a stowaway taking up a little space until he could safely go. Even so, he never thought Lang would want him involved in leadership, so he asks to be sure. "You'll reconsider Ez's arrangement with Zeke if I—what, *work* for you?"

Lang studies him, a faint, almost calculating smile tugging at the corners of his mouth. "I'll consider it. But no half measures. I expect full commitment. If you're ready to take on a role, then yes, your concerns will be considered. Until then, they're just concerns."

The reticence between them stretches taut, a game of chicken neither seems willing to lose. Then Lang's mouth twitches with a flicker of satisfaction, like a man who knows he's already won.

Ulysses promised her.

Why had he promised her?

The look she gave him and her pretty sketches flash in his mind and tug at his heart. She seemed to believe he was someone who could fix things. Someone strong, capable. That's the man who made the promise. But standing here, it's clear to Ulysses that's not the man he brought to this fight.

He slumps slightly, his poise succumbing to the gravity of Lang's challenge. "Fine. I'll consider it. But if I do this, you can't go back on your word. Ez doesn't have to marry Zeke."

Lang clasps his hands behind his back, the power of authority practically radiating from his posture. "I'm a man of my word."

It's dark when Ulysses walks from the Main House to his trailer, a modest sixteen-foot Airstream that gleams like a tin can in the moonlight. The profound stillness is punctuated by faint rustles, the calls of nocturnal creatures, and his too-loud footsteps crunching on the gravel path. But his mind is fixated on one quandary: how had he managed to get Ez's fate mixed up with his own?

If he truly wanted to help her, he'd have to submit to the Order in a way he'd never planned on. Take on a role in an organization he'd spent years running from.

Domino greets him in the yard, leaping and yipping with uncontainable energy. Ulysses unlocks the door to his trailer and stumbles in, letting the dog dart ahead into the pitch-blackness inside. The air still carries the lingering scent of patchouli oil, the kind Sofie wore to complete her free-spirited bohemian aesthetic. The smell twists his stomach with loss every time it hits him, a bittersweet ghost of her presence.

Tonight, it barely registers. Maybe it's the Order pulling at him again, tightening like a noose around his neck, or maybe his mind is just too tangled up to care. A small, nagging part of him wonders if he should have stayed quiet. Minded his own damn business. Yet he remembers the look in Ez's eyes when he told her she'd have a choice. That faint flicker of hope.

She's not his responsibility. Not his burden to carry.

He thought he could help. Turns out he can't.

Fuck. He groans to himself. He can't even fathom it. What kind of man looks for loopholes to excuse his own inaction?

That's not who he is. And if he agrees with anything the Order preaches, it's that people weren't meant to hoard what they have, pretending not to see the ones who have less.

When you can lighten someone's burden—if it doesn't harm you in the process—you should. That's what people are supposed to do for each other. Maybe if he takes on this responsibility he can do some good. Not just for her, but for others like her trapped under the Order's boot.

Striking a match, he lights a beeswax candle on the scratched Formica countertop. Once it's burning, filling the small space with all the light he'll need for the night, he settles onto the creaky dinette bench beneath a panoramic window, where the curtain rod sags in the middle. He looks at his dog.

"What do you think I should do, Domino? Are you ready to go back to Tampa?"

Domino tilts his head, then scratches at his collar with his back leg. He's had a good time running around with the cows and horses. As a Border Collie mix, it's in his nature to herd. He tired himself all day, living out his purpose in ways he never could in Uly's cramped little apartment. *His purpose.*

Damn it.

The revelation that his dog has made better use of his time here than Ulysses sobers him like a bucket of ice water. He lets out a bitter laugh, scrubbing a hand over his face.

All Ulysses ever wanted was to be the person he'd needed when he was at his lowest. It's why he became a counselor, to reach out to the ones who felt like they didn't belong, like they were lost and fighting a battle no one could see. He knew that feeling well. Somehow, he'd found his way through, and he wanted nothing more than to be that steady hand for someone else. So what was he waiting for? If he could make things better for others suffering the way he was, why isn't he?

"You got me there, Domino. When you're right, you're right."

Chapter Six

RETURNING FROM WASHING LINENS, Ez finds bags of flour stacked high on the kitchen counters. Butter and sugar melt in heavy cast-iron pans on the stove, filling the room with the warm, sweet smell as the women move briskly around her, their hands busy, faces focused.

"Y'all are baking a cake?" Ez asks, glancing at Mary, who's stirring a massive bowl of batter. "For what?"

Mary shrugs, her lips twitching into a sly smile. "Father wouldn't say. Just that he has an important announcement." She gives Ez a sidelong, teasing look. "Probably your engagement. I hear Deacon Zeke's pretty eager."

The words strike hard, forcing the air from her lungs and sending her heart into a spasm. No. She hasn't heard from Ulysses or anyone since they spoke in the chapel yesterday. He'd promised he would talk to Father, that he'd try to help her. But now the thought of seeing her name scrawled across a cake next to Zeke's —*Congratulations, Deacon Zeke and Esme*—sends a shiver through her so deep it turns her insides to liquid.

She grips the edge of the counter, and the kitchen's clatter fades into a distorted blur. Images flash through her mind: her mother's skeletal hands in that hospital bed; her father's detached stare as she died; the men from the Order who pulled Ez out of bed in the dead of night like a staged kidnapping. She hadn't known then that it was a life sentence. If she had, she would have fought harder. She wouldn't have let them take her alive.

Is this why I haven't heard from Ulysses? Maybe he can't help me. Maybe he didn't speak to Father after all.

"Ez?" Erma snaps her from her thoughts. "You're on garden duty today. We need the space here in the kitchen."

Ez nods stiffly, keeping her expression blank, but a fresh wave of dread rolls through her. She glances around the kitchen at the mounds of ingredients, the silver icing nozzles lined up like missiles. *Is that why they're sending me out?* she wonders. *So they can pipe my name on the cake without me seeing?*

Her stomach twists as she emerges outside into the harsh sun. She kneels among the rows of squash and carrots, her hands sinking into the dry soil, her palms gritty with dirt. The smell of earth rises around her, but it does nothing to calm the knot of fear tightening in her belly.

When the bell finally rings for dinner, her nerves are frayed thin, each step toward the long table feeling like a march to her own execution.

Under the wide canopy strung with lanterns, the community gathers around a rough-hewn table stretching down the clearing. Torches circle the area, casting flickering shadows over the parishioners.

Ez takes her seat, forcing herself to keep her head down like the other women. But when she glances up, she notices Zeke making a beeline for the seat beside her.

"Well, Ez," he says, settling in close, his shoulder brushing hers as he cranes forward. "Big announcement tonight. You excited?" His breath is hot against her ear, and she stiffens, bile rising in her throat. He chuckles, a sound that rattles the phlegm in his lungs. "Everyone's talking about it. Father's putting something special together. Can't be for nothing, right?"

His hand rests on the table, close enough that his fingers brush hers. She pulls her hand back, pressing it into her lap, heart hammering. She glances up, searching the table for Ulysses, for any sign of help, but he's seated several places down, talking quietly to Father. He doesn't even seem to notice her.

Father rises from his seat at the head of the table, lifting his hand to call for silence. Ez's heart drums as the noise fades. The torchlight flickers over Father's angular face as he looks over the crowd.

"Tonight, we celebrate the strength of a life reclaimed, and we mark a new chapter for this community. A chapter that honors resilience. And there is no one who embodies this quality better than the man I'm proud to welcome to a new role among us."

Ez's gaze drifts back to Ulysses, watching the way his eyes fix on the table, his posture slightly stiff as Father's hand rests heavily on his shoulder. He doesn't look like he wants this. Tension in his hands, faint tightness in his mouth. But Father's hand stays steady, as if it's planting him there.

"I have known this young man since he was a boy," Father says. "Ulysses was brought up among us, in our faith, and he has walked through shadows of grief, hardship, and doubt. These were not light burdens, and they nearly stole him from us."

A ripple of whispers spreads through the crowd, but Ulysses remains still, unfocused, the faintest glint in his eyes beneath the dark line of his brow.

"But it was his faith that brought him back to us. He returned to us stronger, tempered by trials. We need that kind of tenacity in leadership, and Ulysses is that leader. He will serve as Steward of the Order, not only to aid me as my right hand, but to guard and guide the values that hold us together."

Steward of the Order? The title lingers in the air. Murmurs carry across the table. Higher than Deacon. Higher than anything she's known. Father's own second in command.

Father's tone softens, warmth creeping into his words. "I call him my son," he says, his voice filled with pride. "Not by blood, but by faith."

As applause rises around her, Ez joins in, her hands clapping automatically, her mind racing. Turning to Zeke, she finds him stony, not clapping. Glancing around the table, none of the Elders are. They're stiff, eyes dark as they exchange sharp glances.

Ulysses rises to acknowledge the gathering's approval, turning briefly to Father, then sweeping across the congregation.

"Thank you, Father. I came back here because I have hope. Hope that our church can be what we intended all along. That it can lift us up. That we can embody the principles of love and compassion."

Silence hangs over them, every eye on him. "As your Steward, my role is to uphold these values. Not just aspire to be better, but to *be* better."

Ez's heart clenches as she listens. Ulysses's words, talking about a faith based on goodness and kindness, seem out of place here where the Elders only seem to value blind compliance. For a moment she lets herself believe change can happen.

Beside her, Zeke slants closer, his shoulder brushing hers, fingers tapping against the table as if to draw her attention. "Quite the showman, hmm?" he mutters, his voice low enough that only she can hear. "Funny, you'd think he's here to save us all."

Ez tenses, willing herself not to react, but Zeke notices. He shifts even closer, the rough edge of his sleeve scratching her arm. "You're not swayed by that, are you, dear?"

Her skin prickles. She forces herself to nod, keeping her face blank, her hands tight in her lap as her tongue sours. If Zeke is still lurking, does that mean nothing's changed? Did Ulysses really plan to help her, or was he just playing a role now, leaving her to fend for herself?

The applause fades and the gathering begins to break into small groups, a low hum of conversation rising around the table. Ez watches as Ulysses nods, shaking hands with several men. There's a pull to speak to him, to catch a moment of his time, to find some reassurance he hasn't left her to face all this alone.

Rising from her seat, she moves carefully around the edge of the table, trying to approach Ulysses without drawing attention. But before she can get close, three men from the Order step forward, clapping him on the back, engaging him in eager conversation. They close around him, their celebration animated, hands gesturing as they pull him deeper into their circle. She pauses, her path blocked, her heart sinking.

A hand suddenly closes around her wrist. "Where are you sneaking off to?" Zeke's voice is a low rasp, his fingers holding her just tightly enough to keep her from pulling away.

"I just…" she starts, trying to mask the frustration and dread twisting inside her. "I thought I'd say congratulations, that's all."

"Oh, is that all?" he murmurs, his tone thick with condescension. He lets out a low chuckle, stoops in close enough that his breath is hot against her cheek. "Let me tell you something, darlin'. There's only one thing he wants from you, and it ain't a pat on the back."

Ez pulls her hand free, her heart pounding as she looks down, swallowing a scream. She risks a glance back at Ulysses, who is still surrounded. Lingering on him for a second longer, she wills him to turn around with every bit of psychic power she can muster, but when he doesn't budge, dread prickles at her neck as the last flicker of hope fades.

Chapter Seven

ULYSSES DOESN'T BELONG HERE. The thought loops in his mind, growing louder with each measured tick of the clock in Lang's office, where the Order's leaders convene in silence. Opposite Ulysses and Lang, Brother Whitlock, Brother Thomas, and Deacon Zeke—the members of the Elder Council—recline, sunk into well-worn leather sofas and armchairs. Silver threads streak their hair, some nearly white, others gray at the edges. Their features remain inscrutable behind a haze of cigarette smoke—a vice their faith allows in moderation.

At thirty-four, Ulysses is the youngest in the room. He drums his fingers on the chair's tufted leather arm, wondering how he ended up here. Oil lanterns bathe the walls with shifting gold and his thoughts drift to Ez, to his decision, his eyes losing focus until he catches the men's calculating glares. Smirking, he notes the irony of their displeasure that he's risen to the Order's second-highest rank. Ulysses isn't exactly thrilled about it either, and he's still not sure why Lang insisted upon it.

"Brother Thomas, you had business to discuss?" Lang asks.

Thomas, rugged and weathered in his late fifties, ashes his

cigarette into a chipped ashtray on the desk, the ember hissing faintly. He stretches out in his chair, arms crossed over his broad chest, a heavy line carved between his eyebrows. "The younger ones think they can pull the same little stunts they did on the outside." He gestures vaguely toward the window with a dismissive flick of his hand. He goes on at length about teenage troublemakers in the congregation and how they've tested his patience.

Brother Whitlock, a hawk-nosed man in his forties, chimes in. "Perhaps a stronger hand is in order?"

Lang listens in silence, his deep-set eyes giving nothing away.

Clearing his throat, Ulysses speaks up. "With all respect," he begins, glancing around, "I've worked with troubled young people, and I know they can be hard to reach. But I've found a gentler hand often works better than strict discipline."

Brother Whitlock's lip curls, and he lets out a short, humorless laugh. "These kids don't need a gentle hand. Their families sent them here for a reason. They're wayward, disrespectful. No use sugarcoating it; they need correction."

Sent them here? Ulysses frowns slightly, fighting to keep calm. He'd noticed groups of teenagers around but had assumed their parents were congregants. "So these young people didn't move here with their families?"

"No." Brother Thomas sneers as he exhales a thin stream of smoke. "They're here because their families couldn't control them any longer. As Brother Whitlock said, they needed correction." He tuts and shakes his head. "Knuckleheads are more trouble than they're worth sometimes, but we take them in."

Father hunches forward, resting a hand on Ulysses's shoulder. "It's something we started after your time, son. Path to Purpose is a program designed to support troubled teens. An alternative to a youth boot camp, if you will. For spiritual guidance, counseling, and discipline."

A strange hollowness fills him as the meaning of Lang's words sinks in. Their parents just shipped them here. These kids left with strangers.

Before coming back here, Ulysses worked as a counselor at a rehab facility, so entering a program away from home isn't a foreign concept to him. But those young people had addictions to work through. There was clinical oversight, defined timeframes, and visiting days. This…he's not sure what this is.

"It's been an excellent way to grow our numbers," Brother Whitlock says. "Since we started the program, many of the youths have remained here and started families of their own. The Order gets stronger by the day."

A murmur of approval stirs through the room. Feeling Lang's scrutiny, as if he's waiting for Ulysses's reaction, Ulysses keeps his expression blank.

Deacon Zeke crosses one leg over the other, his hands clasped over his belly. "Some families are eager to wash their hands of them. Troubled homes, criminal records, substance abuse—most eliminate all contact."

Lang nods beside him, his calm voice cutting in. "We provide solutions when there's no one else to turn to. They see us as saviors."

"Especially for the more troublesome cases," Zeke continues. "Once we have full control, we can ensure these boys get the training and discipline they need. And for the girls, well…" He trails off with a mischievous smile, glancing sideways at the men leaning in with anticipation. "They give the boys a reason to do better."

Riotous laughter carries through the room until Lang, like an orchestra conductor, holds up his hands to command the room into silence.

"Who looks after them?" Ulysses asks.

Zeke fixes Ulysses with a pointed glare. His face, sharply angled and clean-shaven, save for a meticulously shaped mustache, holds a perpetual look of disdain, as if Ulysses falls short of his standards. "We all do. While you're hidden away in the chapel painting pictures, we're sharing the responsibility. It's taken years to get this right. You might think you know better, but these youths are nothing like what you saw out there in your previous work, I can tell you that."

Ulysses turns away and lets the slight pass. Lang's hand still rests heavy on his shoulder. "Your job, son, is to help us grow the program. You understand, don't you? Our goal is to shape these young people into the next generation of believers."

If his role is to ensure these kids are kept here, bound to the Order, he's not willing to carry it out. But what now? Does he run? He has his Jeep. He's not a prisoner. He could get Domino and leave this heap of dirt in his rearview mirror. But then those dark eyes flash in his mind again, the soft tentative way she spoke about her drawings. Her mysterious arrangement.

"Is Ez a part of this program?"

"Beg your pardon?" Zeke asks, sitting up straighter, as if the mention of her name is an affront to his claim to her. "Esme's none of your concern."

Lang holds up a hand. "Deacon, please." Then he turns to Ulysses. "She was, yes. An early iteration."

Her own family sent her away like sheep to wolves. Ulysses rubs his palms over his knees, the fabric rough under his fingers. He barely knows her, but it doesn't matter. It isn't just about her now, it's about all of them. The boys trained, the girls handed over like rewards. The smug pride in Zeke's voice makes his stomach sink, lead-heavy with the weight of their callousness.

He can't fight this. Not now. If he pushes, if he challenges them outright, he loses any chance to see what's really going on and figure out how to stop it, so he reluctantly agrees.

After the men file out, Lang gestures for Ulysses to stay. He pulls out a thick notebook, flipping it open as he gives Ulysses a sharp, calculating look. "We'll start with work assignments," he says briskly. "No idle hands, no overlap. I need an updated chart by Thursday."

Ulysses nods, but Lang is already moving on. "You'll also oversee the youth program. Meet everyone in the Youth Quarters and get a sense of things. It's manageable now, but we're expecting more soon." Lang pauses, steepling his fingers. "Think you can handle it?"

"Yes, sir," Ulysses replies, his mind racing. After a beat, he asks, "When will I be able to finish the chapel?"

Lang's mouth twitches with dry amusement. "In your free time."

As Lang returns to his notes, Ulysses doubts he'll have any free time at all.

Chapter Eight

EZ WIPES her sweaty hands on her apron, her heart fluttering as Erma's stone-blue eyes bore into her. The striped squash scattered across the butcher block make the reason clear. The other Chosen Daughters have gone to their chores, but Erma kept Ez back. Slowly, Erma picks up a bruised squash, turning it in her hand. Her mouth is pressed into a thin, unforgiving line.

"These squash are damaged."

Ez holds her hands clasped in front of her, back pressed against the edge of the island. "They were like that on the vine, ma'am. It was probably the rabbits."

A flicker of disdain crosses Erma's face. Without warning, the sting of her open hand slaps across Ez's face so sharp it brings tears to Ez's eyes. Ez clamps down her jaw, fighting every impulse in her body to swing back. Been there, done that, had an arm in a cast to prove it.

"Rabbits," Erma mocks. "I was in the garden yesterday, and they were perfectly fine. This is pure laziness on your part, stacking them high in your basket to avoid an extra trip. Now they're fit for soup only, if that." Erma drops the squash onto the counter with a dull thud, giving Ez a hard, measuring look. "I should send you to work with the men, stacking hay bales, if this is the best you can manage."

Maybe if you were in the garden you should have picked them yourself, you miserable bitch.

Ez holds her cheek, heat emanating from it. "I'm sorry, ma'am."

The apology is like spoiled milk in her mouth but she swallows it down. It was true. In the garden yesterday as Zeke watched, all Ez could think about was how soon she'd have to lie down with him and how eager he was to do vile things to her. It made her blood boil so hot she yanked each gourd off the vine imagining herself dismembering that man. Ripping his head right off his neck. Snatching his dick out of his pants and punting it right into that wicker basket.

She'd hoped Ulysses would find her after dinner with good news, but she hadn't even seen him at breakfast this morning. The doubts and questions drift across the sea of her mind as she scrubs the slate kitchen floors by hand. Her punishment for bruising squash. She'd scrub every floor in this place for her freedom.

No. She'd burn this place to the fucking ground.

Years ago, when she still had the will to fight, Father had told her, *"You're free to leave whenever you'd like."* But where? How? She'd left school at thirteen to come here. She had no money, no license, no phone, no idea where "here" even was—just that it was somewhere in Florida, overheard from a complaint about the heat.

The bristles whoosh across the tiles, and the ache in her arms deepens. For years, she's prayed for a way out, but every flicker of hope has been extinguished.

It would be so nice if Ulysses could be different.

After dumping the filthy water, she washes her raw, stinging hands. When she opens the door, Erma is standing there. Ez gasps, the bucket clattering to the floor.

"What are you doing?" Erma demands.

"Sorry, ma'am. I just finished the floor."

"Come with me."

Ez trails after her down the hall to the pantry, where Erma drops a bag of bean pods onto the counter. "You'll shell every last one of these," Erma says, her tone clipped. "If I find even one bruise…" She lets the threat hang before turning sharply, her skirt swirling as she walks away.

Ez stares at the bag, her hands still burning from scrubbing. The thought of prying open each pod feels suffocating. She sinks onto the stool, picks up a pod, and begins. Snap, pull, drop. Her fingers move mechanically, the rhythm monotonous.

Her mind drifts. Her worn skirt is replaced by the airy practice clothes she'd once danced in. She can pretend her mother is just behind her, sitting in a chair against the studio wall, her purse on the ground, watching her dance with a smile. But the fantasy dissolves, replaced by the dry, dusty pantry and the sharp ache in her hands.

Snap, pull, drop.

She tries to picture Ulysses: the way he'd looked at her in the chapel, his kind compliments about her drawings. Maybe she'd read too much into it. Men here didn't help unless they wanted something in return. She thinks of Zeke and his excuses to grope her during his "strolls."

Ulysses is a man, just like the rest of them. She should know better by now.

The beans pile in the bowl, a slowly growing mound that feels mocking. Outside, crickets and cicadas hiss in the twilight. The sound of footsteps interrupts their song.

Mary appears in the doorway, a burlap sack in her arms. Ez's heart sinks as Mary drops it onto the counter with a dull thud. "Sorry, Ez," she says. "Mom says butter beans this time. You have to finish these before you can go to bed."

Ez glances at the last rays of sun sinking beyond the tree line but doesn't argue. She swallows her frustration and nods.

"Can I help?" Mary asks softly.

"No, thanks. I don't want you to get in trouble."

Mary hesitates in the doorway. "Tomorrow will be better," she says before leaving. Ez stares at the sack of butter beans and the mound she's already shelled. A wave of despair washes over her.

Snap, pull, drop.

It goes on long after dusk. Her stomach growls, but she doesn't dare stop. The pantry grows darker as night settles in. Then, she hears a hushed voice.

"Hey."

Kia slips inside, a basket on her hip, her footsteps careful and deliberate. "I saved you some dinner," she says, lifting a layer of freshly dried sheets collected from the clothesline to reveal a small plate with a roll and a drumstick. The scent of baked chicken and spices rises between them, making her gut groan. Kia presses the plate into Ez's hands with a small smile.

"God bless you," Ez mutters, already tearing into the sneaky meal. A mash of chicken and roll bulges in her cheek as Kia raises an eyebrow.

"What's Erma pissed at you for now?"

Ez barely pauses, mumbling through the food. "Bruising stupid squash."

Kia snorts, rolling her eyes. "You'd think you'd pissed in her cornflakes." She drops her basket by the door and props herself up against the counter. "I can't wait for that dusty old witch to get what's coming to her."

Ez doesn't respond, just keeps chewing, her eyes darting toward the hallway. She used to believe in karma—people paying for their sins with some form of divine or natural judgment. Not anymore. Erma will probably live to be a hundred.

The flickering lamp above them casts shadows that make the kitchen feel smaller. Kia glances at the half-empty bowl of beans on the worktable and smirks. "Come on. You don't have much left."

She moves toward the table, playfully nudging Ez aside to make room for herself. Ez shoots her a worried look. "What if Erma sees you?"

"We'll work fast," Kia says, already halfway through a bean pod. Her hands move with practiced speed, flicking shells into the sack at her side. Ez hesitates for a moment, but then picks up the rhythm, the two of them working in tandem. They don't speak, the scrape of fingernails against bean pods the only sound in the pantry.

Kia's stomach is flat, no baby bump to speak of, which is a blessing. No questions to answer or judgments to bear. As close as they are, Ez hasn't pried. She knows Kia will tell her when she's ready. Until then, she lets the silence rest comfortably between them.

Finally, Kia shells the last bean, letting it fall into the bowl. The sense of accomplishment is hollow as Ez surveys the counter. Another task done.

As they head to bed, the rest of the house is silent, everyone long since asleep. They walk the narrow hallway to their room, footsteps echoing like soft breath against the walls. Despite the hopelessness, Ez is grateful for a friend. For Kia. She's the one person who has never let her down.

When they reach the door, Ez slips inside first, her movements weary. Kia follows, letting the door click softly shut behind her. Kicking off her shoes, Kia lets them tumble into the corner. Ez collapses onto her mattress, the springs groaning under her. She drags the thin blanket over herself with hands that tremble from fatigue.

Kia sinks onto her own bed, her body folding under its own exhaustion. The mattress creaks, and she curves forward, resting her elbows on her knees. For a moment, the room is still.

"Thanks, Kia," Ez murmurs, her voice barely audible.

Kia doesn't look up, her hands clasped between her knees. "You don't have to thank me," she says quietly. "You'd do the same for me."

Chapter Nine

"I APPRECIATE THE OFFER, Lang. Really. But I like the trailer."

Lang reclines in his chair, his fingers steepled and his assessing glare flickering over Ulysses, peeling him apart piece by piece. After-noon light captures flecks of dust suspended in the air. He hates the scent in this room—old tobacco, the staleness that lingers in his nose long after he's left this office. Ulysses wrings the end of his note-book, where his handwritten summaries of youth observations are crammed into tight, slanted lines.

"You can't lead from a distance, son. Your presence in the Main House would set an example for everyone. The leaders are expected to live as a community."

In the Main House, eyes were always tracking him. Ulysses didn't need to glance behind him to know there'd always be someone there, scrutinizing his every breath. It's an exhausting thought, never being able to let down the mask he's forced to wear. Searching for a half-decent excuse, he lands on, "Yeah, but…Domino."

Lang's face barely flickers, his expression unreadable. Though Ulysses is certain Lang is displeased by his reluctance, he can't overcome this doubt. The more Ulysses learns about this place, the more challenging it becomes to stay.

Ulysses had visited the Youth Quarters earlier that day, a bleak clutch of portable buildings set far from the main compound, as if the Order wanted to keep them out of sight. Each unit was barely the size of a shipping container, just big enough to house four kids apiece in narrow, bunked beds with thin, threadbare blankets. The only communal space was a squat, concrete structure in the middle of the sleeping areas that provided a kitchen, bathroom, and classroom crammed into a space no larger than five hundred square feet. The thick, musty air clung to Ulysses' throat, leaving a bitter, moldy taste at the back of his tongue.

When he arrived, only boys occupied the classroom, seated in neat rows facing a chalkboard where Brother Whitlock scrawled what looked like an organizational chart. They sat too still, their features drained of anything human, like puppets waiting to be animated.

Whitlock, chalk in hand, paused when he noticed Ulysses, pivoting toward him with narrowed eyes, giving him a slow once-over.

"Steward, to what do we owe this great honor?" he said, making no effort to veil his sarcasm.

The young men, dressed in navy slacks and white collared shirts, turned their gaunt faces toward Ulysses at once, studying him with quiet curiosity. He'd had the foresight to cover his arms, but the tattoos on his hands and neck were visible. As he slipped into an empty desk, he could see the calculations behind their eyes. "Just getting the lay of the land. Pretend I'm not even here."

Whitlock's smile carried no warmth. "You'll find everything in perfect order here, Steward," he said, a hint of challenge in his tone. "These young men aren't just learning logic and reasoning, they're learning discipline and respect. They're becoming the kind of men this world needs."

"And the girls?" he asked. "Are they following a similar curriculum?"

The boys snickered, and Whitlock's features darkened, filling with a subtle controlled tension. "The girls have their own lessons. Modesty, humility, domestic duties. They're learning what they need to know."

Ulysses forced himself to remain calm, remembering the way Ez bowed her head, the way all the Chosen Daughters seemed to avert their eyes in the presence of men, how men like Lang and Whitlock and Zeke could gather in smoke filled rooms to have their pick and plan their wedding nights. It was sadistic.

All the insults and injuries Ulysses had endured at the hands of the women in his life festered inside him like something toxic. Ulysses's mother had enlisted their family in a violent cult. Made him an accessory to atrocities. Sofie had gutted him, abandoned him more times than he could count. Rosario and her fucking podcast nearly got him killed. He could almost understand how a man, poisoned by wounds like his, might be tempted to allow that rage to spill onto an innocent woman. But even as the heat of it smoldered in his soul, there wasn't a bone in his body that could justify it. No more than he'd accept being judged for the failures of worse men than himself.

As Ulysses watched the way these boys recited the Order's pernicious lessons, part of him wanted to turn and run, to make this twisted world a tiny speck behind him. But another part, a stubborn part, wanted to stay and change it.

Back in the Main House, Lang studies him with that unnervingly patient look, as if unraveling Ulysses's reasons for not wanting to move into the Main House thread by thread. "If Domino is the issue, bring him here. But you and I both know he's not the real reason you're hesitating. You wanted change. Now you need to commit to it."

The words hang heavily between them, and Ulysses realizes he has two options: stay and commit to change, or leave and let Ez and all the Order's youth fend for themselves. It's not his responsibility—he knows that— but *fuck*, he thinks, as the pressure at the base of his neck tightens, squeezing around his head like a vise. He wishes he could settle for being a shitty person, or at least someone who wouldn't wallow in guilt for walking away. With a heavy sigh, he concedes. "Fine."

Lang gives a faint, approving nod, and Ulysses can feel the last bit of his freedom slipping away.

There isn't much to move—a few books, a duffel bag of clothes, and Domino's water dish. Ulysses crosses over the threshold of his new room, taking it in slowly. It's more than he expected. A suite complete with a king-sized bed and a private bathroom. Sunlight filters through sheer curtains that billow against the cool breeze from the open window. Outside, flat land stretches as far as he can see, broken up by clusters of oaks and pines, punctuated with cattle and horses. He shifts uncomfortably, feeling a strange sense of displacement. Everything is crisp, clean, and, compared to the Order's usual standards, luxurious.

Domino, padding in beside him, sniffs at the furniture before settling near the bed. Ulysses crouches, running a hand over the dog's fur. "Guess this is home now."

He's barely set down his bag when he hears footsteps in the hallway. Glancing over, he sees Ez passing by with a basket of laundry in her arms. She pauses, surprise flickering across her face.

"You're moving in," she says, more of an astonished acknowledgement than a question. As she meanders closer, that familiar, enchanting floral scent drifts in with her. He's heard the women here make their own perfumes, and his mind takes an unexpected detour, imagining her grinding flower petals, carefully mixing oils, dabbing the blend on her collarbone.

Stray wisps of hair cling to her nape, damp with sweat, and her eyes droop with exhaustion.

"Lang's idea," he replies, forcing a tight smile. "Guess he thinks I'll be more useful here."

She glances around the room, nodding absently, too tired to muster much interest. "Looks nice."

He eases toward her, his voice dropping lower. "Ez, about Zeke.

I haven't forgotten. I talked to Lang, but it's going to take some time."

Her shoulders slump slightly. "I didn't know if you were still working on it," she admits. She glances away, her fingers gripping the basket's handle. "That's okay. Thank you. For trying at least."

"Didn't see you at dinner last night," he says gently, searching her face for a clue. "Everything alright?"

Ez shifts, her fingers tightening around the basket. "I had work to do." Her head lowers in a gesture of submission. "A lot more than usual."

"More than usual?" he asks, frowning. "What do you do around here?"

Her eyes dart back to him and there's a flash of worry. "A little bit of everything," she says, almost like she's rehearsed it. "Cooking, cleaning, helping with—" She shifts the laundry basket on her hip, but the motion sends its contents tumbling loose. A single apple and two oranges roll out, bouncing onto the floor.

"Smuggling fruit," Ulysses teases, unable to stop the grin tugging at his lips.

"Oh!" she gasps, crouching down in an adorable rush, her hands fumbling as she gathers the rogue fruit. Ulysses can't help but notice the way Ez's cheeks turn pink, oblivious to the fact she's the most fascinating thing he's seen all day.

Domino lifts his snout at the commotion, ears twitching as one of the oranges rolls near him. With a slow blink, he gives it an unimpressed sniff before letting out a dramatic sigh, flopping his head back onto the rug.

Ulysses crouches, reaching for the orange that had stopped by his foot. As Ez scrambles for the rest, he notices her hands—small and calloused, clean but raw at the knuckles. He offers the orange, his hand brushing hers as she takes it. "You missed one."

She dusts each piece of fruit with delicate care, her lips pressing into an apologetic smile that does something stupid to him and he doesn't want to look away. He can't explain it, but he's struck by the need to know everything about her.

"Who do you report to?" He tries to keep it light, but the question lands a little harder than he intends.

"Please don't say anything. We're not allowed to have food up here, but my roommate, she's..." She hesitates. "She gets hungry at night."

"No, no. Don't worry, that's not why I asked," he says quickly, wincing at how it sounded. "Sorry. I just meant, I'm in charge of work assignments now, and I was curious. That's all."

"Mostly Erma," she replies, almost cautious. "She's in charge of me."

"Does that make you happy?"

She lowers her head, staring at the basket in her hands. "It's what I'm supposed to do." Her attention flits to him, nodding politely before turning to go. Ulysses hesitates, feeling a surge of urgency as she leaves. He speaks up, hoping to prolong their visit.

"Ez, can I ask you something else?"

She stops, glancing back at him with a hint of wariness. "Sure."

"You mentioned you do a little bit of everything around here," he says carefully. "But what about learning? What were you taught in school?"

Ez drops her gaze, shifting the laundry's awkward heft on her hip. "How to cook, clean, and keep a home." She pauses, choosing her words carefully. "I remember learning things before I came here. Math and science and stuff. Sometimes I wonder who I would be right now if—" She stops herself before daring to say the words. *If she'd never been forced to be here.*

"What do you think you might have done?"

"I don't know." She thinks about it. "I always wondered about those people who work in the art museums and know everything and give tours and stuff."

Ulysses raises an eyebrow, smiling with genuine interest. "A docent. I can see that. Someone who gets to talk about paintings and sculptures all day."

Ez's eyes light up, seeming surprised that he understands. "A docent," she repeats, as if feeling the word against her tongue for the first time. "Yeah, exactly. I've always wondered what it would be like to be around all that. To learn about the artists and why they made things the way they did." She pauses, a little embarrassed. "I don't know much about it, but my mom used to take me to all kinds of museums when I was little."

They've only spoken a few times, but he's already heard about her mother more than once. "Sounds like you and your mom were close."

"Yeah." A silent moment stretches between them before she shakes it off with a forced smile. "Anyway," she says, drawing in a sharp breath. "That was a long time ago."

"What happened to her?"

"She died. Cancer."

He waits, letting her go at her own pace, but when she doesn't say more, he gently presses. "How old were you?"

"Twelve," she replies, her attention fixed somewhere on the floor. "I don't like to talk about it."

Ulysses doesn't miss the way her shoulders stiffen as she says it, like she's bracing for something. "I'm sorry. I won't press," he says, taking a small step closer. "But you know, it's okay to be sad. And if you ever just need someone to talk to about—"

Ez cuts him off with a raised eyebrow and a smirk. "Are you counseling me?"

He laughs reflexively, surprised by her response. "*No*," he says, almost too fast. No, because if he were her counselor, this flutter in his belly whenever their eyes meet would be wrong. The thought roots itself before he can stop it, and his heartbeat falters.

She looks at him like he's someone important, someone worth believing in. And for a man who's spent his whole life seeing himself as a fuckup, it's an illusion he wishes he could hold on to. But it doesn't sit well. It's wrong, like a lie he has no right to let her believe.

"Not officially, anyway. I just want to help."

"I'm okay. She wouldn't want me to spend my life crying about it. She'd want me to be happy, to be kind, to help where I can. So I do. That's how I keep her close."

The certainty in her voice catches him off guard. She's not just saying it. She believes it. It takes the air out of him.

God, she's beautiful.

Not just in the way she looks, but in the way she refuses to break. She's strong, despite everything life and the Order have put her through.

"I know things can be difficult in this place," he says, searching her face. "I'm here because I want to make things better for everyone. I want to help fix it."

Ez lets out a breath, but it's not relief. It's the kind of breath that says she's heard it all before. Her smile is small, polite, but tired. "That's nice." She reaches for the rag she'd tucked into her apron, already moving toward the door. "I have a lot more chores to do."

And just like that, the conversation is over.

She excuses herself and disappears down the hall, her footsteps fading, leaving Ulysses alone in the quiet of his new suite.

He exhales, running a hand through his hair. Words alone won't make a difference. If he's going to help her, it'll take more than promises.

Chapter Ten

EZ MANEUVERS around the kitchen table, her movements unhurried as she refills coffee cups and sets down plates of toast and eggs. The morning sun streams through the window casting warm light over everything, making the room feel more cheerful than it is. Her hands are steady as she pours, but her mind is elsewhere.

As she reaches Ulysses's place at the table, there's a quiet serenity to him. She doesn't expect him to say anything to her, especially not here in front of everyone, but then he looks at her with those dazzling jade eyes. A flash of heat radiates across her chest.

One look, and she's ruined.

"Erma," he says, addressing the room with a confidence that draws everyone's attention. "I'll need help completing the mural in the chapel now that I have other responsibilities. I'll be taking Ez off kitchen duty to assist me."

The words are so unexpected, Ez nearly spills the coffee she's pouring, the carafe clumsily clinking against his cup. She straightens, blinking down at the table, her pulse hammering in her ears. Out of the corner of her eye, she sees Erma's face tighten, lips pressing into a thin line.

For a moment, Ez thinks she's going to protest outright. But then

Erma turns to Lang, as if looking for permission to object. Lang spreads butter over his bread and doesn't say a word. Ulysses is a man, a higher rank than she'll ever hold with the Order, and Erma knows as well as Ez does that she doesn't have the authority to fight this openly.

"Of course," she says, though her voice has a brittle edge to it. "If that's what you need."

Laughter wells up inside Ez, but she swallows it down. She lowers her gaze to the table, biting her lip to keep her expression neutral.

Zeke huffs, shifting in his seat. "I don't see why the chapel would need her help," he says. He furrows his brow, eyes flickering between Ulysses and Ez, mouth pinched. "Seems unnecessary to pull her away from her regular duties."

Ulysses doesn't flinch, and his voice is calm, but there is steel beneath his words. "I've been tasked with new responsibilities," he says, glancing at Lang. "If I'm going to be effective, I'll need someone dedicated to help me with chapel work. Not only is she a capable artist, but Ez has proven herself to be hardworking and reliable, and I'd like to make use of that."

Mary clears her throat. "Ez draws beautifully," she says. "All the angels and flowers in her sketchbook are real nice."

Lang regards Ulysses for a long moment, then nods once. "If that's what you believe will help you fulfill your responsibilities, then so be it."

Zeke shifts again, and Ez can feel him leering at her, something possessive and threatening lurking there. She clenches her hands around the coffee pot as he presses on. "Father, respectfully, a woman's role is to support and nurture. This is a distraction from her sacred duties."

"That's absurd," Ulysses says. "Ez can–"

"Son, I believe I was addressing Father," Zeke interrupts.

Lang holds up a hand to dispel the dispute. "I've made my decision, Deacon. Are you suggesting I would defy God's natural order?"

"I'm suggesting the Steward's motives are transparent."

"What's that supposed to mean?" Ulysses barks back against the clatter of his silverware falling onto his plate. Ez draws into herself, her muscles growing rigid. She would also like to know what that means. *His motives are see-through? Motive… that's like a reason to do something, isn't it?*

"I don't think it's appropriate to have unsupervised time alone in the—"

"Enough," Lang says, cutting him off. "I've made my decision." His tone is resolute. "It is not your place to question the motives of the Order's leadership. And just as I wouldn't permit anyone to challenge your propriety, Deacon, I will not allow a challenge to the Steward."

Ulysses nods, and the room falls into a stiff silence.

Ez wills her face to stay neutral, but inside she's doing cartwheels. Painting a mural. A simple thing, but to her it's a dream.

"Thank you, sir." Ez's words come out in a rush, almost too eager, but she doesn't care. Her pulse thrums with excitement, and for the first time in years, there's a real spark of joy. She risks a quick glance up at Ulysses, catching the faint smile at the edge of his mouth.

"Good," he says. "I'll expect you in the chapel after breakfast then."

Zeke shifts, his fork hovering over his plate as he watches the exchange. Glowering, he says nothing, turning back to his meal with a faint grunt.

After cleaning up breakfast, she breezes across the grounds toward the chapel, a light of hope brightening her from the inside. The fresh morning air fills her lungs. For once, she's not headed toward another day of backbreaking chores. Today, she has a purpose of her own and she can feel the burden of her circumstances lifting.

The chapel's wooden door creaks as she enters. She pauses, letting her eyes adjust to the dim interior light filtering through the high stained-glass windows. Taking in the blank expanse of the ceiling she'll help transform, a ripple of nerves passes through her.

All she's done for years is sketch in her notebook. She hasn't held a paintbrush in years. Is she even capable of doing this?

Ulysses is already there, his back to her as he arranges the supplies they'll need. He glances over his shoulder as she approaches, and his calm expression softens into a smile. He gestures to a set of brushes and paints he's laid out on a table near the wall. "Ready to get started?"

"Yes," she replies, breathless with anticipation. Her fingers twitch at her sides, itching to reach for a brush. "Thank you, sir. Really."

He hands her a paintbrush. Holding it in her hand sends a spark through her, and she hops up on her toes. A grin spreads across his face.

"Wouldn't have asked if I didn't think you were up to it."

She looks away before he can see the flush that's surely rising to her cheeks.

"Ladies first," he says, gesturing toward the ladder. She looks up, counting the many rungs. Taking a breath, she lifts her knee, but the fabric of her skirt catches tight against her thigh, cutting her movement short. She pauses, glancing back at him, her cheeks warming as she tries to shift her leg, the skirt stubbornly refusing to give. She hadn't assumed she'd be climbing ladders when dressing that morning, picking a skirt with a stiff inner lining and little give.

"Hmm," he says through a soft chuckle. "Hadn't considered this."

She notices his amused expression, her face flushing even more. "*Shoot.*"

"Do you have pants?" he asks.

"Women aren't allowed to wear pants."

"Really?"

She gives him a disbelieving look. For a Steward, he really seems to be in the dark about a lot of the Order's rules. With a long exhale, she looks up at the chapel ceiling beyond the ladder. No way she's letting a stupid skirt kill her dream now that she's so close.

"Could you please turn around?" she asks, gathering her resolve.

His eyebrows arch, but he quickly obliges, turning his back to her. She lets out a breath, her fingers slipping to the waistband of her skirt. With one swift motion, she loosens it and tiptoes out, the fabric pooling around her ankles. Stepping out of it, she folds the skirt and neatly hangs it over the back of a nearby pew. Clad in her bloomers, a pair of thin linen shorts that stop at her knees, she grabs the first rung and climbs. When she reaches the top, she looks down to find him watching, his expression unreadable.

"You didn't peek, did you?"

His lips curve into a slight smile. "Wouldn't dream of it."

As he climbs up and settles beside her, his warmth and the faint brush of his shoulder send a shiver down her back. She tries to focus on the unfinished mural, but his closeness knots her thoughts. She studies the delicate lines and shadowed wings, trying to see the angel as he does. Doubt creeps in, heavy in her stomach.

"I don't know if I'm good enough to make it look the way you want."

Ulysses turns to her, and when their eyes meet, she catches the flecks of gold in his gaze. Her heart nearly beats out of her chest.

"Don't worry about making it what I want. I want it to look the way you see it. It doesn't have to be perfect. Just make it yours."

Relief washes over her, mingling with a renewed sense of excitement. "Okay."

"You don't have to continue on with this, but I started with the idea of making something that looks like it's survived."

She thinks about that, scanning the progress again with renewed interest. "A little beaten up," she says.

"Exactly."

"I really like that idea." They sit in silence for a moment, her attention moving from the mural to his hands resting against the platform rail. Then her attention moves to his tattoos. Broken Grecian busts etched into his defined forearm. She wants to ask him about it. About all of it: the art, the story, the reason he's here helping her. But instead, she blurts, "Like these?" and gestures toward it. She doesn't dare touch it, but her fingers twitch slightly at her side, the impulse almost too strong to resist.

"Yeah," he says. "Kind of a common theme in my work."

"Is it 'cause all that stuff Father said? You went down a dark path?"

Ulysses studies her, a gentler expression falling over his features as a soft chuckle escapes his lips. "Yeah. Went through some experiences that left a few cracks. Got lost for a while."

She glances at him, catching the hint of vulnerability in his tone. "Me too."

"After your mom passed?" he asks. There's something in the way he asks—gracious, like he's opening a door and waiting for her to step through it.

She nods, drifting back to the mural. "That's kind of how I ended up here," she says.

Ulysses watches her, his expression thoughtful, and for a moment, neither of them speaks. The quiet stretches, filled with an understanding that's strangely comforting.

"Is it still dark?" He seems like he really cares about knowing the answer.

She toys with a strand of her hair, giving it thought. "Sometimes. But not today. This really means a lot to me. Being able to work on this. I never thought I'd get to do anything like this."

He nods. "You deserve to."

She lets his words settle, her cheeks warming slightly. After a moment, she gestures toward the mural, eager to shift into safer ground. "So, how do you get it so…soft? The edges, I mean. So they don't look like lines. Just shading, I guess?"

"Good question." He picks up a brush from the edge of the landing, giving it a faint dab onto a pool of ochre on the palette. "You use a dry brush, something without much paint. Then you blend it out. Gentle strokes," he says, reaching up to a spot that needs it. "You're not painting so much as you're suggesting."

"Suggesting," she echoes, trying the word out, and finds herself grinning a little. She studies the ceiling again, seeing it with fresh eyes.

He holds out the brush. "You try."

Drawing in a sharp breath, she takes in the scent of turpentine as she summons her confidence. She takes the brush, her fingers grazing his as she does. The contact is brief, but it sparks something in her chest—something that flutters and won't settle. Taking it into her hand, she reaches up, following his lead.

"Good," he says. "You're a natural."

She can't stop the nervous laugh that bubbles up and escapes her lips. Looking back at the image, she examines the spot she's blended, scanning around it to a section of black and brown shades blended together.

"It's about contrast. Caravaggio used shadows to make the light stand out, to make the figures feel like they're emerging from the dark." He sits back, tracing an outline in the air.

Ez watches, captivated by how his expression sharpens, how smart he sounds, how focused he becomes as he explains. She blinks, clueless about Caravaggio or his shadows, but now she's curious. "Coming out of the dark?" She edges forward, trying to see it the way he does.

"You know what? I'll show you," he says, shifting toward the ladder. The thought of scaling the scaffolding again is daunting, but she musters her courage, making a point not to look down as she swings her legs over the edge.

Once on the ground, she finds Ulysses scanning the room, rubbing his jaw thoughtfully before he strides to a lantern, grabbing it. "Not dark enough in here," he says, then turns toward the vestry door at the back of the chapel. "Come with me." He gestures for her to follow.

Past the altar, he opens a door, revealing a narrow room with a single window partially obscured by thick bushes outside. Shadows pool around them, the faint light soft as velvet.

He sets the lantern down in front of a small angel statue, stepping back so only the edges of the figure are kissed with light. "This," he says, gesturing to the statue, "is what I mean. See how only parts of it are visible? The rest stays hidden."

Ez watches the statue, the way the light touches it looks almost alive.

"It makes you look twice," he says. "Makes you wonder what you're missing."

Ez offers a hum of understanding, starting to get it. His face lights up as he talks, like he's gone somewhere else as the lantern's flame dances in his eyes. The glow glimmers across his face, casting parts of him in shadow. He has a beauty she wasn't expecting—strong and rugged, unpolished, with that wild hair tied back.

Ez inches closer, standing just at his side, close enough to catch the slight unsteadiness in his breath. She watches his profile as he looks at the statue, intense and thoughtful. "I think I can see it now," she says.

Slowly, almost tentatively, he turns to face her, and she catches the way his pupils shift, widening just slightly in the low light. A flicker of surprise crosses his face and he draws in a sharp breath, as if he's only just noticed how near she's standing. "Anyway," he says, chuckling softly. His hand moves almost reflexively to rub the back of his neck, his earlier confidence giving way to something shy. "You get the idea."

Before she can stop herself, she presses in just a little closer. "I do," she says. "Thank you for showing me."

He doesn't look away this time, the force of attraction building in the quiet between them. His lips part as if to say something but then he hesitates, his attention briefly falling to her mouth.

"We should get started," he says finally, his voice low.

A silent understanding passes between them, her pulse thundering in her ears. "Yes, sir."

Chapter Eleven

THIS WASN'T THE PLAN. She wasn't the plan.

Ulysses stands alone in the quiet chapel, the image of Ez's face —those wide, dark eyes, the way she'd leaned in, looking at him like that—burned into his mind.

On one hand, he hadn't kissed her, hadn't acted on impulse, and maybe that's a small victory. It took more strength than he'd like to admit. It would have been too easy to close that last bit of space. To bend down and taste her luscious mouth. She would've let him. He saw it in her eyes. Those deep, innocent…

No. You have to stop.

But his body betrays him.

The things that could have happened in that room. Sinful. Reckless. Deeply pleasurable things. Her modest dress made it difficult but not impossible to picture her body underneath. He wondered how the flesh of her hips would yield under his grip. The thought makes his rigidness ache.

Enough.

He hasn't so much as jerked off in months, a means to fortify himself, a test of his willpower. But he hadn't expected Ez to be on the test. His hand goes rogue and rubs against the fabric at his crotch, the small pleasure heightening his temptation. As he considers unzipping his pants, he takes in his surroundings.

You're in a church, you animal. What's the matter with you?

Swallowing hard, he takes a breath, letting himself settle and resisting the urge to find relief. Clearly, months of abstinence have weakened his tolerance, like his first drink after years of sobriety. He's a lightweight. Feeling the warmth radiating from her body so close to his, it took all his willpower not to pounce. Willpower he clung to because this could only end one way: badly. He lets out a bitter laugh, forcing himself to accept the truth as final. He's better off keeping his distance.

After spending the day in the chapel with Ez, he's fallen behind on his other responsibilities. His evening is spent at his desk, reviewing schedules and his notes for his next meeting with Lang. When he hears the dinner bell, he makes his way down the hall.

"Steward," a voice calls. Ulysses turns, finding Whitlock just as a heavy hand claps his back.

"Haven't seen you around today."

His skin crawls at the false camaraderie, but he forces a tight smile. "Still getting used to my new responsibilities."

"And to young women in the chapel, I'm told."

Word travels fast around here. "If you're suggesting anything inappropriate has—"

Whitlock laughs, squeezing Ulysses's shoulder reassuringly. "I prefer the fairer ones. That Mary has skin like milk. Cute little pink nipples."

Ulysses lets the words settle before recoiling, instinctively creating space between them. Mary was almost a sister to him, and the thought makes his lip curl. Whitlock is twice her age and married.

"Don't look so shocked, Steward. You're new, but you'll get it soon enough. That's what they're there for." Whitlock's grin widens, unrepentant. "Just don't spoil Esme for her husband. We have our rules, and we don't need another scandal."

"I haven't spoiled anyone."

Whitlock winks. "Good. But I have to warn you, I don't think

Zeke is interested in sharing. He put that one on ice a long time ago."

Zeke better keep his hands off her.

Had he touched her? Hurt her?

"She's not Zeke's to share," he says, before stomping off toward the dining table, heart pounding hard.

The women have finished serving and are seated. Cicadas hum in the distance. Their song carries on the woodsmoke filled air, mixing with the clatter of plates and hum of voices beneath the pole barn.

Ez sits beside Zeke, who's already lurching toward her, talking close with his hand in her lap. The way Ez shifts away is subtle, but her discomfort and Whitlock's slimy words linger in his mind. This place, these men—they're all too willing to take what they want. The thought of Ez, or any of these women, being used as just another possession for them to pass around sends a blaze of fire straight to his gut. How he'd love to grab that old pervert by his skinny neck and beat his face in.

Calm down. Making a scene won't fix anything.

He could get her away from him. But intervening here in front of everyone will have consequences. He draws in a deep breath. Whatever fallout comes his way, it doesn't matter.

Ez can't fight back, but he can.

He marches toward them, stopping behind Ez and tapping her on the shoulder, his shadow falling across the table. Her head whips around, mouth falling open.

"Ulysses," she says, before stammering, "Uh…sir."

He brings his mouth close to her ear. "Let's go," he says, lifting her plate.

Ez hesitates, her hands fidgeting in her lap. She glances at Zeke.

"It's okay. Get up," Ulysses says. His free hand hovers near her shoulder for a moment before hesitating at the small of her back as she finally rises from her seat. She moves slowly, almost reluctantly, her head ducked low as though trying to avoid the eyes of the congregation. He keeps his movements measured, deliberate, refusing to look back even as Zeke's glare bores into him like a brand. The murmurs around them swell as they walk, whispers rippling across the table. Ulysses ignores them. He focuses on the path ahead, guiding her to an open spot beside him. "Sit here."

Ulysses places her plate down in front of her and takes the seat beside her. Ez looks up at him, her dark eyes searching his face for a long moment. Zeke is still watching them, his face shadowed and tight, fork clutched in his hand like a weapon. Meeting Zeke's glare head-on, Ulysses's cold death stare sends a clear message: Not tonight. Not her.

"Esme," Lang says, a note of surprise in his voice. "Lovely to see you."

She bows her head. "Nice to see you, Father."

Lang smiles warmly at her, but once she's distracted by her meal, he shifts his attention to Ulysses. The warmth in his demeanor fades, replaced by something colder, sharper. His brows lower slightly, his jaw tightening in quiet disapproval. For causing trouble. Disturbing the peace. Fixating on this woman. It makes the hair on Ulysses's neck stand up. He inclines his head in a small, measured gesture, acknowledging the unspoken warning.

Then he turns back to Ez, who is eating quietly now, her hands steady and her shoulders beginning to relax. Whatever this is, this pull between them, it's dangerous. But he can't deny it's there. Can't deny he wishes they were the only two people at this table.

Across the barn, Zeke's glare burns into Ulysses like a hot iron. Ulysses doesn't care. Whatever repercussions come, he'll deal with them. For now, at least, Ez is safe.

Chapter Twelve

WHEN DINNER ENDS, Ulysses rises and lets Ez go ahead of him, hanging back long enough to avoid drawing Lang's eye. She slips into the Main House, pausing in the hallway until he joins her. They walk side by side in silence until they're out of sight beside the stairwell.

Ulysses is unsure of what to say now that he has her alone. He knows he shouldn't be here with her like this, but he doesn't want to walk away just yet. "Heading to bed?" he asks, feeling the question come out stilted and awkward.

Ez's eyes brighten a little at his stupid question—it's not even eight o'clock. "I have some more chores to do before then." She hesitates, then adds, "I had a nice time today."

The way she looks at him, the way her pouty lips perk up makes his heart race. He has to look away for a moment, turning his attention to the worn wood of the staircase beside them. "Me too. It's peaceful, isn't it? In the chapel."

Her hands clutch together in front of her as she looks up at him through thick, dark lashes. "It's one of the few places where people leave you alone. I like the quiet."

He agrees without a word, though he wants to say so many

things. Wants her to know the predicament he's in—how he's captivated by her but woefully wrong for her. He wants to ask about the things Whitlock said, wants to know what she's experienced, what she's seen. But there are few private places here, even when he thinks no one is watching.

"Yeah. It's good for clearing your head." He can't drag his eyes away from her. They stand there, dumb and smiling as the seconds pass by unnoticed, until it flusters him and he offers her an out. "I shouldn't keep you."

"You're not keeping me."

For an instant, he imagines taking her hand and tugging her a step closer, but he doesn't move.

"Do you ever miss it?" she asks.

"Miss what?"

She tilts her head, strands of hair brushing lightly against her cheek as she looks up at him. "The world outside."

As much as he resents this place, he knows there's not much waiting for him out there in the real world. Just temptation. Regret. Sofie had become so embedded in his life for so long there were few places that would be free of her memory. But then something does occur to him.

"I miss my work as a counselor. Sessions. Art therapy. It was meaningful."

"Art therapy," she says slowly, trying out the words like they're foreign. "What's that?"

He drapes himself against the staircase rail, his posture relaxing slightly. "Using art as a way to work through things—emotions, memories, trauma. It helped people. It helped me."

Her hands loosen where they've been clutching together, her fingers brushing her skirt as if she doesn't quite know what to do with them. "I think that's wonderful, using art to help people. It must have been hard to leave something you love like that."

He hadn't thought about it. Not since he'd decided anyway. Maybe because Dr. Okafor was so understanding and he knew he'd always have a home at Palms Waterside whenever he was ready to come back. It didn't feel like an end but a pause. But now that she mentions it, he wonders if a part of him has felt the loss. Suppressed it.

"A little," he admits after a beat. "I never really stopped to think about it."

She laughs softly, as if he'd made a joke.

"What?" he asks, curious.

"It's just funny, I guess. All we have is time to stop and think."

He chuckles, recognizing the irony. "Guess you're right."

Taking a small step closer, she idly rocks onto her heels then back onto her toes. "I understand though. Sometimes you don't know what you'll miss until it's gone."

"That's very insightful, Ez."

A smile lights her face at his acknowledgement. She's incandescent. "I can be sometimes," she says, her bashfulness wrestling with a bit of pride.

It sends a warm ache through him, one he knows he shouldn't entertain and yet can't ignore. "I knew you were clever," he teases, more flirtatious than it should be. "You pulled off a nearly flawless fruit smuggling operation."

Her laughter bursts out in warm, charmed waves, her cheeks blooming with color. "Shhh," she whispers, leaning in and pretending to shield her words as if guarding state secrets. "You'll blow my cover."

He grins, her amusement so infectious that he finds himself laughing too. In her buoyant joy, she almost tumbles against him. For a moment, the rest of the world narrows to their shared joke and the comfortable closeness between them.

"Ulysses."

The abrupt bark of his name jolts them upright, his heart pounding. When he looks up, Lang and the other Elders are marching in a neat line straight for his office and any lightness Ulysses's felt vanishes.

"A word?" Lang says.

It's obvious what he's fired up about. Ulysses looks at Ez, offering her a polite nod. "Goodnight."

"Goodnight," she says, a stitch of concern forming in her brow as her attention flits between the men and Ulysses.

He follows the men into Lang's office, his hands going numb as he wrings them together. The door barely closes before Zeke puffs up, squaring his shoulders to speak. "Father, I'd ask you to help settle a dispute."

"The floor is yours, Deacon."

He takes a step forward, addressing the men. "You'll remember that when Esme arrived here, I expressed an interest in assuming obligations owed by Mr. Perez and taking Esme into my household."

When she arrived here? Ez would have been…twelve? thirteen? He glances at Zeke, whose smugness has taken on a new, sickening hue.

"You mean you've had your eye on her since she was a child?" Ulysses asks, doing nothing to conceal his disgust. Mr. Perez must be Esme's father. Lang had mentioned all the time and energy they'd invested into her. Is that what this arrangement is about? Was that what he meant?

"Beg your pardon?" Brother Thomas says, as if Ulysses were out of line, positioning himself between Zeke and Ulysses and pressing a hostile finger against his chest. "His late wife was in failing health, and it made sense to look ahead."

Ulysses's hands curl into fists, ready to throw a punch if necessary. Ez had been handed over to the Order before she even had a chance to become her own person. And Zeke, waiting for his wife to die, watching Ez like some wolf circling prey, knowing one day she'd be his to defile.

She'd been sheltered, isolated, every decision made for her, every piece of her life orchestrated by others. The realization sinks in his gut. To act on anything he felt for her now, knowing how limited her choices had been, would be nothing short of selfish. It would make him no better than these men who sought to claim her.

"Gentlemen please," Lang says, raising his voice.

Thomas shrinks back, shaking out his hands like he's calming a fight that hasn't even started.

"The Steward wouldn't understand, Brother," Zeke spits. "This isn't the outside world where women run wild. We build families here." He turns to Lang. "Elaine has been gone for months now, and I've been waiting for the announcement, sir. I've been patient while our Steward has been carrying on with my betrothed, and tonight he had the gall to flout his disregard for your decision in all of our faces. This cannot stand, Father."

Lang holds up a hand and looks to Ulysses. "What do you have to say, son?"

"I haven't been carrying anything on other than protecting this young woman from an arrangement she clearly doesn't want. He's been inappropriate with her. How is that at all aligned to the Order's values?"

"Respectfully, sir." Brother Whitlock advances forward. "I saw the Steward and Esme alone in the chapel nights ago. I didn't mention it then because I didn't want to believe it was anything inappropriate, but given recent happenings, I have to come forward."

Ulysses scoffs, surveying the row of men, a firing squad of slighted leaders turning against him for his recent appointment to leadership above their ranks. "We were talking. Nothing more. And you have no room to talk, Whitlock. Just before dinner he was bragging about being intimate with the Chosen Daughters."

"Is that true?" Lang says with a note of shock.

"Of course not," Whitlock says, feigning disgust.

"Father, this is ridiculous. There's nothing going on between me and Ez."

"Enough," Lang says. "Deacon Zeke, Esme has not agreed to the arrangement."

A stunned silence falls over the Elders, their expressions shifting into collective shock. Brother Thomas furrows his brow. "Father, I don't remember us taking the whims of women into consideration when honoring a contract. Are you saying you've gone back on your word?"

Zeke's face flushes with barely controlled rage, his fingers twitching as if restraining the impulse to lunge across the room. The other Elders shift uncomfortably, a murmur of disagreement rippling through the three of them, emboldening Zeke to step forward.

"Father," Zeke begins, the word brimming with indignation, "I trusted your word. I agreed to take on a debt on faith that I would be given what was promised. This retraction undermines my standing. After all our years of loyal service, you make this outsider second in command. A man who thinks he's above our customs, disrupting our order and taking liberties with my fiancée."

"Fiancée," Ulysses mocks bitterly. "And what liberties? I've done nothing but treat Ez with respect, which is more than you can say."

Lang frowns, sizing the men up. "Enough," he says, his tone as final as a gavel, voice cold, carrying a sharpness that leaves no room for protest. "It seems I need to remind each of you exactly who holds authority in this Order."

Zeke's face shifts, a flash of fear breaking through his defiance. He opens his mouth as if to argue, but Lang raises his hand again, silencing him. "Did you think this was a democracy? You will not question my decision as if it were something subject to debate." Lang's words reverberate in the room. The tension thickens as he presses closer, his eyes fixed first on Zeke, then the other Elders who dared to murmur in agreement. "Don't talk about loyalty and obedience then stand here challenging my judgment. Let me make myself perfectly clear." He fixes Zeke and the other men with a hard stare. "The decision to bring Ulysses into the role of Steward was not made lightly. It was strategic."

He pauses, beginning to pace the office as if it were a stage. "As you well know, our Order has been expanding, positioning itself as a refuge. Path to Purpose isn't just a simple mission. It's a business and having a licensed counselor in our leadership, someone who holds real credentials, brings an undeniable credibility that reassures parents, donors, and anyone else who might have doubts about the legitimacy of our operation. Ulysses's experience instills confidence in our ability to reshape lives."

Ulysses's stomach twists as he listens. He'd thought his new role had been based on a long history and trust. Now, the realization settles in with an almost nauseating clarity—they'd used him. He was just a pawn to make the Order's program look credible.

"Tomorrow, Ulysses will accompany me on an assessment visit to Path to Purpose's assimilation facility."

"Assimilation facility?" Ulysses asks.

Lang turns to him, calculating. "Yes. For marketing purposes, it's called the Renewal Center, but in practice, it's a place to help new residents assimilate into our way of life. Before youth are welcomed into the community, we guide them at a separate site—preparing them, breaking down old habits, instilling discipline and humility. That way, they enter with open hearts and minds."

The words hit Ulysses hard as the purpose of this "separate site" sinks in, and he suddenly understands why he hadn't noticed any real unruliness. Their spirits were dead on arrival.

"In the meantime, let this serve as a reminder that my decisions stand. Deacon Zeke, you'll be compensated for the debt. But as for Esme, that arrangement is no longer viable."

Zeke's face darkens, the muscles in his jaw tensing as he struggles to maintain control. He casts a venomous glance at Ulysses before addressing Lang with barely veiled contempt. "Very well," he grits out, his tone simmering with resentment.

Lang's eyes narrow slightly, but he only inclines his head. "See that you remember who leads this Order, Deacon." He pauses, sweeping a glare over the men. "This meeting is over."

The men file out of the room, Ulysses noting their animosity-laden stares trained on him. He swallows hard, ruminating on the idea he's painted a bull's-eye on his back.

As Ulysses moves toward the door, Lang places a firm hand on his shoulder. "I kept my word, son. Now I need you to keep yours."

Chapter Thirteen

THE CHAPEL DOORS are propped open to let in the late afternoon breeze, and Ez crouches twenty feet in the air on the metal scaffolding, a lantern guiding her brush. She can almost hear the trumpets as she paints a golden horn pressed against an angel's lips. She'd done her best to follow Ulysses's method. Dark base. Light lines. *Suggesting* with a dry brush.

Yesterday, he'd taken the time to show her how to build up the light, layer by layer, how to find the right shades to make it look real. He used to teach an art class, he'd told her. *Imagine that,* she thinks. Learning from an actual art teacher.

Today, he'd gone off to attend to his responsibilities, entrusting her with the mural all alone. Her bristles flirt with the wall as her mind drifts to the flex of his tattooed arm. That man, she thinks, drawing in a deep wistful breath. That beautiful man.

"Ez, wow." Ulysses's voice carries from below. She hadn't heard him come in. Peering down, she finds him standing in the aisle, gazing up at her. "You really picked this up fast."

Heat creeps up her neck as she preens. "Guess I had a good teacher." She goes back to painting, humming quietly for only a moment before the dinner bell rings. How is it already six o'clock?

If Ulysses hadn't saved her, she'd be covered in food scraps and flour by now, feeling every minute, counting down until her tasks were done. But up here, the hours slip by unnoticed.

She climbs down, and as he helps gather her supplies, she notices something different in his demeanor, a heaviness she hasn't seen before. "You seem…" she starts, searching for the word. "Sad."

He gathers a drop cloth, folding it tightly against his chest. "It's just this place. It's been weighing on me."

She watches him, waiting, but that's all he offers. A sliver of truth, just enough to satisfy, but not enough to invite further questions.

"Is there anything I can do?"

He shifts the bundled cloth in his arms, already turning toward the vestry. "You're very sweet, but no. It's just the adjustment."

Sweet. The word lingers, making her steps lighter as she glides close behind him. His linen shirt, rumpled from the day's labor, moves with him, the air behind him laced with the scent of hard work. Not harsh, but cleaner somehow, tinged with something earthy and masculine. She breathes it in before she can stop herself.

It makes her head tilt, like she could find the answer if she only inhaled a little deeper. He stops short to shift the scaffolding, and she's so caught up in him that she nearly collides with his back.

He goes on. "Spent the afternoon coordinating work schedules with the Main House, the stables, the Youth Quarters. This place could use a golf cart."

She huffs a quiet chuckle. "You've walked every corner of this place today, haven't you?"

He hums in response, his weariness visible now in the slight drag of his movements. "Would've much rather been here painting with you." A pause. A quiet clearing of his throat. "But you've clearly got it under control. It's coming along beautifully."

Beautifully.

"Thanks. I hoped you'd like it. I appreciate you trusting me with it." She hesitates. "I just hope I didn't get you in trouble."

Ever since he was called away to the Elder Council, she's wondered. Had helping her cost him something?

He shakes his head as if to dismiss the idea. "No. Of course not."

"Good." She bites her lip. "I was worried. Father didn't look happy. Zeke either."

The memory of it seems to pass over him and his beard shifts where his jaw flexes. "Please, that wasn't your fault. I figured getting you away from that sleazeball might turn some heads. People here care too much about silly things like seating arrangements. They can think what they want. I don't regret anything."

They carry the last of the supplies to the vestry in silence. As she sets her brushes down, his voice breaks the quiet.

"Some good news came from that, actually." He glances at her. "I talked to Lang. He settled things."

She stops in place, turning to him. "Settled? You mean with Zeke?"

He raises his eyebrows, his mouth lifting in a small smile. "You don't have to marry him."

For a moment, she can't move, the words settling over her like a dream. Her heart swells, and before she can think better of it, she throws herself forward, wrapping her arms around him.

He stumbles back but catches her, his grip steady. Her palms press against his chest, warmth radiating through his shirt. Her fingers drift to his shoulders, then up, tracing the side of his neck.

"Thank you, Uly," she whispers, looking up at him. Without a second thought, she rises onto her toes, her lips brushing his in a soft, grateful kiss.

The kiss catches her breath, but it's his reaction that steals it entirely. In one blinding moment, his hands seize her neck, her waist —strong, commanding—pulling her so flush against him it's as if gravity itself shifts, forcing them together. It floods her with sensation. Ulysses's mouth on hers, his arms anchoring her, his body heat swallowing her whole. Enveloped by his strength, she's weightless. He draws back, shifts, crouches, his fingers gripping her thighs.

A small gasp escapes her as her feet leave the ground. Her heart races, fingers pressed into his firm shoulders as he strides forward with purpose. Their momentum halts with the cold vestry wall against her back. His mouth captures hers again, his kiss wild and zealous, as if he'd waited forever and couldn't survive another second of restraint. His body pins her in place and a low sound escapes him, something between a groan and a growl, as his arms tighten around her, letting her feel the restrained force of his power.

But then, just as suddenly as he kissed her, he pulls back.

The absence of him is a shock. Her feet hit the floor, unsteady beneath her, as he stumbles back a step. His breathing is ragged, his chest rising and falling like he's just run a marathon.

"Oh God," he mutters, his voice hoarse and full of anguish.

Ez blinks, dazed, her lips still tingling. She reaches for him, but he takes another step back, his hands raised as though to keep her at bay.

"Ez," he says, almost scolding. "We can't."

Her stomach plummets. "I… I don't understand."

He shakes his head, his fists on his hips as if to anchor himself. "I shouldn't have done that," he says, more to himself than to her. "I shouldn't have—" He cuts himself off, his jaw tightening as he struggles to catch his breath.

His panic douses the hot moment like ice water. She staggers back, pins and needles creeping up her neck.

"Ez, you're so special. Y-you're beautiful and talented, but, honey, the Order robbed you of so much. Education, freedom— everything you'd need to stand on your own. You think you know me, but this is all you know. I shouldn't have... I don't want to take advantage of you."

The impact of his words freezes her in place as a flush creeps up her neck, hot and mortifying. Unable to blink away the sting of her tears, a thick knot forms in her throat and she can barely get the words out. "So because all I've ever done is scrub floors and shell beans, I don't know what I feel?"

"I didn't mean it like that. I know this place isn't where you want to be. I know they've taken away things that matter to you." His voice stays annoyingly gentle as his hands rise in defense.

"You don't know anything," she says. "You think I don't know what I've lost because of this place? I was supposed to do things. I never wanted to be here. But it's not who I am. I thought you understood that, that you saw *me*."

He exhales slowly, the tension draining from his posture as his hands drop uselessly to his sides. His gaze flickers to the floor before rising again, his eyes soft in a way she can only see as pity. Before the tears come, before she does something reckless, like punch him for kissing her like that and then breaking her heart, she bolts outside.

Chapter Fourteen

LANTERNS GLOW from under the pole barn, where congregants gather around their tables. A cold sweat gathers at the back of her neck as she gets closer. Where is she supposed to sit? If she returns to her place beside Zeke, these lunatics might take it as a sign she wants to marry him. But if she doesn't sit next to Ulysses, surely people will notice. It will raise questions she doesn't want to answer.

I hate it here.

Maybe he'll have the decency not to show up for dinner, she prays, settling into the seat beside his. Across the table, Erma and her daughter, Mary, are locked in a quiet argument near Father's empty chair. It's difficult not to eavesdrop, but she focuses on the sound, getting only mumbles and hisses.

"Good evening, ma'am. Mary," she says, soft enough they don't seem to hear her.

Place settings have already been set, but something's out of place. A book. Her sketchbook. "Why is my sketchbook on the table?" she asks, a little louder than she'd expected.

There's a slight pause in the hum of conversation as Ez's voice cuts through the air. Heads turn toward her, making the hairs on the back of her neck stand on end.

"Oh, that," Erma says. She lounges back in her chair, the faintest smirk tugging at her mouth. "I found it lying around. Thought you might want to share it with everyone. Such a creative girl shouldn't keep her talents to herself, don't you think?"

Ez holds her breath. *Lying around?* She hadn't left it anywhere. She'd kept it hidden, tucked away under her mattress.

"You went through my things."

Erma's face hardens, her smirk giving way to a cold, imperious glare. "Of course not," she says. "But I'm so happy to have seen it. I'm grateful for the chance to witness the talent I've heard so much about."

Ez's stomach twists as Erma flips open the sketchbook. The motion is lazy, as though the book belongs to her. Her long, thin fingers spread the pages, and Ez's heart drops when she sees a drawing of an angel exposed to the light of the table.

"Look at this," Erma says loud enough for the entire table to hear with a mocking tone that sets Ez's teeth on edge. "Isn't this just precious?"

The table quiets, heads turning toward them. A few of the Chosen Daughters exchange hesitant glances, but no one speaks. Even Mary lowers her eyes, her lips pressed into a tight line, clearly unwilling to challenge her mother.

Erma continues, flipping to another page and holding it aloft like a schoolteacher showing a child's messy homework. "Angels and flowers," she says with a dramatic sigh, shaking her head as though disappointed.

A few of the men at the table chuckle quietly, their laughter like needles piercing Ez's skin. Zeke leans forward, his thin lips curling into a smirk before turning to Ez. "Sweetheart, you're a young woman now. You should be focusing on starting a family, not doodling in a notebook like a child."

The men's laughter grows louder, and though a sting rises to her eyes, a fire stokes in her belly. She wants to scream, to rip the book from Erma's hands and smack her across her stupid face with it. But they'll punish her. Beat her. So instead, she does her best to force their judgment out of her mind.

"Put it down," Ulysses says from behind her.

She doesn't dare turn her head to look at him.

"Oh, Ulysses," Erma says. She tilts her head, her tone turning saccharine. "We were just admiring your assistant's work."

"Put. It. Down," he says again, stepping into the light. His voice is low, steady, and colder than Ez has ever heard it.

The air at the table thickens, the sounds of the table's gossip dying off completely, but Ez can feel their judging eyes on her.

Erma gawks at Ulysses, lips parting like a fish, but doesn't move. When she just sits there, frozen, Ulysses lunges forward and yanks it from her himself. She recoils as if struck, eyes wide, while he hands Ez the sketchbook.

"I'm sorry," he says, but she doesn't look at him. Just his apology is enough to weaken her knees. If their eyes meet, she'll surely burst into tears before the earth opens up and eats her whole. She grabs her book and rises from the table in one fluid motion, her momentum carrying her straight into a march toward the Main House.

Ez rushes inside and back to her room, her heart raw and aching. She needs to escape, to free herself from the grip the Order has on her, squeezing tighter each day.

At the top of the stairs, she stops short. Father approaches from the opposite direction. Their eyes meet, but he isn't really there. He looks like a man who's just stumbled from an explosion, dazed and sifting through invisible wreckage.

"Father?" Her voice is careful. "Is everything okay?"

He doesn't answer. Doesn't even blink. He moves past her as if she's nothing but a ghost, his heavy footsteps thudding down the stairs behind her.

Fuck this place.

She slips through the doorway of the small room she shares with Kia, collapsing onto her narrow bed and curling up against the wall. Every word Ulysses said plays on repeat, digging in deeper until she can't hold back the tears and her shoulders shake with silent sobs.

Not much time passes before a gentle hand touches her arm.

"Are you okay?" Kia asks. Crouching to her knees at her bedside, she strokes Ez's arm. "Don't cry."

"I kissed him." Ez presses her lips together, tasting the salt.

"Kissed who?"

"Ulysses. The Steward. I'm so stupid."

"No, you're not." Kia wraps her arms around her. "It's going to be okay. I've got good news."

Ez draws back, nose clogged, scanning Kia's face. Even in the dark, she's radiant with pregnancy hormones. She smiles and widens her eyes as if she's about to burst if she doesn't let out this secret. "I told him."

She doesn't have to explain more for Ez to know exactly who she means and what he knows. Well, almost exactly. The baby's father, the mysterious man Kia refused to identify. She must have finally broken the news.

"What'd he say?"

"He wants me to keep it. He's going to leave his wife to take care of me."

"Oh, Kia," Ez says. It's not just that Kia carried on with a married man, but that she's naive enough to believe him when he says he'll leave his wife. "But you know how these men are. They say one thing and they do another."

"I know. But this is different. He's so happy. He loves me, and once I'm the one at his side, you won't have to worry about anything ever again. I'll take care of you."

Chapter Fifteen

WHEN THEY STEPPED into the converted strip mall, Ulysses braced for the grim austerity of an inquisition-style dungeon. Instead, polished wood floors and soft lighting greeted him. Modern leather furniture and well-placed plants gave the lobby a corporate feel, and behind the front desk, a sleek metal sign reading *Path to Purpose* glowed with a subtle, golden backlight. Somehow, finding a façade so polished—so completely at odds with what he knew of the Order's lifestyle—was more chilling than any dungeon.

A stout man with a clipboard appeared. Ulysses glanced at Lang, expecting him to make introductions, but he only stared past them. For a man who usually commanded attention, Lang seemed... off.

The man filled the silence. "I'm Carl, the site manager," he said with a tight smile and a faint chin that sloped seamlessly into his neck. "Welcome to the Renewal Center."

He shakes Carl's hand who gestures for them to follow.

They're guided into a colder, more clinical space beyond the lobby, where the intake process is explained: confiscating belongings, testing for drugs, and issuing uniforms. As Ulysses catches glimpses of teenagers in beige seated stiffly under watchful adult eyes, unease coils within him, heightened by the sight of a girl flinching under her handler's looming presence.

"Reintegration classes in session," the man says, catching Ulysses's attention.

Ulysses can't let the girl's fearful reaction go unaddressed. "Are they disciplined with physical punishment?"

"Discipline is part of the program, yes, but always within reason. The goal is to teach obedience, not to harm."

Ulysses's jaw tightens. The girl's thin shoulders stoop forward, her stare eerily blank. "And what does 'within reason' mean here?" Ulysses asks.

Lang's focus lingers on the girl behind the glass, her blank stare almost a mirror to his own. He clears his throat, the movement stiff, as though trying to push something down. "Discipline is always proportional to the behavior," he says, voice weary. "We ensure it's constructive, a way to guide these young people toward better choices. Remember, son, this is about building character and self-control. Surely you understand that from your previous work."

Ulysses doesn't respond immediately. What he saw wasn't guidance, it was distress. "I've found fear isn't the best teacher."

The site manager presses his clipboard to his company polo where the words *Path to Purpose* are embroidered in cheerful letters. "Of course, Steward. I understand this might look intense. But we have health and safety standards. Everything here is perfectly above board."

Though the Order didn't recognize the authority of the government, local sheriffs frequented the Order. Friends of Lang would shoot the shit, propped up against their fancy cruisers funded by the Order's tithes and, apparently, the profits of this teen internment camp. Keeping law enforcement's eyes averted from their compound was a way of assuring their independence. But as far as other people's children are involved, at least, Ulysses assumes there are some additional hoops to jump though.

"What about inspections? Has the state been here? Have they been to the compound?"

Lang sighs, as though Ulysses's incessant questions are a

personal affront to the organization. "Parents can send their children to private programs if they choose, and Florida has religious exemptions for faith-based residential programs like ours. But we're still required to meet certain standards."

"And who checks to make sure you're meeting those standards?"

"We do," Carl says, flashing a troubling grin.

Ulysses turns back to Lang with a look he hopes says, *Are you kidding me?* But for once, Lang stays silent.

No checks or balances. No oversight. "And how long are they kept here?"

"Until they're compliant, sir."

"How long is that?"

"We have two female recruits and one male recruit presently in residence ranging from two to six weeks in training," Carl says.

Recruits? As the tour progresses through cramped bunkrooms and an open-air shower room, it becomes clear that a more accurate term would be maximum security prisoners. A loud buzzing sound followed by a heavy metallic click signals the opening of a door. Teens are brought through in single file to their next approved location—the cafeteria. The men linger, observing as the teens shuffle through the line. The air is damp with steam, the swampy scent of cooked spinach in the air.

Lang turns to face him. "You want to reach them with a gentle hand, I know, but look at these kids." He gestures to a sullen hollow-eyed teen, spearing a spork at a lump of cornbread on a plastic tray. "This young man held his little brother at knifepoint. His family surrendered him to us."

Surrendered, he says, like when someone leaves an unruly dog at the pound. It makes bile rise up Ulysses's throat.

Lang continues. "They're beyond gentleness. Without this, they'll keep hurting themselves and everyone around them."

As the tour concludes, Lang challenges him. "This is the foundation of our work. The future of our faith. I'm willing to be deferential, as long as we see results. But you will be held accountable for the success of this program."

Ulysses doesn't respond. He can't. How can he take part in this?

But if he refuses, what will become of these kids when he walks away?

After their tour of the residential area, they leave Carl behind and Lang guides Ulysses to the administration area. "This will be your office."

The strangest thing about the place is that, despite the Order's rejection of technology, the room is equipped with all the technology one would expect in a normal modern office—a computer, phone, there's even a television mounted on the wall. "Now let me show you why the Path to Purpose program is so critical."

Lang sits at the desk and gestures for Ulysses to take the seat across from him. He opens the laptop, the keys clacking softly for a minute, his face bathed in the pale glow of the screen. The sight is oddly incongruous with every other image Ulysses has of Lang— like a time traveler out of place. He turns the laptop around. "This," Lang says, tapping the screen, "is why the Path to Purpose program is the most important thing we do."

Ulysses moves in closer to the screen, his brow furrowing as he scans. The totals are staggering. Millions of dollars. "You're telling me the families of these kids paid *this* much?"

"Not just the families. It's a combination of things—donations, grants, government benefits, insurance, and, of course, program fees. All tax-free. When people think they're contributing to something bigger than themselves, they give generously. The right cause can open all kinds of wallets. With you involved, the expertise we've been missing is going to take this number into the tens of millions."

Ulysses stares at the screen, still trying to make sense of it. Millions of dollars flowing into a program like this. It turns his stomach.

As the truck rumbles away from the facility, the kids' eerie stoicism lingers in Ulysses's mind. Lang veers off the highway and pulls into a *Git 'n Go*. Its discolored storefront bears the faded shadows of the words **ICE** and **CIGARETTES** smeared and half-erased by time. From the window, an erratic neon sign strobes

LIQUOR | SIDE ENTRANCE, casting a red, flickering glow that pulses with rancor.

"Need a few things," Lang says, stepping out and heading inside. Ulysses follows, grateful for the brief respite.

Inside, Lang heads straight for the counter, where the cashier stacks two cartons of cigarettes. Lang's fingers drum against the counter as the cashier rings him up, his usual ease replaced by a restless energy. He shoves a few bills over to the man at the register before picking at a pile of loose coins cupped in his palm. It's so strange. Back home Lang is almost a deity, but here, he's just a dude fumbling for exact change.

But the power the Order wielded wasn't divine or inherent, it was entirely self-made. Crowns they'd placed on their own heads, bolstered by titles they'd invented to mask their corruption. All of it a smokescreen to justify the unforgivable in exchange for power and wealth.

Ulysses ambles away from Lang, as if space might dull his anger, and he finds himself wandering down the aisles aimlessly.

It's bizarre being among civilization, even just a rural gas station, after months living like a homesteader. Their plain clothes, simple slacks and button-down shirts, compared to the vibrant colors and denim fabrics of others in the shop, the football jerseys and ornamented Crocs. Ulysses and Lang look like time travelers who've wandered in from before the industrial revolution.

It doesn't matter. They can cosplay all they want, but it changes nothing. The old temptations of home are here. Finding himself in front of a wall of refrigerated beer, he stares at the array of logos. Chilled air emanates from the case, and he imagines how nice a cold, sudsy drink would taste. How his skin would feel effervescent and light. His worries would, for a time, float away.

Then, of course, he'd peel himself off the floor the next morning and repeat that cycle until his life spiraled out of control. Struggle to get sober again. Rinse and repeat.

God, he's so tired of boarding that train. As much as he resents the Order, the light of hope narrowing by the day, he's safe there.

Protected from himself. Though what he might become if he stays is a different kind of danger.

He could run. He could even start over somewhere new. But Ez's tearful defense replays in his mind, reminding him how lucky he is to know how to run. All she knows is that cage. How could he leave her behind? How could he leave any of them to be victimized?

His mind travels back to that kiss. How he'd unintentionally humiliated her. His heart floods with an ache at the memory of her rushing from the vestry. Her gentle lips could have done him in, the temptation to take her so powerful he'd rebuked it and insulted her in the process. He hadn't meant to, yet he'd hurt her deeply.

Continuing down the row of cold cases, he finds a freezer stocked with pints of ice cream. He grabs two and, meeting Lang at the register, he sets them on the counter.

Lang eyes him with a smirk. "For Esme?" Lang asks, raising an eyebrow.

Ulysses scoffs, handing over a few bills to the cashier. "You make it sound like something it's not."

Lang chuckles softly, but there's an edge to it. "Oh, it's something. It's obvious you care for her, and if you don't act on it, someone else will." He pauses, looking at Ulysses with a hard, assessing gaze. "I can't keep a young, fertile woman unmarried because you're still figuring things out. You understand what I'm saying, son?"

Ulysses glances at the cashier, offering a tight smile before walking off, wondering how much of the conversation he heard, because the things that pass for small talk in the Order sound batshit crazy to anyone on the outside. They *are* batshit crazy. He pushes through the convenience store doors, jaw tightened, a spike of adrenaline triggered at the idea of Esme being bought and sold like livestock.

Outside, they stop on the sidewalk and Ulysses tries to be firm against the sleepy *whoosh* of passing cars. "If I wanted her hand, I'd ask her for it. Not you."

Lang claps a hand on Ulysses's shoulder, squeezing it with a possessive father's grip. "You're not a boy anymore, Ulysses. It's time to settle down. Build a home. Give the Order a future."

"I barely even—" he starts, but stops himself to take a breath, scraping his palm across his beard. He struggles not to lose his shit, but something in Lang's tone makes his pulse quicken. "Ez and I don't even know each other."

Lang shakes his head. "Look, I get it. You're conflicted. That's natural. But here's the reality—Ez owes a debt."

"What debt?"

"Her father sent her to us," he says, packing a box of cigarettes against the back of his hand. "But after a year, he stopped paying. Disappeared. We've cared for her for years, Ulysses. That support wasn't free."

They part ways and Ulysses trudges toward the passenger side of the truck. The idea that a church was keeping a ledger of an abandoned girl's debt makes him tear the door open harder than necessary. He slams it shut, and once Lang's inside, he challenges him.

"She's been working for you for years without pay. She doesn't owe you anything."

Lang sighs as he unravels the plastic wrapper from the pack, his tone patient, as if explaining something to a child. "Her work offsets some of it, yes. But not all. It's not that simple, son." He glances away, considering his next words carefully. "There are men who'd be willing to help clear her debt and give her a secure place. A future."

What kind of future? Ulysses wonders. They've already taken so much from her, from all the Chosen Daughters like her. Lang draws a cigarette from the box, pressing it between his lips, then lights it. It wiggles as he speaks.

"And once she's married, she'll be focused on what's important. No more late-night chapel rendezvous."

Ulysses shakes his head, his teeth gritted together at the implication. "Nothing happened." He'd made sure that it hadn't.

Lang's jaw twitches, and for a moment, his mask slips. "Do you think I was born yesterday?" he snaps, then pauses, drawing another drag from his cigarette, visibly reining himself back in. "You caused this mess with Zeke when I gave you what you asked for. The Elders are unhappy and that kind of unrest is dangerous for everyone." He takes another drag, his shoulders tightening. "It's bad timing. There are other situations I'm managing. Things that require stability." He sighs. "Adding fuel to the fire doesn't help anyone, Ulysses. Least of all you."

The truck's cabin fills with smoke, and Lang places a heavy hand on Ulysses's shoulder, his grip firm. "You're part of this family now. And with family, there are responsibilities. We all have roles to play."

The fatherly act is a lie, Ulysses knows that. Yet, after years of drifting, of fighting against his own demons, there's still a part of him that craves belonging. A purpose. Maybe even a family. He hates to admit it, but there's a pull, a small part of him that wants to believe Lang's words, that wants to stop fighting and simply fit in.

Lang glances at the ice cream, then back at Ulysses, a knowing glint in his eye. "Decide soon, son. Before someone else does it for you."

Chapter Sixteen

"WHAT ARE YOU DOING HERE?" Erma's question snaps Ez out of her thoughts, and she tenses, her fingers tightening on the broom she's been using to knock clusters of wasp nests from the porch rafters.

Erma's eyes narrow, analyzing Ez's nervous reaction. "I thought you had a special assignment from the Steward in the chapel."

Ez swallows, forcing herself to appear calm.

"He didn't need me today," she says, lying as smoothly as she can. The truth is, she'd rather risk getting stung by a mud dauber than see Ulysses after last night, after everything he'd said, hurting her in a way that didn't just sting but made her question who she was. She barely recognized herself in the mirror, sick with the realization that all the world saw when they looked at her was a dumb, broken girl who didn't know any better. The thought of seeing him again makes her want to collapse into herself. She's not ready yet. Not now.

Erma gives her a dubious look but eventually she loses interest, moving on with the other women trailing behind her. Ez lets out a breath, grateful to be alone, if only for a moment.

But then, as if summoned by her thoughts, Ulysses stops at the porch steps, and her heart skips. She forces herself to turn away, focusing on the broom in her hands, pretending she hasn't seen him. Maybe he'll just leave. Maybe—

"Ez," he says, freezing her in place.

She turns slowly, feeling every nerve in her body flare to life. His voice is gentle, cautious. "Can we talk?"

She hesitates, aware of the lingering women stealing curious glances their way. She doesn't want an audience for this. He flicks a quick look toward the chapel, then motions for her to follow, somewhere out of sight.

Inside, he reaches beneath a cabinet, pulling out a brown paper bag. When he opens it, she blinks in surprise—two small pints of ice cream, half-melted but real. Precious in a way that makes her heart ache. He'd heard her. He remembered.

"I got chocolate and strawberry, but it was chocolate, right?" he confirms, holding out a spoon.

A smile tugs at her lips despite herself. "Always chocolate."

He hands her the pint, and she peels off the lid carefully, as though it might disappear if she's not gentle. She can't remember the last time she had ice cream. She digs in, savoring the cool, creamy sweetness on her tongue, letting it melt there as though she could hold on to it forever. She sneaks a glance at him, watching as he takes a bite of his own, his eyes soft as he studies her.

Finally, he speaks, his voice tentative. "I wanted to apologize. For making assumptions about you. For saying things that made you feel less. I didn't mean that. It's the last thing I'd want."

She stops mid-bite, the spoon resting between her lips.

"But, Ez, I don't know if I'm the person you think I am. I don't want you to have a picture of me that isn't real." His look is serious, unflinching, and for a moment she feels silly with her mouth full of ice cream.

She pulls the spoon out, resting it beside her pint, and swallows. "I want to get to know you. Who you really are."

He exhales, a hint of something fragile in his eyes. "I'm an alcoholic, for starters."

Oh.

The admission hangs in the air, and she nods calmly, as if it's not even slightly surprising that he'd drop something so heavy just like that. But it is. Searching his face, she finds vulnerability there, like he's bracing himself and waiting for her to react.

She chooses her words carefully. "So, is that like…something you're working on?"

"Yeah. Six months sober."

"That's good. Is it something you have to fight every day? Like, wanting it?"

A weary smile tugs at his lips. "Some days are easier than others. But I work at it every day, because I don't like the person I become when I'm drinking."

She doesn't have experience with addiction, but she knows what it's like to battle something that feels too big to overcome. The kind of burdens that greet her at sunrise and tuck her into bed each night. "That must be hard. Having to fight it every day. But you're doing so good. You should be proud of that."

He responds with a tender look that feels like a *"thank you."* Setting his ice cream aside, he reaches over to take her hand, his thumb grazing her knuckles. For a moment, all she can feel is his gentle touch. It wakes something she hadn't realized was at rest, and not the kind of waking that slowly opens its eyes under the sunlight, but a jolt, the way shock paddles revive a dying man.

"You're very kind."

"I mean it. And you know," she starts, glancing down at their joined hands, her fingers curled around his. "Just 'cause you struggle with that stuff, it doesn't make me like you any less."

He shifts closer, the heat of his body nearer to hers. "Good."

They sit in silence, his thumb tracing slow, careful circles over her hand. Their eyes meet, her heart pounding like a drum.

"Ez, I'm so sorry. I never should've tried to make you doubt your feelings or make you think you don't know your own heart. I just didn't want to be like these men who take whatever they want without caring who they hurt."

"You're not like them. You're the only one who's ever asked me what I want."

"I did. And you told me. I should've listened. I'd like a chance to do better." He shifts, turning toward her, inching closer. "Would that be okay?"

The answer is so obvious, an unstoppable grin unfurls across her face. She's drawn to him, like the tide pulled by the moon. Their lips brush softly at first, careful, testing. But then his fingers thread through her hair, reeling her in, and their kiss deepens into something all-consuming.

The chapel pew creaks beneath them as they move together. He lets out a low, contented sound that rumbles against her lips, tingling up her spine and spreading like cool water over hot skin. The faint sweetness of strawberry ice cream lingers on his tongue. She tastes it, loses herself in it. And for a moment, she swears her soul tries to slip free from her body.

Rough hands drift down from her cheeks, resting gently on her waist, pulling her closer as if he can't bear to let any space remain between them. Her fingertips need to explore him, finding the hard planes of his chest, the firm curves of his biceps, the muscular ridges beneath his shirt. When they finally part, his hands cradle her face. It's as if he's seeing her in a way no one else ever has. "Remember how I said things move fast out in the world?"

She agrees, though she doesn't fully understand.

"There's one area where things move a lot slower than they do here."

"What do you mean?"

He sweeps her hair back, tucking it behind her ears. His fingertips trail down her arms before his hands settle in his lap. "I mean that I got you away from Zeke, but Lang's going to marry you off to the next highest bidder. I can't take that chance." He hesitates. "Ez, I'm not ready for marriage. We hardly know each other."

She hadn't realized that was even an option, but once the premise clicks, her body is certain. Even though he's right, they don't know each other well enough to make a lifelong commitment, the thought of another Zeke buying her to be his bride makes her queasy.

"But I want to protect you," he continues, "and I can't risk you being married off to someone else."

She blinks, her heart fluttering in her throat. "So does that mean…"

He reaches for her hand, clasping it gently. "I'd like to ask for your hand anyway."

She looks up, hope flickering to life. "Really?"

"Would that be okay?"

"Yes," she says, breathless. "Yes, that would be wonderful."

His face softens with relief. "I need you to understand, Ez, I can't make any guarantees. If this wasn't an emergency, I'd take you on a real date first. Let you get to know me for a while before, you know…" His voice trails off, leaving the rest unsaid.

A *real date*. A giddy laugh escapes her lips, a sound of pure joy. "What kind of date would you take me on?"

He grins, a glint of humor in his eyes. "An art museum. Then dinner by the gulf. We could watch the sunset."

Her heart swells, the image as beautiful as any dream she's ever imagined. "I'd love that." Warmth spreads in her chest as she squeezes his hand a little tighter. Ulysses, beautiful sweet gentle Ulysses, will be her husband. She could float right out of her shoes. He'd already fascinated her, but suddenly her curiosity has multiplied. "I want to know you," she says as excitement bubbles up. "Tell me everything."

Ulysses raises an eyebrow, a smile playing at the corner of his mouth. "Everything?"

"Yes!" She laughs, surprised at how bold she sounds. "I want to know all the things about you. Like your favorite food, your favorite color, what you were like when you were a little kid. Everything," she says, feeling a little embarrassed but unable to stop herself.

He chuckles, his thumb brushing over her knuckles in a slow, calming rhythm. "Alright," he says, his tone playful, "but you'll have to narrow it down. I wouldn't even know where to start."

She thinks for a moment, glancing at his hand in hers as she considers. Finally, she blurts, "What's your favorite food?"

He lets out a warm, easy laugh, his shoulders relaxing a little.

"Favorite food?" He tilts his head, like he's reaching back to a memory he hasn't touched in a long time. "Love a good salmon roll."

Ez's eyebrows shoot up, and she stares at him, baffled. "A what?"

"Salmon roll," he says, smiling at her reaction. "Sushi."

"Oh." She blinks, trying to picture it. "I don't know how to make that. But I can learn." The idea of preparing something so exotic is thrilling. "What about your family? Do you have any brothers or sisters?"

His smile slowly fades. "No. Well, yes but no. My sister…it's a long story but she disappeared when I was a kid."

Her stomach sinks and she curses herself for bringing up a topic that would darken the mood. "Oh no, I'm so sorry."

"You don't have to apologize. But family is kind of a sore subject for me."

She understands more than he knows. "Me too."

He was clear when he said he's not ready to be married, that he can't make any guarantees. But her heart can't help but hold out hope. "Maybe we can be each other's family."

The way Ulysses's shoulders sink ever so slightly makes her stomach twist. He shifts slightly, his hand still wrapped around hers, but his thumb has stopped its gentle tracing. For a moment, she worries she's said too much, moved too fast.

"Maybe. But, Ez, there's still a lot to know about each other."

Of course he's right. But it's been so dark for so long that she's holding on to this bit of light. "I know." She shakes her head, squeezing his hand a little tighter. "I know it's an emergency marriage. But I feel like we've been through so much, remember? Dark paths? Maybe we could make something good out of all of this."

He lets out a small sigh, looking down at their joined hands as if he's gathering his thoughts. Then something occurs to her. She doesn't want to upset him, but she needs to know and there won't be a better time to ask than right now. "Can I ask one more thing?"

"You can ask anything you want."

She hesitates, then asks the question that's been lingering on the edge of her mind. "That woman…the one who left?"

A dark cloud drifts over him. "Sofie."

"Yeah."

He sighs. "I wish I knew what happened. She never told me, she just left."

An ache swells in her chest at the thought of Ulysses finding himself abandoned. "That's not right. You don't just abandon someone without a word. Not when they matter to you." It was too easy for her father to forget she was ever born. She knows now it had nothing to do with her and everything to do with him.

"It's not the first time." He lets out a humorless laugh. "It's not even the second time. It's what she does when things get hard. She runs."

The words hit her like a strong gust, knocking her back a little. She almost regrets asking. This has happened before? More than once? The thought makes her heart sink. "What happens when she comes back?"

Ulysses's jaw tightens for a moment, his brow furrowing. "She won't," he says, meeting her eyes.

"How do you know?"

He shifts forward, his elbows resting on his knees as he rubs his palms together slowly, as though working out the words. She watches his demeanor change, like he knows why she's asking and doesn't like what it implies.

"I won't let her." He exhales sharply, dragging a hand through his hair, his posture slumping back. "It's not like I was perfect; the drinking had a lot to do with it before." He glances at her, and for a moment, she sees hesitation flicker in his eyes. "For a long time, I was carrying this enormous weight that no one outside our past could ever fully understand. The fear, the shame. We didn't even have to explain it to each other. We just knew. She was the only person in the world I didn't have to pretend with."

The pain in his voice cuts deep and she's struck by the realization that Ulysses and Sofie's history is a larger threat than she'd ever imagined. He looks at her, his eyes heavy, and Ez wraps her arms around herself.

"I thought that meant we were supposed to be together," he says. "Like we were the only two people who could ever make sense of the mess we'd both become. I thought it was fate, or destiny, or whatever you want to call it. But what I didn't see was that we weren't helping each other heal. We were just hurting each other in a way that felt familiar.

"When she came back this last time, I thought it was proof I'd been right all along, that all the drinking, all the pain, all the times she left and came back were leading to this moment where we'd finally figure it out. But nothing changed. She was still running from herself, and I was still breaking myself into pieces trying to hold her together."

He hesitates, lowering his head, his voice soft but steady. "I know why you're worried. But you don't have to worry about her. There are plenty of unknowns, but that's not one of them." His gaze lifts, meeting hers, and there's an earnestness in it that steadies her racing thoughts. "Ez, I promise you. If you're willing to give this, whatever this is, a chance, then so am I."

Her breath catches, his words sinking into her chest before effervescence rises—relief so overwhelming it feels like laughter and tears at once. Without thinking, she reaches up, her fingers grazing his cheek.

"I'm in," she whispers. "All in."

Chapter Seventeen

JAX LOOKS like he's already given up on himself. Battered knuckles, a stubborn set to his jaw, slouched in his chair like he's waiting for this to be over. Ulysses knows that look well. Sitting across from Jax in the Renewal Center feels like counseling a younger version of himself.

Closed off. Angry. So damn reckless it's a miracle he hasn't broken every bone in his body.

Ulysses relaxes in his chair, studying him. Adjusting his seat, he folds his hands on his knee, searching for a way in. "So," he says slowly, "wanna tell me why you decided the answer to your problems was punching through a window?"

Jax's eyes flicker to him—quick, dismissive—before dropping back to the floor. "Didn't have anything else to hit."

Ulysses resists the urge to crack a smile, not wanting to encourage the little smartass. The fact is, it's not funny, it's dangerous, and until Jax can rein in his anger issues, it would be irresponsible to move him into the Youth Quarters. "Yeah, I get that. But I'm guessing all you got out of it were stitches."

Jax shrugs, his face unreadable. Ulysses watches him, waiting.

He knows better than to push. Sometimes you have to give people space to open up on their own, but Jax's walls are fortified.

"Look, you hate it here. I don't blame you. But the sooner you can show us that you're not a danger to yourself and others, the sooner you can move on from here."

"Yeah, and go live in the fucking woods with you nutjobs. I'd rather beat my head against a wall."

It's the first time Jax has spoken this openly about his feelings toward the Order. The first time he's spoken much at all. His voice is still in that awkward stage where it dips too low one moment and cracks the next. Ulysses remembers that age. The weight of his trauma and self-contempt were only magnified by existing in a body he could no longer recognize or control. He understands. A heaviness swells in his chest.

He decides to try a different approach.

"When I leave our session today, I'm going back home," Ulysses says, "and I'm getting married."

"Whoop-de-doo," Jax mutters, though his eyes turn upward with the faintest trace of curiosity betraying him.

Ulysses rests his forearms on his knees, smiling slightly. "I'm not just making small talk, Jax. I have a point I'm getting to, hear me out." He pauses, collecting his thoughts, thinking about Ez and the strange, tangled mix of feelings she stirs in him. "I didn't expect to meet her. I didn't want anything to do with the Order, if I'm being honest, and I'm still on the fence. But remember when we talked about finding bright spots?"

Jax's defenses recede, just a fraction. Ulysses can tell he's listening, even if he would never admit it.

"The Order is far from perfect. I know that," Ulysses continues, choosing his words carefully. "But if you try—if you look hard enough—there are bright spots. People worth knowing. Things worth seeing." He pauses, looking Jax directly in the eye. "At the end of the day, Jax, you're going to thrive a hell of a lot better out in the sunshine, with other kids your age. And I'm working as hard as I can to make it a better place. For you. For everyone."

Jax looks away, a shadow passing over his face, his posture relaxing. "I just want to go home."

It hits Ulysses like a kick to the ribs. Before Jax joined them, he'd had an emotional meltdown, threatening to kill his little brother, holding a knife to his throat. The police were called, but after he was released from psychiatric hold, his parents didn't know what more to do. They sent him here, signed paperwork agreeing to no contact, to keep him here under Path to Purpose's religious instruction until he was of age to leave on his own. After a hefty "treatment program" fee, Jax was effectively theirs. There was no home to return to.

He forces himself to hold the teen's attention, to give him something real. "I know. And if that were an option, I'd gladly help you get there. But we've talked about this, Jax. This is where you are. You're stronger than you give yourself credit for. Channel that energy into building something that has meaning for you. I know it's not easy, but it's worth it."

Jax doesn't respond, but the tension in his posture eases just a bit. Ulysses takes it as a sign he'd at least planted a seed.

As Jax gets up to leave, Ulysses watches him go, his thoughts melancholy. The truth is, he doesn't know how much longer he can play along with the Order himself. But as long as they're responsible for kids like Jax, he has to find a way to stay true to his word.

This is all supposed to be part of a larger plan, a cause he's dedicated to support with irrational commitment, and yet he could piss himself every time he thinks of standing at the end of that aisle. Ez in a white dress gliding toward him. It's all happening so fast.

When he'd informed Lang that he'd asked for Ez's hand and she'd accepted, Ulysses expected a lengthy process, some kind of deliberation or formality. But he was caught off guard by the eagerness with which Lang had approved the union. Almost before he could blink, the wedding had been scheduled for that very week, hastily arranged for dusk in the chapel.

Ulysses had tried to push back, suggesting they take more time, but Lang had waved away his concerns with a dismissive smile. "No sense in waiting, Uly. You're a man of action. You want her, she's yours. That's the way it's supposed to be." And just like that, it was decided.

The more he thinks about it, the further the trap closes in around him. The Order has a way of claiming people, binding them up in commitments and promises. Debts. He wondered if Lang thought marrying Ez would be the final tether, the thing that would secure Ulysses's place there, too entangled to ever walk away.

But then he thinks of Ez, her bright smile and her quiet strength. She was the reason he'd agreed, the reason he doesn't pull back even as the Order rushes him forward. This is about protecting her, about giving her a life that's not dictated by the whims of men who only see her as a pawn.

Still, as he makes his way through the dim hallways of the Main House to see her before the ceremony, a small knot of doubt tightens in his stomach. Is he making the right choice, or is he letting himself get swept up in something he can't control?

When he finally reaches the door to the room where Ez is getting ready, he pauses, taking a deep breath. He knows he shouldn't be here and the women will scold him for daring to see his bride before the ceremony, but he needs to reassure himself. A final gut check before making one of the most insane decisions of his life.

As he enters the room, the Chosen Daughters cluster around Ez and gasp, one of them stepping forward to block his way. "Steward!" she whispers harshly, her brows knitting in disapproval. "You can't be here. This is supposed to be her time to prepare, and you're breaking with tradition by—"

"Just one minute," he interrupts, pleading. "I just need to talk to her. Please. Then I'll leave."

The woman scowls, muttering under her breath, but jerks her head, motioning for the others to shuffle out. They cast him disapproving glances as they go. When the door finally closes, Ulysses turns to Ez, feeling some of the tension in his shoulders ease the moment he sees her.

She stands by the mirror in a white lace dress, her hair pulled back in a loose braid. She looks both devastatingly beautiful and vulnerable, her fingers nervously fiddling with the fabric of her bodice. "Ulysses."

He edges forward, unsure what to do with his hands. "Ez," he says, awed. "You look…stunning."

She breaks into a smile. "You're not supposed to be here."

"I know. But I couldn't wait." He hesitates, searching her face. "Everything's happening so fast, and I just want to make sure we're doing the right thing."

Ez lets out a small, shaky laugh, looking down at her hands. "I didn't think we'd get here so quickly." She looks up. "But I'm sure, Ulysses. I'm sure about you."

Her words settle something inside him, a balm for wounds he hadn't realized were still bleeding. She has a way of doing that. But he knows better than to take it at face value. He's always been the fuckup, the one who couldn't quite get it right. No matter how hard he tried in the outside world, his failings followed him. It's a pattern he knows too well, a cycle he could never seem to break.

But with Ez, it's different. She looks at him like he's a hero, like he's something good, something solid. Like he can do no wrong. And even if she's naive for believing it, and he's just as naive for wanting to believe it too, it still makes him feel something he hasn't felt in…maybe ever. It makes him feel worthy.

He reaches out, taking her hands in his. As he looks into her eyes, there's a flicker of hope, a sense that maybe they could make something real out of this. Ulysses considers it, his thumb sweeping over her hand. He brings his face close to hers. "This marriage, it's for you, Ez. Not for Father or the Order. It's for you. Whatever happens now happens together. Okay?"

Her chest rises sharply with a held breath. "Okay."

The door creaks open, and one of the women pokes her head in. "Time's up. You've seen her. Now go so she can finish getting ready."

He glances at Ez, giving her hand one last squeeze. "I'll be waiting for you in the chapel."

Making his way toward the church, the weight of the decision strangely lifts from his shoulders. Lang might think he was binding him to the Order, that he was locking Ulysses into a life he couldn't escape. But Lang didn't understand one thing: Ulysses wasn't marrying Ez to stay, he was marrying her so they could leave *together*. But only after he could be sure the people he's leaving behind would be safe.

When he reaches the chapel, he takes a deep breath, steadying himself. He hears the low chatter of voices inside, the shuffling of people waiting for the ceremony to begin. As he pushes open the door and crosses into the dim, candle-lit space, heads turning toward him, he thinks about the weight of Ez's hand in his own, her dark eyes that reflected only goodness and worthiness, to remind him why he's here.

As she promenades between the pews in her lace veil, he draws in a breath. Real or not, permanent or temporary, in that moment his heart doesn't know a difference, and a sting rises to his eyes at their inscrutable fate. Esme. She's his bright spot, the thing that makes the darkness bearable. And as they stand before each other exchanging vows beneath Lang's watchful eye, the Chosen Daughters lining the chapel clutching their hand-picked bouquets, he makes her a silent promise, one that goes beyond any words spoken in this room.

Lifting her lace veil reveals her natural beauty, radiant like sunlight piercing through clouds. His palm settles on her cheek, tender and reverent, as he lowers his face to hers. They'd kissed before, here in this chapel, but the rapture of their lips meeting now, as husband and wife, is entirely new. It blinds him to the shadows of the past, leaving only her light. In that sacred moment, she is his beginning.

As Ulysses and Ez walk out of the chapel, hand in hand, they step outside into the twilight, the night air prickling his skin as he takes in the dimming sky. There's a moment of stillness, a brief respite as they stand together on the chapel steps. Ez squeezes his hand, and that same glimmer of warmth he'd tried to pass on to Jax in the bleak little counseling room courses through him.

Bright spots. He'd told Jax to look for them, to search for meaning, even in a place as dark as this. And here Ulysses is, finding his own in the woman at his side.

Ez rises on her toes, her voice barely a whisper. "What's my last name?"

He looks down at her, naked laughter breaking through. "Katsaros."

She tilts her head, curious. "Esme Katsaros."

Chapter Eighteen

THE ROOM IS BEAUTIFUL. Vases overflow with jasmine and hibiscus, filling the air with their delicate perfume. Candles flicker, casting warm light over the space the Chosen Daughters had carefully prepared for her—the space she now shares with Ulysses as husband and wife. It would almost feel romantic, if not for the Elders lurking in the hall outside.

Outside the Main House, the celebration continues. A spire of flames rises into the night, and through the window, the faint sound of chanting filters in. Prayers for fertility.

Blessings upon her womb. Blessings upon his seed.

Ez sits on the edge of the bed, fingers twisting in her lap. Ulysses closes the door behind him, hesitating. For a moment, he just looks at her, hand still on the handle like he's unsure what to do next. She can tell he's nervous too. Somehow, that makes her feel a little better.

"I'd overlooked this tradition," he says finally. "I guess kids don't really think about what happens after a wedding at a place like this."

Ez tries to steady her breath, but her heart races.

"Ez," he begins. There's a wrinkle in his brow, like he's picking his way through the words. "I, uh, I just want you to know you don't have to do anything tonight. Just because we're married now. I'll play along." He hesitates, glancing away before meeting her eyes again. "I know it all happened fast, and if you're not ready, that's okay."

It takes her a moment to find her voice. Of course the Elders are just outside the door. These people never let her have a moment to herself, not in a decade. But it doesn't matter. She's spent half her life being watched and judged. This is different. This is hers. Ulysses is hers.

"You don't want to?"

"No." Then, realizing how that sounds, he laughs nervously. "I mean, yes. I do. I just don't want you to feel like you have to."

A glint of worry flashes in his eyes. What can she say when she has no words for what she feels? At least, not words that would make sense. But she tries.

"I know it happened fast, and…" She trails off, feeling heat rush to her cheeks, but forces herself to go on. "I don't know much about this. But I know I want to be with you. I trust you. I don't feel scared when I'm with you."

A flutter in her belly and the quickening of her pulse call her a liar. A small, shaky laugh slips out as she glances up at him. "Well, maybe a little scared."

Ulysses softens in a way that makes her heart feel light. He takes her hand, letting it relax into his. "What are you scared of?" His thumb brushes over her palm, slow and careful.

The candlelight casts a warm glow over his face, the shadows framing him in a way she wasn't used to seeing. He looked gentle, his eyes deep lagoons, peaceful and serene.

"It's just," she whispers, barely able to look at him, "I don't know if I'll be any good."

He raises his hand to brush his thumb softly over her cheek. "You've never done this before?"

She shakes her head.

"Have you done…anything?" He dampens the question with a shrug and a subtle wince.

"No."

"Wow."

"Is that bad?"

"No. It's just, I don't think I've ever been someone's first."

Ez's cheeks flush even warmer as Ulysses's words settle between them. He holds her hand over his heart, keeping a strong and steady beat under her palm. The idea that she could be a first for him too, in some way, is a small comfort.

"I'm your first wife," she says, a teasing edge to her voice.

"That's true," he replies, his lips curving into a playful smile. "I've never made love to my wife before."

A thrill ripples through her. *Made love.* She can hardly draw in a breath at the thought of it.

Sitting back, he begins to unbutton his shirt. Each bit of him revealed makes her heart beat faster, a mixture of nerves and curiosity. Intricate tattoos swirl over his bare chest and arms, symbols she doesn't understand but can't look away from. There's a strength to him, his muscular body holding a kind of quiet power. Tracing over the muscles in his arms, the fine hair blanketing his torso, her hands itch to touch him.

Then she notices something out of place. A small patch of skin above his heart interrupts the tattoo—a pale, fresh scar. Her breath catches, not from nerves this time, but a strange ache at the thought of him getting hurt. This isn't some old scar from years ago. This was recent, like it's only just begun to settle into his skin. She can't help but wonder what kind of pain he must have gone through.

"What happened?"

Ulysses glances down and gives a wry smile. "I ran into a little… misunderstanding." His voice is light, like he's trying to brush it off, but there's something in his eyes that looks darker, a weight he's still carrying. "Long story."

Her hand trembles a little, but she lets her fingertips sweep over the edge of the scar, feeling the warmth of his skin under her touch. For a moment, his guard drops, and a kind of sadness or regret washes over him. He reaches out, delicately lifting her chin to look at him. "Let's not talk about that." He gives her a reassuring smile, his hands gliding down her sides, holding her at her waist. "Can I help you out of this?"

The look in his eyes, the tenderness she discovers there, steals her breath. She swallows hard. "There's buttons," she says, gesturing over her shoulder and twisting. He shifts slightly to sit at her back, his fingers beginning the delicate work of undoing her. With each inch of skin exposed, he presses a light kiss down her spine, each sending shivers through her. Heat flashes across her skin as he glides the fabric down her arms.

"I've thought about this, Ez," he murmurs, dragging the tip of his nose along her shoulder. "About you. Your soft skin."

His breath warms her ear. "Those deep, dark eyes on me."

He inhales her scent, his lips finding the crook of her neck. The heat of his mouth almost makes her gasp. He lingers there, traveling up to her ear, turning her bones to jelly. "I wanted you for myself. I can admit that now."

Goosebumps rise at the low timbre of his voice in her ear, and a deep, unfamiliar longing unfurls within her. She tilts her head, his breath warm against her neck. Her dress has already slipped from her shoulders, linen gathered at her waist. Cool air kisses her bare skin before his fingers do, skimming over the rosy peaks of her breasts and making her shiver.

With deliberate care, he guides her onto her back. His eyes move over her exposed skin with a sort of reverence, as though she's something sacred. He eases closer, his lips grazing the shell of her ear. "There's not a man here who deserves you. Me included."

She holds her breath, her heart thudding so hard she wonders if he can hear it. "Don't say that."

The linen at her waist loosens under his touch as his fingers gather the fabric. With a gentle tug, he slides it lower, raising her hips to guide the dress past her thighs. The motion is smooth, the fabric pooling onto the floor in a soft heap of white lace.

Her breaths grow shallow as she wonders what he'll do next. But whatever it will be, it's right. Like the universe had always planned this for them. Every injury she's endured, every wound, meant to lead her here, to this moment, to him.

His hands glide down her torso, fingertips tracing a delicate, absentminded circle over her skin. "You're so beautiful," he says, his voice barely above a whisper. "Inside and out. I mean it, Ez. I know we rushed this, but I want it to be real so bad."

She reaches up, her hand resting against the side of his face, her thumb stroking his cheekbone. "It is real," she says, her voice steady. "I was meant to be yours, Uly."

The words hit him like a spark to dry kindling and he lets out a low, pleased hum, his chest rising as he stares at her. "God I love to hear you say my name like that." He pulls back just slightly, enough to drink her in with his gaze—awed and hungry.

"Tell me you're mine. Say it again."

"I'm yours, Uly," she whispers, her voice trembling.

The corner of his mouth twitches with an almost imperceptible smile, his fingertips sprawled and dragged like a feather down her belly, making her suck in a sharp breath, forcing every muscle in her body not to squirm. His thumb grazes her bottom lip before his mouth captures hers, hard and unyielding. It's a kiss she pours every burning cell of her body into. His lips blaze a trail from jaw to neck and collarbone before he takes her breast into his mouth.

She's waited so long for her reward. Done everything that's been asked of her, suffered everything that's been forced on her. Ulysses, her husband, with his compassion and protection, is a gift from God.

The heat of his breath hovers by her navel, his lips dragging against the bone of her hip, her thighs, which, until he says, "Are you okay?" she hadn't realized she'd been squeezing so rigidly together.

Her eyes flutter as she draws in a deep breath, then exhales slowly, thinking through loosening every muscle and relaxing into the cotton blanket. He parts her legs, his mouth lingering danger-ously close to…

Oh my God. Sucking in a sharp gasp, her efforts to still herself are abandoned and she can't help but arch her back. This was not in the Order's marital curriculum, and it's so good, she wonders if it's even allowed, but she surrenders to it.

How is it possible to feel relief and torture at the same time? Surely if the other girls knew about this they would have told her. Closing her eyes, it's like she's floating in the mineral springs with the sun on her face, peaceful and relaxed, except something more, something stronger that grows and wanes with each movement of Ulysses's tongue.

She wants to curse. To shout. The Elders are lurking the halls for sounds of consummation, and women weren't meant to feel this much pleasure. She bites her hand, stifling the sounds she wants to make but she can't help but whimper. He's feasting on her like a man starved, with a hunger that feels insatiable. Each wave grows more powerful until she shudders, a strange but wonderful rush of bubbles flooding her brain. Her legs seize and she's light, buoyant. Her head flies up, realizing her seizing thighs could have suffocated him.

Considering the pleased grin on his face, he seems okay. Better than okay. His feathered breath falls against her and makes her quiver, and all she can manage in response is a giddy laugh. It's odd seeing him there, between her legs, studying her. He presses a final possessive kiss against her flesh before returning to her, face-to-face.

Their mouths meet in a sweet kiss, and she's taken by how connected she is to him right now. She'd married a near stranger, but he'd been so careful with her, she's not sure she's ever trusted anyone more. She didn't know it was possible to want someone this much, to crave him, to be desperate to connect with him. Her fingers move to unbutton his pants before her mind can catch up with her body. As his pants slide away, she sees him completely.

She's seen them before. Penises. Several, actually. All unsolicited. Her first instinct those times was to look away, to run away. But she can't take her eyes off him.

"Have you thought about me?" he asks, his voice dropping an octave as he strokes himself. The question, the way he looks at her, sends a chill through her.

Her voice wavers. "I thought about you a lot."

He beckons her with his free hand. She sits up, and his fingertips trail down her arm before curling around her hand, guiding it toward him in an unspoken invitation to touch. She pulls in a deep breath, hoping to settle the nerves vibrating under her skin, as her fingers brush against its length in soft, rhythmic strokes. Aside from being surprised at his skin's velvety feel, she wonders mid-motion if she's doing this right, a thought that makes her freeze for a split second, her cheeks warming. Wrapping her hand around him, she applies gentle pressure and mirrors the motion she'd just watched.

His eyes flutter and his breath hitches. There's an odd sense of power in watching his belly quiver under her touch. "Did you think about this?" she asks, looking up at him, a smile tugging at the corners of her mouth.

"After that night in the chapel, it was all I could think about," he says, moving toward her until there's nowhere left to go but down. Lowering himself over her, he hovers and they lock eyes. "I'll go slow."

Men of the Order take whatever they want without asking, but Ulysses is tender. Even so, she's surprised by the pain. They kiss as he inches into her, and she sucks in air. She'd been warned, but nothing prepared her for the sensation of being torn at the seam.

Ulysses lets out a long shaky breath, pressing deeper in a slow thrust until there's no space between them. The pain subsides, replaced with the pleasure of fullness. His mouth finds hers again, gentler this time. Her mind clears, focusing on the weight of him, all the deep places his rigidness touches as he rocks back and forth, making her whole.

Once he starts to move, she can't help but move with him, her body yielding to his like a brush to a canvas. After a while, it's like a dance—rise and fall, rise and fall. Feathering her fingertips down his back, everything else seems to disappear and it's just them in their cocoon. But there's something else. It's different from floating in the springs, but there's nothing she can compare it to. The part of watching him get lost in her, hearing his breath, feeling his pleasure as if it's her own.

She'd learned from the Order's teachings on marriage that lying together is like becoming one flesh. She'd always thought it was a metaphor for their lifetime connection, like Adam's rib or something like that. But now she sees it's real. It's physical and spiritual. She can feel it from her fingertips to her toes, electric light striking through darkness.

His hands grip her thighs, mouth at her breast as his movements lose rhythm. He seizes up, a pained sound escaping his lips as his heartbeat pulses inside her. He shudders, his face flush. Holding in place, he seems to catch his breath.

"Fuck," he says, and it's the first time she's ever heard him curse. "Fuck. *Fuck.*"

Second. Third. Each time growing in emphasis as he sits up and rakes a hand through his hair, his chest still heaving.

Her heart sinks.

Chapter Nineteen

"DID I DO SOMETHING WRONG?" she asks, eyes wide. She clutches the sheet, pulling it over her nakedness.

Once the euphoria of his climax ebbs, a swell of fear crashes into him. He's not sure how to explain the flurry of anxiety churning through his head. The point of this marriage was to give her a way out. To leave her options open once they've made it out into the world and she realizes that when stacked against her other options—men not addled with trauma and abandonment issues and addiction—she won't want Ulysses anymore.

But he wasn't thinking clearly. *This is the problem with abstinence,* he thinks. Weeks of pent-up tension clouded his judgment, and now, with his needs sated, the weight of his actions become terrifyingly clear.

He holds her, pulling her close to him. "I'm sorry. You didn't do anything wrong. If anything, you were very, *very* right."

Her fingers twist in the sheet as she tilts her head up to look at him, her wide eyes searching his face, then she sits up a little straighter, clutching the sheet tightly. She blinks at him, her lips parting slightly, but she doesn't say anything as he goes on.

"I should have been more careful."

"What do you mean?"

"Well," he says, trying to think of more tactful words and failing. "You haven't even had a chance to see what else is out there for you."

"But I don't need anything else. I'm happy with you."

Her words break something in him. He closes his eyes, his hands still cradling her face. "I didn't say that right," he whispers, his voice thick. "I just mean, you think this is enough now, but you don't know what the world has to offer. I want you to have the chance to choose. Not because of me. Not because of something we didn't plan for."

She studies him for a long moment, then lifts her chin. "Who's out there for me that you think is so special?"

It makes him laugh as he settles beside her. "It's not like I had anybody specific in mind. But I'm not exactly the best the world has to offer."

"You're kind, and you care about people. You really listen to them, and you always try to help. You're good, and you're mine. You're my husband. I don't care if the King of England comes knocking on the door and asks me to marry him—I'd still pick you, every time."

Her unwavering earnestness almost undoes him. He swallows hard, his hand tightening over hers, holding it against the steady thrum of his heartbeat. Ulysses doesn't say anything for a long moment, just pulls her close, wrapping her tight. The sheet rustles as they settle together in each other's arms.

"I'm sorry I ruined this for you. Your first time."

She shifts, tilting her head to look up at him. "You didn't ruin anything."

"Yes, I did." He sighs, dragging his hand gently through her hair. "I got in my own head, like I always do. I wanted it to be about you, but I couldn't stop thinking about everything else. That's just me, I guess. I get caught up in my own bullshit."

She presses her cheek over his heart. "I don't think it's bullshit. It was nice."

"It was nice," he agrees. "I don't deserve you."

She presses her cheek into his hand. "You deserve more than you think. You just don't let yourself see it."

For a fleeting moment, Ulysses lets himself buy into the hope she's offering him. He lets himself believe maybe she's right. Maybe this can work, they can make this real.

And then, there's a knock.

The sound jolts him, splintering their fragile moment. He tenses, every muscle in his body coiled tight as his mind races. What now?

Ulysses slips out of bed, fumbling to pull on his pants before turning toward the door. When he opens it, he's met with the sight of one of the Chosen Daughters standing in the dim hallway, a neatly folded bundle of fresh linens in her arms. Her presence is almost businesslike. Behind her, Lang, Zeke, Thomas, and Whitlock stand in a silent row.

Lang's gaze is piercing, his eyes sweeping over Ulysses as if he's judging whether he's fulfilled his marital duties to the Order's satisfaction.

Zeke's posture is stiff, and his eyes dart past Ulysses, straining to see into the room behind him. Ulysses catches the flicker of resentment there, the way Zeke's jaw tightens as though the act of restraint is physically painful. Ulysses knows exactly what he's looking for. The thought churns in Ulysses's gut, an unpleasant mix of pity and disgust. If their roles were reversed, if it were him standing in the hall while someone else deflowered the woman he'd pined after, he'd be humiliated.

But whatever pity he might feel for Zeke is quickly overshadowed by the invasive cruelty of this ritual.

The Chosen Daughter clears her throat, drawing his attention back to her. "I'm here for the linens," she says simply, her voice calm and practiced, as if this were no more significant than collecting the mail.

"The linens?"

"Tradition, son," Lang says, his tone measured and authoritative. "The congregation is waiting. Kia will replace them with fresh ones and then you'll have your privacy. I promise."

Lang's words are meant to sound reassuring, but all Ulysses can hear is the thinly veiled threat beneath them. He grips the edge of the doorframe, his knuckles white as his mind races. Every fiber of him wants to tell Lang, Zeke, all of them, to go to hell. That this is obscene. That they have no right to this moment. His lips part, the words burning at the back of his throat, but before he can speak, the woman shifts slightly.

"Ez," she calls gently, bending just enough to peek around Ulysses. Her tone is warm, careful, as though she's trying to soften the blow. "It's me."

"Kia?"

He looks back into the room where Ez is watching him now, still clutching a sheet for modesty, and when she catches sight of Kia, some of the tension in her shoulders melts away. She nods faintly, and Ulysses finally moves aside, opening the door enough for Kia to slip through before shutting it behind her.

"Hey," Kia says softly, approaching the bed. She crouches down next to Ez, her voice low enough to create a bubble of privacy despite the circumstances. "I'm sorry about this. They need the bed linen. It's stupid. I know."

"I'm glad they sent you," Ez says, shifting out of bed, still wrapped in a sheet.

Kia smiles faintly, her eyes warm. "I asked to come," she admits. "I didn't want them sending someone else in here. I figured this way, it'd be easier."

Ez agrees, running her hand over the sheet absently, smoothing out a crease. "It is," she says. "Thank you."

Kia starts to strip the bed with careful movements, pulling up the sheet the two of them had lain on. Ez watches for a moment then turns to Ulysses.

"Kia's my roommate," Ez explains. "Well, she *was*." She glances back at Kia, watching her work quickly, a wistful look crossing her face. "They're all out there waiting, huh?"

Kia doesn't look up. "Oh, you know they are," she whispers. "Nasty bitches."

Ez's head rolls back with silent laughter, and all Ulysses can do is observe, grateful for this small kindness. If they're going to be humiliated this way, at least it's Kia who makes it bearable.

As she folds the fabric in her hands, the slight smear of blood near the center catches his eye. Ez's lips part in the faintest exhale, her shoulders falling as though she'd been holding her breath this whole time. Ulysses notices the subtle shift, the way her fingers briefly tighten on the edge of the sheet she's clutching against herself before relaxing. A relieved look passes between Ez and Kia.

"Thank God," Kia says. She glances at Ez, and her relieved smile is met with a matching one from Ez. Finishing the fold with precise care, shielding the stain from view, she straightens, tucking the sheet under her arm, and exhales quietly. "They'll leave you alone now."

Ez's shoulders relax, the tension appearing to fully leave her. "Thanks, Kia," she says, her voice lighter than before.

"You're welcome, love. I'll see you in the morning." She turns, soiled linen folded over her arm and holds Ulysses in a stern glare.

"You take care of her."

"I will."

Kia returns to the hallway, presenting the stain to the men. Lang regards it with a smirk. "Good girl," he says, craning his neck to peek into the room around Ulysses. Ulysses shifts slightly, blocking most of the doorway with his broad shoulders, but Lang still manages to angle his head just enough to peer inside before turning to Ulysses. "You've done well."

It makes Ulysses's skin crawl, and he wants to tell Lang where he can shove his approval. But instead, he grits his teeth at the indignity of handing over a fluid-stained sheet like a trophy. He doesn't miss how Zeke winces, presented with the evidence of their deed. But now, having seen Ez's relief, it hits him. He'd been so focused on the absurdity of the ritual, he hadn't stopped to think about what might have happened if there hadn't been blood. What would they have done to her?

The door clicks shut, and Ulysses exhales. Returning to bed, he reaches out to touch Ez's shoulder, his fingers brushing against her sheet as he settles beside her, and he pulls her into his arms. She feels fragile, tension still thrumming beneath her skin. Once the congregation's chants and cheers at the sight of their bloodied sheet die down outside, Ulysses and Ez relax in their bed. But his thoughts are far from restful.

The assimilation center is the last place he wants his mind to be on his wedding night, and were it not for their perverse ritual, it probably wouldn't be. But the more he learns, the more he believes that allowing young people to be brought here to be molded by this bizarre cast is depraved.

"You seemed so relieved by the blood," he says.

Ez doesn't answer right away. When she does, her tone is flat, detached. "Have you ever seen a purification ceremony?"

He shakes his head.

"When a woman's declared impure," she says slowly, "she has to fast for a week. And then they do a bloodletting ceremony. To get the impurities out."

The barbarity of it unsettles him. What's worse is he knows Lang is smart enough not to believe this shit. "That's complete nonsense."

Ez doesn't flinch. Instead, she presses on, describing the ritual: A woman is brought before the congregation, made to disrobe. The prayers spill into the silent shame of her body. They open a vein in her arm, and blood pours into a vessel, as if it could carry away her sins. The vessel, set on fire, turns the room acrid with smoke. As Ez speaks, it becomes clear to Ulysses the Elders don't really believe in "cleansing," only in breaking these women—reminding them what happens when she fails to be virtuous.

He swallows hard, his thoughts churning. He doesn't remember any of these "traditions" from his childhood. His mother was never subjected to anything like this. She wore pants, studied astronomy, philosophy, and lived an independent life.

"I hate this place," Ulysses mumbles against Ez's hair. "I'd love to leave. To take you with me." He sighs, dragging a hand through his hair, resting it at the top of his head. "But there are kids here who've been hurt, left behind. They need help. They need someone to protect them."

Her fingertips twitch slightly against his side, like she's working through her own thoughts. "If you can protect them," she whispers finally, "you should. If you can keep them from feeling the way I did, the way I do sometimes…" Her voice trails off, and she doesn't finish the thought.

"I know I have to stay," he says after a moment. "As much as I want to take you and run, I can't. Not yet."

She traces a fingers softly against his chest. "I understand. I wish somebody had wanted to protect me."

It occurs to him he has no idea what happened to her. Only bits and pieces. He's not sure if he should ask, if she wants him to know, though the fact she's mentioned it makes him think maybe she wants to open that door. "Do you want to talk about it?"

"Nothing to talk about. My dad was never around much to begin with. When my mom died, I was left alone a lot. I ended up hanging around with people who got into trouble, and I got into some fights."

"That's a lot for a kid to go through. You must have felt so alone."

"I did," she admits. "But my dad didn't care. It was just easier to send me here and forget I exist."

He closes his eyes for a moment, his hand coming up to stroke her hair. The thought of her being abandoned, so young and left to fend for herself, makes his chest ache. He presses a kiss to the top of her head, his lips lingering.

"I'll never abandon you. Not as long as I'm breathing. I promise you."

She presses closer, curling against him like she's found something steady in him she doesn't want to let go of. "I believe you."

Three simple words, soft and sincere, unravel him completely. In trusting him with her most deeply rooted fear, the kind of pain that reshaped her and the betrayal that altered the course of her life, she handed him the most vulnerable part of herself. The weight of her faith in him leaves him awed and humbled. In that moment, he swears to himself he will never let her down.

She exhales, her body melting into his. "That scar. What happened?"

He sighs, the subject still as tender as the healing wound from months earlier. "Yeah. It was a mistake. A cop shot me, actually."

"Why?"

"He thought I was a bad guy. It was a misunderstanding. But I'm lucky—at least he didn't hit anything vital. It was a clean shot."

She traces a finger around the spot. "There's so much I don't know about you."

That's exactly what he's afraid of. He watches her delicate hand as it lingers over the jagged edge of the scar. A reminder of all the pain he's tried to bury and all the ugly parts of himself he's terrified she'll discover.

"We have a lifetime to learn each other." He rests his head back against the headboard and watches her as her eyes grow heavy. "Sleep," he says, pressing a kiss against her hair. "I've got you."

He lets himself enjoy the peace with her just a little while longer. The silence envelopes them, and the warm coziness of their bed delivers him into dreamless sleep.

Chapter Twenty

A BLOOD-CHILLING SCREAM shatters the stillness.

Ez's head jerks up, her wide eyes meeting his in the dark. Ulysses's heart slams against his ribs, a chill rushing down his back. He's already moving. The sheet is gone, his hands fumbling for his pants.

"Get dressed," he says sharply.

Ez scrambles to obey, her fingers shaking as she fumbles with her clothes. The scream still rings in his ears. His mind swarms with chaos as he yanks his shirt over his head.

By the time they rush into the hall, candlelight flickers through the dark, framing the others as they stir, their voices hushed and panicked. The air still carries the scent of charred wood from last night's festivities, sharpened by the bite of lamp fuel.

"What's going on?" Ez whispers, clinging to his arm.

"I don't know," he mutters, gripping her hand tightly. The muffled sound of sobbing rises over the whispers, raw and frantic. They follow it, his pulse hammering as they move toward the source.

They round the corner. A crowd hovers near the open bathroom door, lanterns in hand, their faces pale and stricken.

"What's going on?" he calls, pushing forward.

The moment barely registers before the scene hits him. A woman lies in the standing clawfoot tub, her face drained of life. Streaks of crimson drip down the white porcelain, pooling on the floor. The metallic scent clings to the air, thick and suffocating.

He stares, unable to believe what he's seeing—so surreal, so impossible that it takes a second to even recognize her.

Oh my God.

"Kia!" Ez screams.

Ulysses's arms snap open, blocking her view, shielding her. She lurches forward, but he grips her firmly, locking his arms around her waist as she struggles against him.

"I...I heard a noise. It was a loud thud," Mary says with a tremor. "I didn't know what it was. I found her like this." Her eyes glaze over, seeing something far more distant than the horror of the scene.

What happened? Why would this woman, who mere hours ago seemed overjoyed at her friend's wedding, who'd lovingly offered to help Ez and Ulysses through the awkwardness of the Order's ritual, choose to take her own life? He knows that what others show the world isn't always a reflection of the pain they might hold inside, but after all this time working with people in crisis, wouldn't he have seen it? It doesn't make sense.

The group of Daughters murmur, then Zeke, in his robe and slippers, chimes in. "Shame. Suicides won't enter the kingdom of heaven."

The sound of that man's voice alone could throw Ulysses into a rage, but his audacity to pass judgment while her body still lies warm in her own blood sends a rush of fire through Ulysses's veins.

"What the fuck is your problem?" Ulysses shouts without a second thought to hold his tongue. It elicits a round of gasps and murmurs from the onlookers.

"Steward!" Lang barks, approaching fast from the hall past the pajamaed Main House residents in his dress shirt and slacks. "May I remind you, you're in a house of God."

They're in a plantation mansion in rural Florida, he thinks to himself, drawing in a sharp breath. It's hardly a holy site.

"I would expect an outsider to slip so easily into his sinful ways," Zeke says, curling his lip. "Esme, the Lord would forgive you to not follow in your husband's example."

Esme sobs in Ulysses's comforting embrace as he glares at Zeke. "You will not address my wife," Ulysses says, his arms instinctively tightening around her. "Do not speak to her. Do not even look at her, you demented old fuck."

"Enough," Lang says. "Zeke, this is hardly the time for judgment. Ulysses, watch your mouth." He turns to the women gathered outside the bathroom door. Mary stands at the threshold, pale and stoic.

"This is a tragedy, but we must remain strong as a family. Let's focus on healing and prayer. I'll ensure everything is handled appropriately."

Lang turns back to Ulysses, his earlier edge dulled "See that Esme is comforted," Lang says, looking briefly to the bloodied floor before turning back to Ulysses. "She's been through enough already."

Ez's body shakes against Ulysses, her wails muffled against his chest.

"Yes, of course, Father."

Turning back to the Daughters and Elders gathered in the hall, Lang straightens his cuffs. "Let's not allow this tragedy to disrupt the good work we're doing here. We'll pray for her soul, but let us not dwell on sorrow."

* * *

THE DAYS after Kia's death pass in a suffocating haze. Ez drifts through them like a ghost, her smile and laughter gone entirely. She hardly eats, hardly speaks. Ulysses stays close, offering whatever comfort he can, but the light in her eyes has dimmed, snuffed out by the stark, unrelenting reality of this terrible place. No one wants to talk about what happened. The whispers die the moment Lang enters the room, and any questions are swallowed up by the community's need to move forward without looking back.

On the fifth morning, over breakfast, the silence finally breaks. The dining room smells of burnt biscuits, the usual sounds of cutlery scraping against plates louder than ever in the absence of conversation. Mary speaks first. "The girls have been asking about a service. Have you selected a date, Father?"

Lang doesn't hesitate. "There won't be a service," he says, his tone clipped.

Across the table, Esme flinches, her hands going still in her lap, a faint break in her otherwise catatonic state. Ulysses straightens, staring at Lang as though he hasn't heard him correctly. "What?"

Lang exhales slowly, setting his fork down with deliberate care, as though the conversation itself is a nuisance. "Suicide is an affront to God. We cannot glorify that, no matter how painful this is for those left behind. To do so would endanger the spiritual health of the entire community."

"She was loved," Ulysses says, jaw tightening as anger coils tighter around his heart. "She mattered to people here. You can't just pretend she didn't exist."

Lang's eyes narrow, his tone growing harder. "As usual, you're emotional, Ulysses. This isn't about what you or Esme want. It's about what's best for the community. My decision is final."

For a moment, the room is still, the air thick with unspoken tension. Ulysses opens his mouth to argue again, but before he can, the sudden clatter of Esme's spoon hitting the table breaks the silence. Every head turns to her as she stands abruptly, her hands trembling at her sides. She doesn't look at anyone, her shoulders rising and falling with uneven breaths. Then, with a sudden jerking motion, she grabs her teacup and hurls it across the room. It shatters against the far wall, the sharp sound of splintered china reverberating through the stunned room. The liquid from the cup splatters down the floral wallpaper.

No one speaks. No one moves.

Esme's whole frame pulsates, her cheeks tinged pink. Then she turns on her heel and storms out of the room, her footsteps echoing down the hall and up the stairs. A door slams, and a few seconds later, a muffled scream rings out from the hallway, raw and primal. The sound makes the room shift uncomfortably.

Ulysses pushes back his chair, the legs scraping loudly against the floor. He rises, his gaze darting between the door Ez stormed through and Lang, who sits unbothered, cutting into his food with infuriating precision. He strides out, the weight of the room's collective stares trailing behind him.

Zeke calls out to him. "You need to get control of your wife. She's embarrassing herself, and you."

Ulysses freezes for half a second, his hands clenching into fists. He doesn't trust himself to look at Zeke. If he does, he might not stop at words. He's supposed to be strong for her, for everyone. But each time he sees Lang's smug expression, hears Zeke's venomous words, it chips away at his resolve. How much longer can he pretend this place is salvageable?

The hallway is quieter now, but he hears her upstairs—the faint creak of floorboards followed by muffled sobs. He takes the stairs two at a time, pausing briefly outside their door. "Ez," he calls softly, his knuckles rapping lightly against the wood. No response.

Trying the handle, the door gives way, revealing her curled on the bed, her back to the door, motionless except for the faint trembling of her shoulders. Her face is buried in the pillow, and her breaths come sharp and uneven. He sits on the edge of the bed, the mattress dipping under his weight. "Honey."

She doesn't move.

"I'm here," he says. "Whatever you need, I'm here."

Still nothing.

He's supposed to know how to help people. But here, now, with Ez retreating further into herself, he's powerless. He slips off his shoes and slides into bed beside her, gathering her into his arms.

"We don't have to talk. Is it okay if I hold you?"

For a moment, he thinks she won't answer. Then she responds with a faint hum, her face still hidden in the pillow. He rests his chin against the top of her head, holding her tightly as her breathing hitches. Whatever is breaking inside her, he can't reach it. Not yet.

He knows Lang expects him to tend to his responsibilities today, to handle the youth program, to keep things running. But the idea of letting her go, of stepping away and walking out the door seems cruel. He can't leave her alone like this.

She needs air. She needs to get out of this house, away from this place, from the people who have only made everything worse. And maybe he does too.

He'll take her to work with him. Just for a few hours. She's barely seen the world outside these walls, and maybe a change of scenery will help. After, he could take her to lunch, run some errands, something simple. At the very least, it'll give him a chance to watch over her. Of course Lang will watch their comings and goings like a hawk, but for now, Ulysses doesn't care. Let him notice. Let him question.

He presses a kiss to the top of her head and Ez's sobs begin to subside, her breathing slowing as her body softens against him. "Let's get out of here for a bit," he says gently, fingers combing through her hair. "No pressure, no talking if you don't want to. Just a break."

For a long moment, there's no response. Then she shifts, offering a subtle dip of her chin in agreement and relief floods through him.

"Take your time getting ready. I'll wait."

She doesn't answer, but that small movement is enough. It's a start.

Chapter Twenty-One

THE BLOOD WON'T LEAVE her. The tub, the stillness of Kia's body, the lifelessness in her eyes. Every time Ez blinks, the images rush back.

She should be happy. On any other day, she would be overjoyed to ride in a car, to feel the wind on her skin, to watch the world blur past her. She should be reveling in the relief of never having to serve under Erma's oppressive supervision again. That alone should be enough to fill her with a lifetime of happiness.

But Kia is dead, and nothing makes sense.

Ez spends the morning in Ulysses's office. Before today, she didn't even know this building existed. There's a desk, a sofa, and things she hasn't seen in years. Things forbidden for women to touch. A television. A computer. A phone.

She sits stiffly, hands clasped in her lap, while Ulysses types away at his desk. The click of keys, the faint smell of coffee, the shifting sunlight through the blinds—mundane details she clings to, desperate for something solid. But it doesn't work. Her stomach churns with the same question over and over: What really happened to Kia?

"You okay?"

Ulysses's voice cuts through the fog. She startles slightly, looking up to find him watching her, his brow furrowed.

"I'm fine."

He doesn't look convinced, but he doesn't press. Instead, he leans back, rubbing a hand over his face. "We don't have to stay much longer. I just need to wrap up a few things."

Ez nods stiffly, eyes fixed on the floor. Ulysses turns back to the computer, the soft clicking filling the silence. She folds her arms tightly across her stomach, as if that could quiet the twisting inside her.

Should she say something? Could she? The words hover on the edge of her tongue, but the weight of them, the consequences, clamp her jaw shut. If she told him what she suspects…

No. Not yet.

Later, in the passenger seat of Ulysses's Jeep, the last conversations she had with Kia swirl in her mind. She was the happiest she'd ever been. If something were wrong, Ez would have known. They shared everything. Kia was the first person Ez thought of when something good happened.

God requires there be no secrets between husband and wife. Ez wants to honor Ulysses in every way possible. But the weight of what she knows feels too big to say out loud. Yet keeping it inside is like swallowing poison.

* * *

THE MENU IS JUST a jumble of letters. A mess of nonsensical shapes. Ez stares at the page, her breath quickening. Ulysses is going to ask her what she wants. She squints, searching for anything familiar. Pizza. Chicken. Those stand out, but the rest? *Tusca… ana. Mar… mar… sa.* The letters might as well be shifting on the page just to mock her.

The restaurant hums around her—low music, clinking glasses, quiet bursts of laughter from nearby tables. The air smells like garlic and warm bread. She should be excited. She's in a real restaurant, sitting in a booth beside Ulysses, about to order a meal she didn't have to cook herself.

It's not like she can't read. She can. And it's not like she's never eaten at a restaurant. She has. But she was just a kid then, and it's been a decade since anyone's expected her to read anything more than a recipe. A lump rises in her throat. She shoves the menu away with a clipped, "I'll have whatever you have."

Ulysses turns to her, but she refuses to meet his eyes. She doesn't want to see what's in them. Pity. Disappointment. Understanding. Any of it would be too much.

"Are you sure?" His voice is gentle, almost drowned out by the restaurant noise.

She blinks fast, a rogue tear slips free before she can stop it. She wipes it away just as fast, pretending to adjust her hair.

Ulysses watches her carefully. Then, just as gently, he moves her hair off her shoulder. "Do you want to go?"

What she wants is to scream. Cry. Her best friend is dead. Ulysses is letting her experience things she's only dreamed about and it should feel magical, but she's numb. The Order did this. The Order ruined her.

"No," she says, almost a whisper. "Thank you for bringing me here."

"Of course," he says, returning to his menu. "Do you like pizza?"

She's almost forgotten what proper pizza tastes like. Her seventh grade English class won a pizza party once for reading more books than any other class in the school. She used to read books. Stacks of them. Now she can barely read a menu. A sting rises to her eyes. "Pizza's good."

Holding it in, she wills every muscle in her body to still. To stop. To hold together. The waiter comes and Ulysses orders. She catches the words *pizza* and *margarita*. The word takes her back to a sip she'd had of her mom's margarita, back before the cancer changed everything. It was sweet and salty, and the tang of alcohol warmed her tongue. That memory stirs another, the day Ulysses proposed in the chapel, how he'd confessed his struggles with alcohol. How he fights the urges every day. The waiter disappears and Ez leans closer. Has he been struggling under the weight of this week as much as she has?

"You ordered a margarita?"

"Margherita pizza."

She wasn't sure how it was possible to mix the two. "Does it… have alcohol in it?"

"No, honey, it's a different kind of margherita," he says, his smile warm but restrained, like he's trying not to make a big deal of it. But despite his effort, a familiar heat rises in her cheeks. She acts as if she understands and forces a tight smile, but only because there's no energy to struggle through this, not with Kia's lifeless eyes burned into her mind, not with the things her best friend might have seen before she died, churning in Ez's gut.

Ulysses leans closer. "Hey," he says, low and coaxing, tilting his head to catch her eye. "I appreciate that you were listening, and that you were looking out for me. That's sweet." Ulysses leans closer until his lips meet hers.

It's a lovely kiss, and she appreciates that he's trying to comfort her, but as far as romantic feelings go, her heart is a clod of dirt. She sips her soda, sharp syrupy bubbles making her eyes water. But even as she swallows, the feeling sours. Kia won't ever drink soda, and Ez can never tell her about her night with Ulysses, or how she rode in a car and ate at a restaurant. She'll never tell her anything again.

The waiter sets the pizza on their table, and it's a work of art— an imperfect circle of vibrant tomato, melted cheese, and fragrant basil. She doesn't do it on purpose, but a sigh escapes her, her shoulders falling. Once she realizes it, she straightens up to not appear ungrateful. Turning to Ulysses, she sees he's watching her. She looks away, forcing her hands to still, pressing her palms flat against the smooth fabric of her dress.

"I'm sorry. I'm okay," she assures him.

Ulysses studies her for a moment, his brow furrowing slightly. "You don't have to be," he says. "It's okay to feel sad. Or angry. Or both."

Ez finally looks at him, spiritless, her grief an anchor plummeting to her depths. "I don't even know what I feel," she admits, the words slipping out before she can stop them. "Kia's gone, and I can't—" She stops herself, swallowing hard, the rest of the sentence dying in her throat.

"You can't make sense of it," Ulysses finishes for her, tucking a lock of hair behind her ear. He leans back slightly, giving her space. "Because it doesn't make sense. It's not fair. It's not right. And you're allowed to feel that."

Ez presses her lips together, her throat burning. She doesn't respond right away, doesn't know if Kia would want her to honor this secret or if her responsibility to Ulysses makes it necessary to reveal, but she can't hold it in. The way he's looking at her with compassion and understanding, inviting her to put the weight she's been holding in his hands.

"Remember how I brought her fruit?"

He nods, attention honed on her.

"She wasn't just hungry," she says, her mind at war with itself until the words finally leave her mouth. "She was pregnant."

He holds perfectly still, the information freezing him in place as horror flashes in his eyes. "Oh my God."

"She was so excited, Uly. It doesn't make sense. She didn't want to die."

He wipes his hands with a napkin, eyes going distant. "She was pregnant," he says, tone laced with disbelief. "How do you know?"

"She told me. I promised I'd keep it a secret until she was ready."

Ulysses leans forward slightly, careful now. "Did she tell you who the father was?"

Ez looks down at her lap, her throat tightening. She hadn't expected him to ask, though she should have. It's the first thing anyone would wonder. The name gets lodged in her throat, threatens to choke her, but if she speaks it, there'd be no taking it back. What if he doesn't understand?

"She told him," she says softly, avoiding his eyes. "And me. That's it."

Ulysses's brow furrows, his attention sharpening. "So he knew?"

Ez's hands twist together. "She said he promised to take care of her. That he'd make things right." She hesitates, trembling as she forces herself to keep going. "She loved him, Uly. She really believed he'd protect her."

Ulysses's jaw tightens, his hand curling into a loose fist on the table. "Ez," he says, her name loaded with caution, "who was it?"

Her breath catches, and she shakes her head, tears pricking her eyes. "I don't know what happens if I tell you," she whispers.

"You can trust me."

Ez takes a shaky breath, her fingers woven together. "It was Father."

She watches the name hit him like a physical blow, how he flinches and turns away in disbelief. Hunching over, he rubs his forehead as if the thought itself is painful before turning back to her. "Are you sure?"

"Yes. That's what she told me."

"And she wouldn't lie?"

"What? No," Ez snaps, surprising herself. But she doesn't pull it back. "She wouldn't lie about something like that."

Her mind goes back to that night. The night Ez and Ulysses kissed and he rejected her. The same night Erma stole her sketchbook. The culmination of embarrassment and heartbreak had made her sick enough to skip dinner and rush upstairs, where she'd passed Father heading downstairs, shell-shocked and in a daze having just learned his misdeeds had life-altering consequences.

That night, Kia's words had spilled like water from a faucet. Now, Ez tells Ulysses as much as she can remember. "It started after a sermon. Kia knew something was different from the way he looked at her from across the chapel. She wondered if she just imagined it, but then Father woke her one night, and told her that she came to him in a dream. Said it was a vision from God. That's when it started, she said, but it went on for months. After sermons, sneaking away to meet in his office."

Telling him now, Ez can't believe she didn't notice. All that time, Ez and Kia were so close. How could she not see what was happening?

"When the baby comes," Kia had said, "everything will be different."

The memory of her voice is almost too much to bear. She was so hopeful about the future. Kia wouldn't do this. Now, waiting for Ulysses to respond, Ez's insides twist with unease.

Ulysses hisses a breath through his teeth, his face falling into his hands. "That piece of shit," he mutters, almost to himself. "Ez, I'm so sorry. It's just—I can't believe it." He shakes his head. "I mean I can, but God, I'm such a fucking idiot."

"Stop it," Ez says sharply.

"Not just with Lang, but with this place. I knew not to trust him, and still I pushed past every instinct. It was like watching my own execution and I didn't do anything to stop it." His anger accelerates slowly, but whatever is brewing inside him has its foot on the gas and it's gaining momentum fast. She shrinks into the booth, her teeth gnawing at her bottom lip.

He laughs bitterly, a humorless sound that makes her flinch. "It's pathetic how easily I bought into this stupid fucking father-son thing. You know, because I didn't know my father and I—" His words catch just slightly before he cuts himself off. He glances around the room, at the other tables, and draws in a deep, shuddering breath.

She's never seen him like this before. Wounded. Spiraling out of control.

"I'm sorry," he mutters, straightening slightly as he pulls out his wallet. He flips it open, counts out a few bills, and tosses them on the table with too much force, the edges crumpling as they land. "We need to go."

"Okay," she says, abandoning their pizza.

Ulysses is already halfway to the door before she can move. He walks fast, his shoulders tense, pacing ahead of her. She trails behind, unsure if she should try to catch up, until she sees him climb into the driver's seat. It's as if the ground disappears and she's suddenly in a free fall. Just for a moment, she thinks he might leave without her. She sprints to the passenger door and slips inside, breathless.

His hands grip the steering wheel so tightly his knuckles whiten, and as soon as the tires hit the asphalt, he picks up where he left off, his voice low but venomous.

"You know, it's important that you find out who you married," he says, staring straight ahead, his words bitter and hard. "And this is it. This idiot here."

Ez doesn't respond. She doesn't know if she could even if she wanted to.

"I was fucking elated," he continues, louder now, then faltering with disgust. "And I hated myself for how elated I was that Lang was proud of me. That he put me in this meaningless-fucking-position." His grip on the wheel tightens, his jaw flexing. "What a joke."

Ez watches him carefully, her hands clasped tightly in her lap, unsure if she should speak or just let him tire himself out.

"Probably because he realized he could use me," Ulysses says, colder. "Because, oh, look, here's a licensed mental health counselor. Here's someone he can use to legitimize this fucking internment camp for kids he's running. I won't be shocked by how insane the Order is because I've already lived through it. And I bought it. I'm so fucking stupid."

He hisses the last word like it physically hurts to say it. His foot presses a little harder on the gas and the car picks up speed, the air inside the cab growing heavier with each word.

She wants to reach out, to touch his arm, to say something—anything—that might steady him, but the thunder in his voice keeps her frozen in place.

Chapter Twenty-Two

HE SHOULD HAVE BLOWN Lang's head off when he had the chance.

Thoughts of destruction burn through his mind as the Jeep's tires skim the asphalt like a stone skipping water. The compound is close now, but Ulysses is far from solid ground, his thoughts careening in a blur. Every nerve in his body screams for sedation.

He believes Ez. Ulysses knows it's the most obvious conclusion. He remembers sitting in a public health seminar, stunned as the presenter clicked to the next slide. Homicide. The leading cause of death for pregnant women in this country. It felt impossible then, and he was desperate to disprove it, sickened to confirm it.

At the hands of men.

Men who claim to value life. Men who sermonize about its preciousness until it threatens to complicate their own.

And Lang. Lang wasn't just one of them. He was worse. He'd shielded himself in righteousness, used God like a weapon, only to prove himself a coward.

That flickering neon sign **LIQUOR | SIDE ENTRANCE** strobes behind his eyes. He can taste it. Feel it rippling over his skin, warm and calm like slipping into a bath. Something to numb the pain of his stupidity. To destroy himself for being so gullible.

"Uly," Ez whimpers.

He turns his head. She's gripping tight to the oh-shit handle, her other hand braced against the seat. Her chest rises and falls in shallow gasps, and her cheeks are streaked with tears.

"Please slow down."

The air rushes out of him, as if someone had punched him in the gut. She looks terrified. Terrified of him. Of his spiraling rage and the way he's letting it consume him.

His grip on the steering wheel loosens slightly, and he eases his foot off the gas. "I'm sorry."

What the hell is he doing? Ez just lost her best friend. Her world has been cracked open, the one person who truly understood her ripped away. And now here he is, barely keeping it together, frightening the one person he's supposed to protect.

He exhales. "I'm sorry."

Ez wipes her face, her voice steady despite the raw edge of grief.

"He didn't just lie to you. Father lied to everyone. He fooled *everyone*. This isn't about you."

"I know it's not," he says with a sigh. She's right. A prickle of pins and needles tingle up his neck, and he scrubs a hand down his beard. "I'm so sorry. How about we stop and let me cool off a little before we go back. Okay? Before I end up doing something even more stupid."

"Okay," she says, seeming relieved.

* * *

DOWN SLEEPY COUNTRY roads he barely recognizes, without a GPS to guide him, he drives aimlessly until a road sign for a nature preserve catches his eye—**Cockroach Swamp.**

Sounds charming, he thinks.

He turns onto a long dirt road that kicks up a trail of dust behind them. At the end of the road, a wood pavilion comes into view, its metal roof dented and rusted in patches. He pulls up to a concrete parking barrier and kills the engine. They sit there for a few moments, enveloped by the hiss of cicadas and the caws of crows, all mingling in rural Florida's bleak cacophony.

Sparse pines and southern oaks dripping with Spanish moss line a pool of murky placid water. A breeze carries crisp winter air that feels amiss in the swamp and rustles through the leaves. The cold keeps the mosquitos at bay, at least.

He lets out a long, morose breath. "Ez, I don't know what to do." Ulysses stares straight ahead. He doesn't dare to look at her, afraid of what he might find in her eyes. Disappointment. Or worse, pity.

"I don't know either," she says. "I've been thinking about it. About what happens next. I know what I want to happen." She pauses, and he hears her shift in her seat. "But I don't know how to get there."

Her words are careful, like she's trying not to upset him. Ulysses glances at her out of the corner of his eye. She's sitting with her arms wrapped around herself, staring out at the knees of cypress emerging from the swamp.

"What do you want to happen?" he asks.

Ez shifts again, smoothing the fabric of her dress with one hand. "I want him gone," she says, her fingers trembling slightly. Finally, she looks at him, her dark eyes wide and serious. "Father. I want him to pay for what he did. To Kia. To all of us."

Ulysses stiffens slightly, his hands tightening on the steering wheel. "Pay how?"

"I just keep thinking about how scared she probably was and…" She trails off for a moment, chewing on her bottom lip. "I think he needs to die."

The bluntness of her words lands like a blow, and for a moment, he's speechless. Her look is intense, unflinching but there's no anger there, rather, something almost pleading. What does she want him to do?

"Ez," he says carefully, sitting up straighter. "You don't mean that."

Ez looks over at him, eyes shimmering with tears she seems too angry to let fall. "He killed her, Uly."

"We don't know that. What if…what if he ended things. Do you think she would have—"

"Never. She'd sooner run away."

As much as he wants to find doubt, he can't deny that Ez and Kia were close. If anyone would know the truth, it's her. He just wishes there were some kind of proof.

"There was a time when I thought Lang was involved in my sister's disappearance. Had I acted on the impulse then…" He trails off, letting the catastrophic permutations linger in the air.

Ez's brows draw together, her fingers clutching the fabric of her dress. "Your sister," she says, as if she's afraid to ask but knows she has to. "What happened to her?"

Ulysses's knuckles whiten on the steering wheel. The swamp outside seems quieter, the hum of cicadas fading beneath the buzzing in his ears. He leans forward slightly, resting his elbows on the wheel, his focus fixed on the horizon. "Calliope," he says, his hand brushing his neck, fingers grazing the inked cursive letters there. "She was my sister. She's gone now." He hesitates, staring out at the water.

Ez tilts her head slightly. "I'm sorry. You don't have to tell me if it's too hard."

He knows Ez would let it go if he said nothing. She'd stop pressing, give him space to shove all his baggage back where it belongs. But it doesn't work like that, does it? Not with things like this.

Ez deserves to know. If she's going to keep trusting him, she should know what kind of man she's dealing with. What he's still dragging behind him. Maybe if she sees it, the whole mess of him, she'll walk away now before he falls any deeper.

"We were part of the Order then," he says finally. "My mom believed everything Thorne said came straight from God. I guess I did too, for a while." He hesitates for half a beat, but he doesn't stop. He lets it all spill out—the Order, that bloody Easter Sunday, the truth about Calliope's disappearance, and the *Mysteries of the Southern Gothic* podcast that brought the most wretched parts of his past to light. How it almost destroyed him and nearly got him killed.

Ez's leans over the center console, rubbing his thigh. "Oh, Uly. I'm so sorry."

His voice falters, and he closes his eyes. "After Calliope disappeared, I was in so much pain. I just wanted it to stop—or at least to feel something else. That's where it started.

"That's part of why I stayed. The feelings about all of it. About Sofie. They were too intense. I was afraid that if I went back, losing her again, falling for her bullshit, letting myself get sucked back into that place, it would put me right back in that cycle. So I figured the only way to force myself to deal with it was to stay. No distractions. Just me and the pain. I threw myself into my art in the chapel, and then…" He trails off, letting the rest of the story speak for itself.

"All this time, I thought you and Lang were so close."

Ulysses shrugs. "I grew up around him. He just knows where I'm weak. Knows how to manipulate me." He takes a beat. "And I *am* weak, Ez. Too emotional, too sensitive. Always have been. I blew up earlier and—"

"Stop," she says, cutting him off. "You're human. You said yourself, you're allowed to be angry. But look at where we are."

Wisps of moss slant against the wind. Branches bow, and leaves rustle. Amid the peacefulness of it all, he looks back at her, finding her dark eyes full of warmth and love. She goes on. "You stopped here. Took a breath. Now we're talking about it. You're okay. I'm okay. Everything's okay."

Ulysses exhales, the tension in his shoulders loosening slightly. After making this all about him, scaring her after all she's already been through, he doesn't deserve her kindness or her understanding. Yet here she is, sitting beside him, offering both without hesitation. It's not just what she says, profound despite its simplicity, it's how unshakably certain she seems. It's disarming in a way that makes him believe it.

"How do you do that?" he says, grazing her cheek with his thumb. "How do you know how to make everything better?"

She blinks at him, a look of concern fading slowly with a slight upturn of her lips. Their eyes meet, and suddenly the world outside the Jeep is distant, fading into the background. There's only her now. Only her affection that anchors him.

There's a pull between them now, magnetic and electric, the space between their seats suddenly feeling unbearable. Her free hand comes up, fingertips brushing lightly against his jaw. It's such a gentle touch, and yet he can feel it healing him.

She closes the distance between them, leaning in, and the moment her lips touch his, it's like lifting a shade, letting the light flood into a dark room. Ulysses doesn't just kiss her, he plummets, loses himself in her, in the way her fingers disappear into his hair, in the soft, urgent sounds she makes.

The kiss deepens quickly, all hesitation burning away. There's just her. Just this. Just the way she exists in his arms.

He reaches for the lever at the side of his seat and sharply pulls it. The seat reclines with a soft click, and Ez shifts back slightly, just enough to meet his eyes, her flushed with color, lips swollen from the kiss.

"What are you doing?"

"Get over here," he says, his arms already attempting to lift her out of her seat.

Her long dress gathers around her thighs as she climbs over the center console, settling into his lap. Ulysses's breath falters when she presses against him, her hands cupping his face as she leans in for another kiss.

His hands slide up her back, fingers tangling in her hair as her lips move against his, as her body presses closer, as the world outside fades completely. There's only this now, her body pressed against his, the quiet, desperate need growing inside him.

Intent on shifting her panties aside, his hands glide up her dress, but his mind stumbles over the sensation of cotton on her thighs. "You're wearing those shorts?"

"Bloomers?" she asks simply, like it's the most natural thing in the world.

A childish giggle escapes him before he can stop it, a low, startled sound that quickly escalates into something uncontrollable, before he finally settles enough to say, "We need to get you some modern underwear."

She presses a playful shove against his chest. "Do you think Erma's taking us on field trips to Victoria's Secret?"

Ulysses tries to keep a straight face, but it's useless. He drops his head against the seat, laughter shaking his body, until he catches her unamused pout. Sitting up slightly, he smothers the last of his grin, his hands still fumbling with the fabric beneath her dress. "Alright, how do we get these things off?"

"They tie in the back."

"Okay," he says, waving a hand. "Lean forward."

She sighs dramatically but does as he says, bowing so he can reach behind her. His fingers grope awkwardly at the ties, fumbling to undo the bows.

"Fuck's sake, how many bows do they put in these things?" he says, and a puff of air escapes his lips, half grunt, half laugh. "This is like trying to disarm a bomb."

Ez groans again, louder this time. "I have to…ugh." She pushes herself up slightly, trying to shift her weight off his lap, but the limited space in the Jeep makes it clumsy and awkward. Her dress gets caught in the process, catching around the gear stick as she tries to maneuver the bloomers down her legs.

Ulysses bites his lip as she wiggles and twists with difficulty. She finally manages to wrestle the fabric off, tossing them into the passenger seat with a frustrated huff before collapsing back onto his lap, her hair a mess, her dress askew.

Shifting, he undoes his belt and unzips his fly. Something about the way she reaches to free him, paired with the knowledge she's never done anything like this before, adds a level of excitement. It's an adventure, and it's clear she wants this just as much as he does when she maneuvers to make them fit together.

In a heartbeat, she sinks onto him. The sensation of being enveloped in her tight heat makes him groan as he holds her at her waist. The weight of her body is in her hands, pressed against his shoulders to steady herself as she rocks her hips.

My God, those hips, he thinks, gripping them.

She's watching him with a smile dancing on her lips, and he knows she loves the way she unravels him, the way her body renders him stupid. How talented she is at fraying his edges and tugging him apart one thread at a time.

Ez's affection had calmed the storm inside him. It's a pattern he knows too well: it brews, spinning tighter and tighter, the eye narrowing as it builds force. Then it crashes, violent and indiscriminate, tearing through whatever's unlucky enough to be in his path before finally breaking apart, leaving nothing but wreckage in its wake.

But she was right. This time, he'd felt it brewing—darkened skies threatening to form a storm. It spun briefly, gathering momentum, but then it cooled. It passed.

And for the first time in forever, he was okay. It was okay.

Ez didn't need to fix his jagged pieces. All she did was hold them in her hands and somehow made him feel they were still worth something, just as broken as they were.

"Ez," he breathes, his arms drawing her closer, his movements urgent. The air inside the jeep grows dense, the windows fogging over in a slow blur as their bodies move together. His hands slide up her dress, gliding over the slick heat of her thighs. They flex under his palms as she rises and lowers, her eyes locked on his, burning into him. Finally, her head rolls back, her breaths rough and ragged as a bead of sweat traces the curve of her throat.

"That's it," he says, thrusting up, driving deeper. He wants to get her there. She deserves a reprieve more than anyone he's ever known—deserves every comfort, every pleasure. Reaching between them to where their bodies join, he sweeps his thumb over the spot that makes her breath hitch. Her fingernails dig into his shoulders, a moan escaping her lips as she clenches around him. He can feel her on the brink. "That's it," he whispers again, thumb stroking, circling. "Come for me."

"Oh my God," she says, voice hoarse, arching her back and crying out.

Bowing forward, her mouth captures his. Her body trembles around him, every breath ragged as she shudders in his arms.

Ulysses holds her close, his grip tightening at her waist as a low groan escapes him. At the last moment, he releases a hard breath, his fingers tensing as he pulls back, barely managing to put space between them.

For a moment, there's nothing but the sound of their breathing, the slow return to reality. Ez exhales a soft, contented sigh, her forehead resting against his. His heartbeat pounds against her palm where it rests on his chest, a rhythm steadying with every second.

Chapter Twenty-Three

HER RELEASE IS A BALM, soothing a wound she's carried since that terrible morning. Collapsed against Uly's torso, the buzz of the swamp outside hisses into the Jeep's cabin and she lies still, her body rising and falling with his every breath.

The damp heat of his body fades as she pushes herself upright. She reaches for the edge of the seat and pulls herself up, her fingers brushing the rough fabric as her knees tremble slightly, unsteady from the intensity of the moment. Climbing back into the passenger seat feels heavier than it should, her limbs sluggish as she settles in. Looking at Ulysses, he's steadier, eyes half-lidded as he lies back with a sigh. He seems relaxed, satisfied.

They fall into a cozy silence, the kind that comes only after shared intimacy, and it naturally gives way to quiet conversation.

"I've been trying to make changes where I can," he says, words teeming with a kind of hope Ez lost long ago. "Do whatever I can within my limited power to spark change. I've changed policies at the center, and before all this, I was working on getting Lang to agree to update the girls' curriculum." He pauses, recognizing the pointlessness of it all now. "I don't know where we go from here."

Listening to him talk about the limitations of his power conjures up thoughts of her own. The women of the Order have no power. At least, that's the lie they've heard so often they forgot how to question it. But it isn't true, is it? The women hold the community together. They grow the food, prepare the meals, care for the children. Not just the Chosen Daughters, but the wives, the girls. And yet they're all treated like possessions, unable to stand up for themselves, unable to be whole.

They'll have to leave this park eventually and return to the roles the Order's designed for them. But as much as Father would love for them to let Kia go, to fall in line, she knows that's not possible now.

"I don't either."

The question figure eights in her mind the entire drive home. She searches for answers in the wide-open blue sky stretching overhead. When Ulysses pulls into the dirt lot and cuts the engine, the sudden quiet startles her. He reaches for her hand, his touch momentarily breaking the restless loop of thoughts skating in her head.

"I have kids I need to check in on," he says, brushing his thumb across her knuckles. "Why don't you take your mind off things? Get some quiet time in the chapel. Work on your painting."

Ez agrees. The quiet always has a way of making things clear and helping her find focus. He kisses her hand before they part ways at the Main House, and she heads to the chapel.

Inside, sunlight filters through the high, narrow windows, painting streaks of gold across the floor. Ez gazes up at the ceiling, at the progress she's made so far, the story they've been trying to tell. A journey from the Order's dark past toward a brighter future.

It's total bullshit.

From what Ulysses told her, nothing has changed. They've only grown greedier, fattening their wallets with broken children. Keeping receipts of good deeds and burdening kids abandoned by their families with debts they can never repay. Once they've feasted on their last drops of blood, the Order tosses their bodies aside without so much as a prayer.

An idea occurs to her, striking like a bolt of lightning, and she nearly trips over herself rushing to the vestry. Standing there, paint and brushes scattered around her, she lets the plan take shape.

She can see it already in her mind, the colors and lines drawn together. This is the story that needs to be told. Ez drags the scaffolding to the center of the room beneath the unfinished mural with a screech. She climbs, balancing precariously on the rickety ladder, her fingers tightening around the handle of the paintbrush.

She starts with Kia's face. Strong, kind eyes. They comforted her, assured her, warned her, and made her laugh. They would be sad, now, *forsaken*, she thinks. Ez's vision blurs with tears and a raw tightness clenches her throat.

Wiping her eyes with her sleeve, she paints with broad strokes. Soft, full cheeks. Lips just slightly parted, as if she's about to tell a secret. Ez paints her arms and hands next, outstretched and open, fingers delicate. Her sniffles echo in the empty chapel as the daylight begins to fade.

Ez pauses, the brush hovering mid-air as the image becomes clearer. Dipping the brush into the red paint, she traces a path down from Kia's wrists and feet to a pool of blood at her bare, swollen belly. The paint runs in jagged lines until it's as if the ceiling itself is bleeding.

Shoulders aching like she's done a thousand push-ups, dress streaked with paint, hair damp with sweat, she descends the ladder then paces back to study her work on the ceiling.

It's unmistakably Kia. Her best friend, high above her, looking down with hurt. Ez hopes Father recognizes the betrayal on her face. She lets out a shuddering breath, her hand gripping the back of a pew to steady herself. When she hears the door open behind her, her stomach twists, a cold knot of dread evaporating whatever sense of triumph she might have felt. She doesn't turn around.

"Ez?"

She turns her head just enough to watch Ulysses take a tentative step inside, eyebrows drawn together at the image on the ceiling as the realization of what he's seeing sets in. She swallows hard, her grip tightening on the pew. His tall frame and hair bundled up on his head are silhouetted by the pale, fading light streaming in from the open door. For a moment, he doesn't move. His eyes are wide, his mouth slightly open, as if the words he wants to say are caught somewhere in his throat.

She tries to speak but no words come. Facing him, she searches for something—anything—to explain. Slowly, she turns back to the mural, letting it say what she can't.

Ulysses shuffles further into the chapel, his boots dragging softly against the floor. He moves with deliberation, absorbing every detail. She glances at him from the corner of her eye, her pulse quickening with each step he takes. When he finally reaches her, he stops, still staring at the mural, his face unreadable.

"Say something," she says, breaking the silence. It comes out sharper than she intended, but the tension in her chest is unbearable.

He turns to her with a grave look, eyes dark. "You know what this is going to do, right?"

"Yes," she says without hesitation. "It's going to make them see her. Father won't like it, but I don't care."

Ulysses glances back at the mural, his jaw tightening again. He's quiet for a moment, his attention on the bleeding figure of Kia.

Finally, he turns back to her, pleading. "The Order I remember would have you beaten you for this, or worse."

"I know."

"And not just you, but probably me too."

His brow furrows, and for a moment, she wonders if she's pushed him too far. She hadn't considered how Ulysses might be punished for her act of protest. She winces at the thought. After all he's done for her, it wouldn't be right to drag him into this. But doesn't he believe her? Lang killed an innocent woman, and Ulysses should be just as mad about it as Ez is.

"We should have talked about this. This is just going to make things worse, honey. We don't know how the Elders will react, and Lang—"

"I don't care about the Elders," she says. She takes a step closer to him, her hands trembling. "How can you just stand there and pretend he didn't do this?"

"I'm not saying he's innocent, but Ez, we don't know for—"

He finally looks at her, and the doubt in his eyes only makes her angrier. She cuts him off. "She didn't kill herself!"

The volume of her voice seems to freeze him in place.

"Why don't you believe me?" she asks, voice breaking.

"I *do* believe you." His voice is calm, too calm for all the pressure threatening to explode in her, and his even-keeled counselor tone only makes her temper smolder. "I want to protect you, but if you do this, it might be bigger than what I can stop."

Ez stares at him, her throat burning, her sense of grief swelling into something too monstrous to define. "You're afraid," she says. "Afraid of what this means. You can't just admit that you're never going to change this place while asking for Lang's permission."

He pauses, letting the impact of her words settle, but he doesn't deny it. "I can't protect you from all of them," he says, his hands resting on his head. He faces the mural once more, as if he's trying to force himself to accept it, but he shakes his head. "You can't leave this up. It's too dangerous."

Her heart clenches, but her resolve hardens as she takes a step closer, holding firm as she insists, "I'm not painting over it."

"Ez, please think—"

"No." She gestures up at the mural. "I'm standing up for the truth. I'm standing up for Kia."

"You think they care about the truth?" he shouts. "Lang won't feel guilt. He'll punish you. And me. And anyone else he can make an example of."

She takes a step back, her voice rising. "So we just stay quiet forever? Pretend it didn't happen? Pretend she didn't matter?"

"That's not what I'm saying," he snaps. "I'm begging you, Ez. Please. Paint over it. Just for now. We'll figure out another way."

She stands taller, accepting no argument. "No."

He takes a deep breath, his trimmed beard shifting slightly as he clenches his jaw. "You're being stubborn."

"And you're being scared."

Pressing his fingers to the bridge of his nose, he closes his eyes briefly as if trying to pull himself together. Without another word, he turns and walks out, the chapel door swinging shut behind him. Ez stares after him, her eyes burning with unshed tears.

She turns back to the mural, the bleeding figure of Kia staring down at her. Her hands tremble as she grips the back of the pew. "I'm not painting over it, Kia," she whispers. "I won't let them forget you."

Chapter Twenty-Four

TWO GUARDS STAND rigid outside Lang's office, rifles slung over their shoulders. Their scowls give nothing away as Ulysses knocks on the door. A voice calls from inside. One of the guards pushes it open, and Ulysses steps through, his pulse hammering. He has no plan. The heavy click of the latch behind him seals his fate. Too late to turn back. Candlelight flickers across the polished desk where Lang sits, pen in hand.

Lang doesn't look up, scribbling a line before setting the pen down neatly. "Something on your mind, Ulysses?"

"Kia," Ulysses says, the single word speaking volumes.

Lang leans back in his chair, his mask firmly in place. "I've already made my decision. There will be no service. I trust that was made clear at breakfast."

"She was one of your Chosen Daughters," Ulysses says, stepping closer. "Don't you think she deserves better than this? At least to be remembered?"

Lang sighs softly, as though the conversation itself is an inconvenience. "Her actions were selfish and sinful," he says. "You know as well as I do that glorifying her would be an affront to God. It would endanger the spiritual health of this community."

"And what about the people she left behind? The ones who loved her?"

Lang tilts his head. "This is about Esme, isn't it?"

"This is about what's right."

Lang rises from his chair, his movements slow and deliberate as he rounds the desk. "What's right," Lang echoes, "is ensuring this community survives. That means putting its needs above personal grievances."

"She wasn't a grievance. She was a person. She mattered."

Narrowing his eyes with a piercing glare, Lang pushes closer. "Careful, Ulysses," he says softly. "Your emotions are clouding your judgment."

Ulysses doesn't step back. "What are you afraid of, Father?"

"Afraid?" A thin, calculated smile spreads across his face. "I'm not afraid of anything. But perhaps you should be." He pauses, studying Ulysses, lingering just long enough to unsettle. "Emotions have a way of making people reckless. I hope you saw to it that Esme learned her outburst was inappropriate."

"She's grieving."

"You cannot lead with a weak hand. Coddling your wife breeds insolence. Handle it, or someone else will. I cannot continue to intervene in your affairs. It's causing dissent in our ranks."

Ulysses's jaw locks, his teeth clenching. "If anyone lays a hand on Ez, they'll answer to me."

Lang brushes him off with a dismissive wave, his smile returning, thin and cutting. "Don't be dramatic, Ulysses. No one wants things to escalate. But understand this, if you cannot maintain order in your household, the leadership will step in. And trust me when I say, their methods will not be as kind as mine."

The remark lingers, but Ulysses refuses to be intimidated. If they ever harm Ez, the Elders have no idea what kind of hell he'll unleash on them. Lang continues. "We're all grieving. But grief is no excuse for defiance."

"*Are you* grieving, Father?"

Lang's smile falters for the briefest moment, a flicker of something sharp and unguarded flashing in his eyes. Ulysses catches it—a glint of something knowing. It's gone as quickly as it appears, replaced by Lang's usual controlled demeanor. But in that split second, Ulysses finds the confirmation he'd sought.

Lang straightens, smoothing his hands over his shirt, brushing away invisible creases. "Grief manifests in many ways, Ulysses," he says, "Some we endure privately. That is what leadership demands."

"She was pregnant," Ulysses says, the words slipping out before he can think better of it.

Lang freezes. "What did you say?" His voice is quiet, deadly.

"You heard me," Ulysses says, his voice steady despite the way his heart pounds. "She was carrying your child, wasn't she? That's why you couldn't let her live. Because if people found out, it would've undermined you. People would see that you're no different than Thorne."

Lang offers a faint smile, though it never reaches his eyes. "I assume Esme fabricated this story after she didn't get her way?"

Ulysses expected him to deflect, to place the blame anywhere but on himself. He feared Lang had the capacity for evil, but he'd wanted to be wrong so badly. That small hope dies a painful death.

"I saw her here. Leaving your office the day I'd come to ask you to reconsider Ez's engagement to Zeke. You'd played it off as a girl reporting a silly squabble. I didn't give it a second thought until now."

"Nonsense."

"You've been acting strange. Distracted." The facts shift into focus. The details he'd tucked into the back of his mind.

"Ulysses, I'm warning—"

"Why'd you make me second in command?" Ulysses interrupts. "You could have just hired someone for Path to Purpose. Why would you try to keep me here?"

Lang exhales slowly, the fire of their argument cooling, settling like ash.

"I told you why. My children. They don't care about the Order. You know that."

"What does that have to do with me?"

Lang leans forward, his voice softer now. "I've known you since you were a boy. We don't share blood but we share a history. I've watched you grow up. Prayed for you. Prayed for your recovery."

It's as if someone wrings him out, and though he'd held on tight, tears begin to blur his vision. "Don't patronize me."

"Haven't I always tried to protect you, son?"

"I'm not your son." His voice shakes with fury. "I don't know why I ever trusted you." He wipes away a stray tear, cursing himself for letting it fall.

Lang's eyes darken. "You are not a victim here. Were it not for your love affair, none of this would have happened."

"Excuse me?"

"My men," he says, his words dropping with spite. "Do you think they would have concerned themselves with my affairs before all this? Behind closed doors, we all have our little indulgences. We're men. But now? They won't forget. They won't forgive me for giving you Esme. If Kia had spoken out, they'd seize the chance to undermine my authority. The entire congregation would be in jeopardy. I cannot sacrifice a flock for a lamb that's already lost."

A *lamb?* The confession turns Ulysses's stomach. Facing Lang with conviction, Ulysses vows, "You *will* answer for this."

"Be careful. There are limits to my patience. What I've given I can easily take away."

The threat chills him.

The door creaks open, and both men whip around toward the sound. Zeke enters the room, his face pale and his hand still on the knob. He freezes mid-step, his eyes darting between Lang and Ulysses.

"Deacon," Lang says smoothly, recovering his composure with unnerving speed. "What brings you here?"

Zeke hesitates, his gaze lingering on Ulysses for a beat too long. "The guards said you were in here, Father," he says slowly. "I... I didn't mean to interrupt."

Lang's smile tightens, his eyes hardening. "Not at all. Ulysses was just leaving."

Ulysses doesn't move immediately, his eyes locked on Zeke, searching for any sign of what he might have overheard. Finally, he forces his hands to unclench at his sides. Ulysses turns, his boots heavy against the floor as he exits to the hallway.

Outside, the guards' eyes follow him, but Ulysses pays them no mind. Lang's words churn in his head, as does the darkness in his eyes, the magnitude of his threat.

Ez was right. Of course she was. But what now? If holding Lang accountable wasn't dangerous, his men would have already removed him from power. He doesn't know what to do, but Ez is his priority and keeping her safe is his only focus.

The vestry is dim, the scent of old wood in the air. His bones feel hollowed by the agony of his decision. As Ez's husband, it's Ulysses's duty to protect her, and with a gallon of paint and large paint roller in hand, he crosses into the main chapel to fulfill it.

Ez has gone, but Kia's pregnant figure still bleeds on the ceiling. It's unfinished and yet beautiful in its simplicity. She'd perfectly captured the emotion, a look that says *How could you?* A look that challenges him even now.

Despite the potential violent consequences playing out in his mind, his heart swells for Ez thinking of the night she showed him notebooks full of angels she drew because, even in her private moments, she complied with the Order's oppressive limitations.

Yet, she did this. Either because she felt safe enough with him to express her pain and sense of injustice, or because she no longer cared to live this way.

Emotion claws its way up his throat. He's supposed to protect her, but what does that mean in a place like this? A church where the guards carry rifles? How do you protect someone from something so pervasive, so deeply rooted, without cutting yourself down in the process?

He sets the metal can on a pew. This is what Lang wants. He wants Ulysses to silence Ez, and like a loyal servant, Ulysses rushed to the chapel to blot out her voice with this paint. To bring her back into line.

No. Not for Lang. For Ez. Because she's right. He is scared.

Scared of what might happen to her, scared of having to watch her suffer for her grief.

He should start painting. He knows it. Every instinct in him screams to cover it up, to spare her the inevitable wrath, to restore the illusion of obedience just long enough to keep her safe. But his feet feel encased in concrete, his attention locked in on the ceiling.

Ez's work isn't just defiance. It's faith. Faith in the idea that something better is possible, that the truth matters, even here. Even now. Ulysses has spent his life helping people find that kind of strength. He's spent his life seeking it in himself. How could he take it from her?

A vise seems to clamp around his ribs, his mind racing through the possible tragic outcomes. If he leaves it, Ez will bear the brunt of whatever comes next. But painting over it is a betrayal.

He exhales a shaky breath, the roller lowering to his side as he turns away from the mural. His thoughts drift to Ez and the way her hands shook when she showed him her drawings for the first time, the raw pain in her voice when she spoke of Kia, the fire in her eyes when she said she wouldn't be silent. This isn't about obedience. It's about something far more important. If she chose this, if she chose to speak her truth, who is he to take that from her?

Ulysses sets the roller down beside the can of paint, the quiet clink echoing through the chapel. His heart pounds as he backs away, his eyes locking on the mural one last time. *God, please protect her.*

Just before dinner, he finds her descending the stairs of the Main House. Her steps falter when she sees him, her mouth pressing into a line.

He clasps his hands in front of him, hoping to look contrite. "I'm sorry."

Stopping at the landing, Ez's dark eyes search his face for an explanation. He draws nearer to her. "I know what this means. For you. For both of us." He reaches, his hand closing gently around her wrist. "But if you're brave enough to stand up, the least I can do is stand beside you."

"Uly, I don't want you to get hurt because of me, but someone has to do something."

He closes the remaining distance between them, his hands coming to rest on her waist. "Whatever happens, happens together. Remember? What kind of man would I be if I let my wife fight this on her own?"

A Chosen Daughter's footsteps crunch down the old wooden stairs behind them, and Ulysses guides Ez by the hand to the parlor. Tucked in a shadowed corner, he whispers to her. "You want justice for Kia because you can't stand to see something so innocent destroyed. You can't stand to see people broken, or used, or forgotten. That's goodness. You don't even see it, but you're pure light, Ez. Simple as that. I know why this is important to you, and even though I'm terrified of what will happen, if this is what you need, then I'm in."

* * *

UNDER THE BARN, lanterns sway gently from overhead beams casting flickering light over the tables. Families and Chosen Daughters are scattered in their usual groups, heads bowed over plates or murmuring quietly to one another. The Elders cluster together at one end, their heads bent in tight conversation. Lang isn't among them, but the intensity of their discussion is unmistakable. Ulysses slows as he takes it in, his gut tightening. Whatever they're discussing, it isn't idle talk. Ulysses can feel the grievousness of it from where he stands. One of the Elders—Whitlock—glances up, his eyes catching on Ulysses for a fraction of a second before flicking away again.

Then, like the sudden hush before a storm, the atmosphere shifts. Lang strides into the barn, the murmur of conversation dimming as heads turn. Ulysses's spine stiffens as Lang crosses the clearing, his hands clasped lightly behind his back. Ez lets out a tense breath, growing rigid beside him. A chill slides down Ulysses's spine as Lang pulls out the chair beside him and lowers himself into it with deliberate ease.

"Steward," Lang says, his tone silky as ever. He doesn't look directly at Ulysses, instead picking up his fork. "Esme." His voice sharpens, her name loaded with gunpowder.

Ez's fingers tighten around Ulysses's under the table. "Father," she replies.

Lang leans back in his chair, his hands resting lightly on the table as he surveys the barn. The congregation has resumed their conversations, but quieter now, their voices carrying a cautious undertone. Even the Elders have shifted their attention to Lang, their secretive huddle dissolving as they take their seats.

Chapter Twenty-Five

SUNDAY MORNING, Ez's heart patters like a frantic drum, a flutter caught in her throat. Her hands twist in her lap as whispers and mumbles rise around her, the voices rumbling against the chapel walls like rolling thunder. Beside the altar, Zeke, Whitlock and Brother Thomas speak to the guards. Are they going to have her removed?

"What is this?" Erma asks, sliding into the pew beside Ulysses.

He doesn't answer. He's stiff, jaw clenched, eyes locked forward. Erma surveys the room for an explanation before noticing the mural. Ez closes her eyes to measure her breath, just for a moment as the adrenaline flooding through her veins warns her this was a mistake.

"This was you, wasn't it?" Erma bites, turning to Ez. "Father isn't going to like this at all."

"I don't care what Father likes," Ez says, though her stomach turns at the inevitable consequences that approach sooner by the second. Erma stares at her, stunned, before looking to Ulysses like he's supposed to fix this. But when he says nothing, Erma sinks back, shaking her head as if she's questioning whether water is wet.

When Lang finally emerges, cloaked in his white satin garments and red stole, he looks upward with a hardened glower. With each deliberate step, the guards and Elders start to move, heading for the doors, the aisles, the exits. Ez grips Ulysses's hand, clinging to it.

There's no way out.

"Silence please," Lang says, and the room goes soundless in a heartbeat.

His attention turns to Ez. She can feel his fury burning into her, but she looks back at him unflinching, refusing to look away. "I must address the spectacle," he starts, his voice echoing in the space. "This childish act of defiance seeks not only to defile this sacred place of worship, but to interfere with the Order's divine purpose. Steward, I expect you to explain why your wife has chosen to humiliate you and the Order in such a shameful way."

Ez's body stiffens, and before Ulysses can open his mouth, she stands. Her knees shake, but she forces herself to raise her voice. "I'll speak for myself."

Her voice echoes in the silence. The crowd stirs, and a ripple of murmurs rolls through the chapel. Ez's mouth dries, but she keeps going, her words tumbling out in a rush.

"Kia was my best friend," she says. "She didn't keep secrets from me."

Erma bolts up from her seat, moving toward Ez, her face flushed red, her hand reaching out like she's about to grab Ez and force her back down. But Ulysses gets there first, stepping in front of her and blocking her path with his body and a firm arm. Erma freezes, her mouth opening and closing, unsure of what to do next.

"Let her speak," he warns.

Ez's voice rises, though it shakes. "Kia was pregnant. She told me. She said you told her you were gonna take care of her. That you would leave your wife to be with her."

Erma gasps. "That is ridiculous!" She struggles against Ulysses, who shields Ez from her attempts to strike.

"Enough!" Lang's voice booms, but Ez doesn't stop.

"She didn't kill herself!" Ez shouts, spinning to face the congregation now. Her eyes dart between their faces, desperate to make them understand. "Father doesn't want us to remember her. He doesn't want us to remember any of the girls the Order's hurt. But I'm not gonna forget her. I will never forget her."

The guards move now, a blur of camo and olive garb, their combat boots heavy against the chapel floor. Ez's pulse spikes as they close in. Grabbing her arms, they yank her back, and she cries out, struggling against their hold. Time blurs, slowing down and racing by all at once.

"Don't touch her!" Ulysses shouts and shoves one of the guards hard, sending the man stumbling back. Another guard rushes him. Ulysses swings, his fist smashing into the man's cheek with a sickening thud. Ez flinches at the sound, her heart pounding in her ears as the man falls back. The other guard doesn't hesitate—he raises his rifle, slamming the butt of it into Ulysses's temple. The crack of bone reverberates and her stomach twists in horror.

"Ulysses!" she cries as he crumples to the floor in a heap, blood streaking down his face. Her body jerks forward instinctively, but the guard's hands grip her shoulders, yanking her back. Tears blur her vision as she kicks at their legs, their boots, anything she can reach. "Let me go!"

"Stop!" Zeke's booming voice cuts through the chaos. He shoves his way to the center of the room, then gestures to the guard. "It's alright. Let her go." He turns, pointing an accusing finger at Lang. "You will not conceal this evil! Why would a girl carrying a child kill herself? Answer that!"

The guards release Ez and she slumps to her knees, scrambling to Ulysses's side. Her hands tremble as she cradles his head, brushing back blood-soaked locks. "Uly," she whispers. "Please wake up. Please."

Mary crouches, approaching quietly. "Ulysses," she whispers. She produces a handkerchief from her pocket and presses it against the wound near his ear. His eyes flutter.

"Fuck," he groans, struggling to sit up, but Mary presses his shoulders.

"Don't. Please."

Whitlock steps forward. "We cannot tolerate evil at our helm, one who knowingly extinguished not just one life but two. An innocent unborn child."

Lang slams a hand on the pulpit, his face twisted with fury. "This is nonsense! Lies meant to divide us! Do not listen to—"

Whitlock cuts him off. "What the girl says is true. Kia wasn't carrying just anyone's child," he says, addressing the congregation, his voice clear and cold. "She was carrying Father Lang's child."

Gasps ripple through the room, then the congregation erupts into chaos, shouts, cries, and frantic whispers. Lang tries to speak, but his words are drowned out by the noise. How could the Elders know?

Brother Thomas stands slowly, his face pale. "The girl confessed to me," he says. "Before she died. I stayed quiet to protect the Order, but I cannot hold this secret anymore." He turns to address the congregation. "God forgive me."

That can't be true, Ez thinks. Kia would never confide in Brother Thomas. None of the Chosen Daughters would be stupid enough to share their secrets with the Elders. The idea is absurd.

Ulysses stirs again beneath Ez's hands. His lips part, his voice faint. "Ez."

"I'm here," she whispers, leaning close. Her tears drip onto the chapel floor as she strokes his hair. "I'm right here."

"Run." His voice is soft, barely audible.

She shakes her head, her voice breaking as she holds him tighter. "I'm not leaving you."

Brother Thomas advances again, raising his hands as if calling for calm. "We must protect this community from further harm. The time has come for new leadership."

Lang finally emerges from behind the pulpit, storming the line of Elders rising against him. "You dare challenge me in the house of God?"

"I dare," Zeke says, his voice cold. "Because you're no man of God. You're a fraud. And the people see it now."

Ulysses shifts beside Ez, his voice hoarse, "Ez... please. Go."

Lang's voice booms again, his desperation evident. "Guards! Remove these traitors!"

But the guards don't budge, their hands gripping their rifles, standing before the congregation. The tide has turned, and Lang's authority is crumbling before their eyes.

Zeke seizes the moment, raising his voice to the congregation. "The time has come to reclaim the Order. To purge it of corruption and rebuild it in the light of God's truth. Who will stand with us?"

A wave of voices ripples through the room, hesitant at first, but then a few more rise in agreement, their confidence building. Turning to face Lang, Zeke glares at him. "We can do this peacefully, or we can do this the hard way."

Lang stalks closer, his eyes narrowing into slits. His voice drops, low and venomous. "I answer to a higher authority than you, Deacon. Don't you dare think you can strip me of what God Himself has ordained."

Before anyone can react, Lang lunges toward one of the guards. The sudden movement draws startled gasps and terrified screams from the congregation. His hand jerks to the guard's sidearm, yanking it free from its holster in a blur. The room explodes into chaos as Lang raises the weapon, his face twisted with rage.

A single shot cracks through the chapel.

The sound echoes against the walls, and Whitlock falls backward onto the floor like a rag doll. The collective gasp of the congregation turns into a roar of panic as pandemonium erupts. Deafening shrieks reverberate in Ez's ears.

Ulysses reaches for Ez, cradling the back of her head and pulling her against him. "Get down," he says, wriggling them both under a pew. On the ground, between the pews, Whitlock lies on his belly, lifeless eyes staring back at Ez as blood pools beneath his head. "Oh my God, he's dead," she whispers.

"Get the gun!" someone shouts.

The guards react too late. One of them dives for Lang, but he fires again, the shot going wide and striking a window, sending shards of stained glass raining down around them.

"Father, stop this!" Zeke shouts, drawing his own weapon from beneath his jacket. The gleam of the pistol catches the morning light as he raises it.

Before Zeke can fire, one of the guards takes aim at Lang. Another shot rings out, striking Lang in the shoulder. He stumbles back, his grip on the sidearm faltering, but he doesn't drop it. Instead, he turns, firing wildly. The bullets ricochet off pews, splintering the wood and sending the congregation ducking for cover.

"Enough!" Zeke bellows.

Lang pivots toward him, blood staining his white garments, the gun trembling in his hand. Another deafening pop rings out and Lang jerks back, the weapon falling from his hand as a dark stain blooms across his chest. His body crumples to the floor beside the chapel doors, motionless.

For a moment, the chapel is eerily silent except for the faint, panicked breaths of the congregation. Then a wail cuts through the stillness—Erma, collapsing to her knees in the front pew, her face buried in her hands.

Zeke marches forward, his gun still in hand, boots clicking against the floor. He stands over Lang's lifeless body, regarding it a moment before he slowly holsters his pistol. Then, he turns, raising his hands to address the congregation.

"It didn't have to come to this," he says, his voice steady and commanding. "But this is what corruption brings. This is what happens when a leader strays from God's path."

The parishioners stir as Zeke rises to the pulpit, standing in the very spot Lang had occupied moments before. He spreads his arms wide, his voice rising to fill the space.

"Today, we take back the Order. No more secrets. No more lies. We will cleanse this community of its sins and restore it to the light."

His words elicit a mumblage of agreement, though fear and shock still linger in the room like a heavy fog. He turns to the guards. "Lower your weapons. No more blood will be shed today."

The guards exchange looks, then slowly comply, slinging their rifles back over their shoulders.

Ez watches all of this from the floor, her hands still cradling Ulysses's face. Her heart thunders inside her as she processes what just happened. She doesn't trust Zeke, but right now, she doesn't have time to think about the future.

Ulysses groans softly. "Ez," he whispers.

She leans closer, tears spilling down her face. "I'm here," she says, voice wavering. "We're okay."

Zeke's voice booms again, stealing her attention. "Those who stand with me, together, we will rebuild. Those who don't, you are free to leave. But know this, there is no place for corruption here anymore."

The congregation begin to shift, some rising hesitantly, others remaining seated, their reactions a mix of fear and doubt. Leaving the pulpit, Zeke's footsteps close in.

"Esme," Zeke says, sending a shiver through her. She freezes, her eyes locked on Ulysses.

"Look at me," Zeke insists, his voice darkening. She draws in a breath, slowly turning toward his voice. His eyes are wide, warm like shallow water in the sun.

"Esme, your courage was essential to the happenings here today," he rasps, his tone almost reverent. His eyes narrow, a gleam in them that turns her blood to ice with doubt. "You spoke the truth when others would not. You proved your loyalty to this community. To God."

Ez doesn't speak, her throat tightening. Lowering to a crouch, Zeke meets her at eye level. "What happened today marks the beginning of a new chapter for the Order. Lang was corrupt, but his sins do not define us. You, Esme, were instrumental in exposing his lies. You stood up for the truth, and because of that, I know you'll do what's necessary for the good of our community."

Zeke stands slowly, towering over her now. "Lang's death changes many things," he says, his voice rising just enough for the remaining congregants to hear. "His corruption poisoned every corner of this house, even the unions he blessed in God's name."

Ez's stomach drops as Zeke looks down at her again with a smirk. "Your marriage to Ulysses is nullified in the eyes of the Order."

Her breath catches. "What? You can't do that."

Zeke shakes his head slowly, his tone almost pitying. "Your marriage is tainted by Lang's corruption. You know as well as I do that he married you and Ulysses to protect his own interests. The union is not blessed by God."

Ez's heart pounds in her ears as Zeke gestures to the guards. "Take him."

The guards step forward, grabbing Ulysses by the arms and pulling him to his feet. He stumbles, groaning in pain, but manages to fix a glare on Zeke. "If you lay one finger on her, I will fucking kill you."

"Careful now, boy. I'm sparing your life out of respect for the work you've done for this community. But if you challenge me again, I won't hesitate to make you Lang's second in hell."

Ez leaps to her feet, her voice cracking as she cries out, "No! You can't take him, he's hurt!"

"He'll receive care," Zeke replies. "But he will no longer reside in the Main House. He will return to the congregants, where he can work to support the youth programs and nothing more."

Ulysses struggles against the guards, shouting back to Ez. "Run! Ez, don't let him—"

One of the guards slams the butt of a rifle into Ulysses's side, cutting off his words with a pained grunt.

"Stop!" Ez screams, lurching toward him, but another guard intervenes, grabbing her arm and yanking her back.

Zeke raises a hand. "Enough."

Ez thrashes against the grip on her arm. "Ulysses! Don't take him, please!"

"He's no longer your husband, Esme," Zeke says coldly.

Ez turns on him, her fists trembling at her sides. "You're a monster," she spits, her voice shaking.

Zeke inches closer, his voice dropping to a low rasp. "You'll thank me in time. A woman like you deserves a partner worthy of her strength and courage. Someone who can lead alongside her. Someone chosen by God."

A bitter taste spreads across her tongue, bile rising in her throat as his meaning sinks in.

"You belong here, Esme," Zeke continues, admiring her like a predator sizing up its prey. His words are calm, convicted, as if this was all meant to be. "With me. Together, we'll rebuild the Order in God's image."

"No," she whispers. "I belong with Ulysses."

Any trace of false warmth in Zeke's eyes evaporates. He gestures sharply to the remaining guards. "Take her to my quarters. She needs time to reflect on her role in our new future."

Ez jerks back, trying to pull free, but the guards' grips tighten, forcing her forward. "You can't do this!" she screams, her voice breaking.

Zeke doesn't respond. Instead, he addresses the congregation. "The old ways have fallen. Today, we rebuild."

Ez's cries echo through the chapel as she's dragged toward the door, her heart shattering with every step. She twists, catching one last glimpse of Ulysses as he's pulled in the opposite direction. Their eyes meet, and the pain there mirrors her own.

"Ulysses!" she screams, her voice raw.

Two guards drag Ulysses toward the open church doors, the bright morning light silhouetting his bloodied form struggling between them. "I'll come back for you, Ez!"

Chapter Twenty-Six

ULYSSES'S EYES FLUTTER OPEN. The familiar heft of Domino curled against his side in the bed gives him pause, an ephemeral moment of comfort that vanishes as quickly as it comes. Inhaling deeply, he takes in stale air of a space that's been sealed mixed with the familiar scent of patchouli. He's in his trailer. Could it all have been a dream?

All uncertainty dissolves as he sits up. A sharp ache blooms in his skull as the horrific memories of blood and chaos rush back. The blinds are drawn, casting the room in shadow, though faint lines of light seep through the cracks, cutting the darkness into slivers. His ribs throb with a burning ache.

"You're awake," Mary says.

"Where's Ez?" he asks, his throat dry. He swings his legs over the side of the bed, desperate to push past the dizziness.

"I don't know," Mary replies. The mattress dips under her weight as she sits down at the edge of the bed, the familiar creak of the worn springs jarring in the silence. "The guards took her. I haven't seen her since. I was told to tend to you."

"How long have I been out?"

"A few hours."

A few hours. His stomach twists violently. What could Zeke do to her in a few hours? Ulysses doesn't want to imagine it, but the thoughts come anyway—Ez at the mercy of Zeke's cruelty, the monster hurting her, breaking her. He jolts to his feet, the sudden motion sending a wave of nausea through him. His knees buckle almost immediately, and he grabs the wall to steady himself.

"I need to get to her," he says, breathless.

"There are guards at the door," Mary says. She rises with him, resting her hands on his shoulders to stop him. "There's nothing you can do right now." Her touch is steady, grounding, but it only fuels his frustration.

"Every second I'm here, she's out there with him," he snaps, shaking her hands off him. Strain ripples through his torso as he forces himself to stay upright, every muscle tensed as if sheer willpower will carry him to her.

"Ez will be okay," Mary says, as much to him as to herself. "You don't know her like I do. There wasn't an assimilation center back when she arrived. *Mother* was the one who had to take it all—her kicking, screaming, spitting in her face. Ez isn't as delicate as she looks."

It's little consolation, but right now, he's struggling just to stand. He allows himself a minute to sit on the edge of the bed, his mind racing with thoughts of Ez and the aftermath of the shootout. The smell of gunpowder mixed with the citrus oil that polishes the oak pews. Lang's blood darkening the crimson runner.

Lang is dead.

As much as Ulysses mistrusted Lang, as corrupt, selfish, and cruel as he was, Ulysses can't deny that Lang was the closest thing to a father he's ever known. That thought sickened him, but it was true. And Mary, he suspected, must feel the same way, whether she'd admit it or not. She sits beside him now, her eyes glassy with unshed tears.

There's an odd, bitter pang of loss at Lang's absence, oscillating to the relief of knowing Lang couldn't hurt anyone ever again, and back again.

But his death wasn't justice, it was strategy. The Elders didn't give a shit about Kia. They just dogpiled on Ez's cause to sow division, to steal power. Whitlock. That son of a bitch. A welcome casualty of the Elders' coup d'état. Though, watching Mary's distant stare, he wonders if she's grieving him too.

"I know it isn't like, blood, or anything, but since we've met, I've looked at you like a sister," he says.

She softens, her gentle nod knocking loose a tear that spills down her cheek. She clears it with an efficient sweep of her hand. Offering a tight smile, she rests a soft hand on his cheek. "I know. And I feel the same."

"You and Whitlock," he starts, testing the waters on the subject and watching her reaction closely. A stitch forms in her brow and she winces with revulsion.

"Whitlock was a disgusting man."

He blinks through the moment of confusion, recalling Whitlock's crude comments about Mary's nipples. He'd thought Whitlock was just a douchebag bragging about his sexual pursuits and assumed whatever he and Mary might have done together was consensual. He hunches over, pressing the heels of his hands into his eyes. He should have asked. He should have talked to her. Protected her. He sits up, ready to apologize.

"I didn't know. I thought maybe… I don't know. I'm so sorry."

Mary is quiet for a moment, smoothing the edge of her dress with slow, deliberate movements. She doesn't look at him, her posture perfectly straight, letting her hands fall still in her lap. "It's done now." She exhales slowly, the sound barely audible, and her fingers twitch in her lap before she forces them still again.

"There's no one forcing you to endure this place now," he says, trying to find a silver lining. "You can leave. Start your life."

"Where would I go? This is where I belong. I know everyone here. I don't know anything about the world out there." She brushes a hand affectionately over his head before rising to her feet. "Rest. You're no good to Ez like this. We'll get this sorted once you're feeling up to it."

Chapter Twenty-Seven

"ESME," Zeke says, voice a low rasp. "Thank you for waiting. Sorting things with the bloodshed has taken some time. Erma is beside herself, as you could imagine." The wood barely creaks under his soft footsteps. He takes her in with a reverent look in his eye.

Standing near the bed, Ez recedes into herself, rigid, refusing to unfurl. Zeke had entered his quarters as covert as an assassin, yet that same false warmth painted his face. The too-easy curve of his mouth is unnervingly placid, his polished exterior as hollow as the man beneath it. She watches him long enough to assess his energy, the intent behind his movements. She drops her head, her jaw clenched.

The faint creak of the floorboards under his shined loafers is barely audible over the relentless thrumming in her ears. She doesn't look up as he moves closer, but she feels it, as if this man is charged with dark energy.

"My dear, you have no idea how many nights I longed for you in this room."

Her breath quickens, shallow and rapid as her mind scrambles for escape routes that don't exist. The suite is eerily similar to

Ulysses's bedroom, but it's cluttered with old trunks, maps, and insects framed behind glass. The smell of varnish, aged wood, and oil clings to the air, fueling lanterns that burn on the dresser. The flames flicker in the dim room, casting long, jagged shadows over the floor.

Erasing the distance between them, he stands so close now she can smell the faint tang of yeast on his sweat. A bitterness sours the back of her tongue, and she forces her attention to fall anywhere but his face. The urge to recoil grips her, but she resists, willing herself to remain still, to betray nothing.

"I know you must feel a bit awkward," he says. "That's only natural. After all, you were placed in a very precarious situation. Used as a pawn by Lang to control Ulysses. It was unfair to you. To us."

There is no us, she thinks, but swallows the words down; they won't do her any good.

"As a result, you entered into an unholy union with that man. Esme, my sweet girl, I am so sorry, and I want you to know that I forgive you."

She glares at him. "Forgive me for what?" The words fire from her lips before she can stop them.

He rests his hands on her hips. "For your lost virtue. It pained me deeply to witness it firsthand, waiting outside the door. But all the while, I reminded myself you'd have remained pure for me were it not for Lang's interference. You were simply doing what was asked of you." He leans closer, pressing a kiss to her shoulder.

His hand leaves her hip, and pushing against the billowed fabric of her skirt, he firmly cups the tender meeting of her thighs. She shoves him, but her arms strain against him. Forcing her back, he presses her against the wall by her throat.

"Now, now," he says, his face so close the foul heat of his breath dampens her cheek. "Forgiveness cannot unpick an apple, my dear. Unblemished fruit tastes sweetest, but you're already bruised, already bitten. It's time I take what's left for myself."

"I'd rather die," she says.

He scoffs. "You're not thinking clearly, my girl," he says, pressing his forehead to hers. "I'm taking my rightful place at the head of the Order. I will give you the life you want. That tattooed fool you called a husband is a broken man, hiding his weakness behind soft words and empty gestures. A failure masquerading as a savior."

"Get off me!"

His false patience snaps. He grabs her roughly by the arms and whips her away from the wall. She staggers, her knees giving, and before she can steady herself, he swings her sideways, slamming her onto the bed.

The mattress creaks under her impact as she falls, and in an instant, he's on top of her, pinning her down. One hand clamps around her wrists, holding them above her head, while the other presses against her hip. She thrashes beneath him, a tide that won't recede.

"No," she chokes, her voice breaking.

"Stop fighting," he hisses, his breath seeping into her skin.

She thrashes against him, desperate to find something—anything—to fight back. Her vision swims, her thoughts splintering as his hand drifts lower, fingers grazing the hem of her skirt.

Digging into the mattress, she arches back, coiling tight before surging forward with all her strength. Her forehead slams into his with a sickening crack. The impact reverberates through them both, a sharp jolt flashing through her skull. Pain flares, but the sting is nothing compared to her rising panic.

Blinded by pain and terror, she wildly drives her leg upward with every ounce of strength she has. It connects squarely with his groin, and a howl tears from his throat. His grip falters and he reels back, clutching himself. She doesn't hesitate. Scrambling out from under him, her elbow strikes the dresser as she twists, and the lantern tips over. It smashes against the floor, spilling oil that ignites in a flash. Flames roar to life on the rug. The old fabric of the curtains dissolves like wet sugar under the licking tongues of fire.

"Stupid woman," he gasps, his voice raw with pain. His face twists with rage as he straightens. "Look what you've done."

He lunges, seizing her arm as they crash into the nearby shelf. The impact sends his insect specimens tumbling to the floor, glass shattering on impact. Shards scatter across the wooden boards, gleaming like tiny beacons. She grabs for one, her fingers struggling to pluck a jagged piece from the floor. The sharp edges bite into her palm, but she grips it tightly despite the pain. With a desperate cry, she swings upward, plunging it into his throat.

The blaze reflects in his widened eyes, a guttural, choking sound spilling from his lips as blood spurts in violent bursts. His grasp loosens and he stumbles back, hands clawing at his neck. The flames behind him spread, crawling up the walls.

Ez doesn't move. Her body shudders watching the thick crimson pool spread beneath him, steady and slow. It's not until the sting of smoke hits her eyes that she realizes how fast the fire is spreading.

Ez can't think, can't breathe. The room is suffocating, a cauldron of searing heat and choking smoke. She inspects the wound in her palm left by the shard of glass. It's bleeding, sticky and hot, but there's no time to treat it. She needs to move. Now.

She forces herself to step back, her bare feet sliding over the shards of glass littering the floor. They bite into her soles, but she barely notices over the relentless throb in her hand and the oppressive heat that broils her.

Pulling open the door and staggering into the hallway, smoke billows past her, obscuring her vision and sending her into a fit of coughing so violent it's as if her ribs will crack.

There are children here. The other Chosen Daughters.

"Fire!" she screams, gripping the wall for balance, her bloodied hand leaving smears against the wallpaper. Every step is an ordeal, her knees trembling as adrenaline surges through her, as she fights to keep moving. A Chosen Daughter lingers near the stairwell, head dipped in exhaustion as she sweeps, barely listening.

Ez shouts again. "There's a fire, you need to get out!"

Residents emerge from nearby rooms, scrambling at the sight of smoke, and Ez calls to them, warning them.

When she bursts outside, the sun hits her like another wall of heat, but the open air is a relief so sharp it nearly knocks her to her knees. She gulps down breaths, though they taste of smoke and ash, and stumbles away from the house. Her hand throbs fiercely, blood trickling between her fingers as she moves.

Ulysses. She needs to get to Ulysses.

Through the haze of smoke and terror, she spots a familiar figure—Mary, her sharp posture cutting through the chaos. She'll know where Ulysses is.

"Mary!" Ez's voice cracks as she calls out. She staggers toward her, every step unsteady, her good hand pressed tight to her injured palm.

Mary turns, her eyes widening as she takes in Ez's bloodied appearance. For a moment, Mary is unreadable, her reaction caught somewhere between shock and suspicion.

"Ez? What happened?" Mary's voice is sharp, demanding.

Ez shakes her head, her chest heaving. "I need to find Ulysses. Where is he?"

The woman's head jerks up, her eyes narrowing as she sniffs the air. Her focus shifts toward the rising smoke curling into the bright afternoon sky. She moves past Ez, her movements stiff and slow, like her body hasn't caught up with her mind yet. A hand flies to her mouth. "Oh no. Oh my God."

Ez turns just in time to see bright flames leap from the windows, consuming the walls. Smoke billows upward in thick, black waves, darkening the sun as residents rush outside.

"The house." Mary stumbles a step forward.

"It was an accident, Zeke—"

But before she can explain further, Mary stumbles back and takes another disbelieving look at her. "Why are you covered in blood? My God." Mary's eyes flutter, her attention shifting between Ez's blood-covered figure and the burning house.

"I need to get to Ulysses. *Please,* Mary."

Mary hesitates, glancing at the growing panic around them. "You're bleeding," she says, as though she's weighing her choices, trying to decide which emergency to manage first. "Stay here." Mary strides toward the two guards stationed near a trailer.

Until now, the panic had kept Ez alert. But each pump of her heart seems to draw life out from her. The horizon wobbles, and she closes her eyes to stop it. Opening them again, the lush green landscape is less vibrant, shaded in gray. The distant trees smudge together.

"You two," Mary calls, her voice sharp and commanding, cutting through the discordance of screams and crackling flames. "The Main House is on fire, it's spreading fast. You need to get people out now. Make sure everyone's accounted for."

The guards exchange uncertain looks. "Our orders are to—"

"To stand there while the Order burns down?" Mary snaps. "If you don't act, people will die. Move!"

The older guard blinks, visibly shaken, then turns to his partner. "Let's go," he mutters, gripping his rifle.

Mary watches them go, then turns sharply back to Ez. "Go."

Ez stumbles forward, her legs unsteady with each step. The path to the trailer stretches endlessly, farther than it had just moments ago. Her bleeding hand throbs in time with her pulse. Every step is agony, but the sight of Ulysses's trailer ahead keeps her moving.

Chapter Twenty-Eight

THE TRAILER DOOR CREAKS OPEN, and Ulysses's head snaps up, his body going rigid. Have the guards come to finish what Zeke started? He swings his legs off the bed, every movement dragging fire through his muscles. Domino stirs at his feet, letting out a low, uneasy growl, but doesn't rise.

Then he hears a voice.

"Uly?"

It's soft. Familiar.

"Ez?"

Her figure crosses into the dim light filtering through the blinds, and Ulysses freezes, the breath punched from his lungs. Blood streaks her dress, soaking the fabric all the way down to the hem. Her face is pale as bone.

"Oh my God, are you alright?" Crossing the room in a quick stride, he pulls her into his arms, cradling her gently against his body.

"It's Zeke's blood," she says, flinching, the motion sharp and involuntary.

"Ez, what happened?" He brushes the hair back from her face where a faint sheen of sweat glistens on her brow.

"I killed him," she says, her voice so faint it's almost lost.

"What?"

"Zeke. He wouldn't stop. I didn't mean to, but the lantern…it started the fire."

"What fire?" Moving to the window, he pulls the kitchen curtain back. Outside, curls of smoke drift across the sky. *What the hell is going on?* This is no small emergency, this is catastrophic. If Zeke is dead… Lang, Whitlock… then who's in charge? There are people out there who probably need help. He's ready to rush out the door when Ez raises her hand and blood trickles down her wrist.

"You're bleeding," he says, voice softening, focus honed to her again. "Come here. Sit down." He leads her to the bed, easing her onto the mattress.

Ez doesn't respond. Her attention stays fixed on the window, where the world beyond the blinds burns. For a moment, Ulysses doesn't think she's heard him, but slowly, she blinks, her rigid posture relaxing. She catches sight of her hand as if noticing the blood for the first time.

"I'll take care of it," he says.

He grabs a clean towel hanging by the sink and wets it under the faucet. The water runs cold and clear, a seemingly small blessing for which he finds himself immensely grateful. Grabbing a second, dry towel, he sets it beside her on the bed before pulling a bottle of iodine from under the sink.

Kneeling in front of her, he unscrews the cap. "This might sting," he warns.

Ez doesn't flinch as he pours the liquid over her hand, watching the wound yellow. It's not pretty, but it should close on its own.

Blood swirls into the brown liquid, and Ulysses rounds his lips to blow gently over the skin, hoping to dull the pain. "That's not so bad, huh?" he says, though she doesn't answer. If she's in pain, she doesn't show it. Her stillness worries him more than anything.

Dark possibilities churn through his mind, unsettled by the hollow look in her eyes. He starts dabbing her hand gently with the wet towel, his movements and his words soft and careful. "Did he hurt you?"

Half-lidded eyes flick weakly to his. "He tried."

The words hit like a blow, sending his heart plummeting deep into his stomach—not just for what Zeke did, but for what Ulysses didn't do. He wasn't there. He hadn't stopped it.

And yet, beneath the guilt, there's a bitter kind of relief. Zeke didn't win. Ez had fought back like Mary said she would, the way she had before the Order had broken her. At least, they thought they had.

He dries her hand with the second towel, then grabs a folded linen sheet from the cabinet. Tearing a strip from the fabric, he creates a long bandage and wraps it tightly around her hand. He ties a firm knot before pressing a kiss to it.

"You're safe now," he murmurs. "I've got you."

Outside, the sound of shouting grows louder. The faint bite of smoke seeps through the seams of the trailer windows and doors. Ez's bloodied dress clings to her, the dark stains standing stark against her olive skin. She shifts, the ruined fabric rustling faintly. Ulysses frowns, brushing a hand over her arm. She needs more than a bandaged hand. She needs to feel human again. Clean.

"Wait here."

She doesn't respond, but her shoulders loosen slightly.

He crosses to the closet, yanking the door open. It smells of stale air and dust. As he rifles through the shelves, his hand brushes against something soft. A small stack of clothes crammed in a corner of a high shelf.

He vaguely remembers seeing a few clothes left behind when he first arrived, forgotten pieces from whoever stayed here last. Rifling through them, he pulls out a folded dress. It's simple, pale yellow and cottony to the touch. He has no idea who it belonged to, but right now, that doesn't matter.

He brings it back to the bed, kneeling opposite her again with the dress in hand. "Let's get you cleaned up."

Ez doesn't resist, but lets him lift her hand, swabbing the blood from her skin with careful strokes. His touch dwells longer than it needs to, his thumb tracing along her wrist as though he could smooth away the hurt with his hands alone.

Setting the dress beside her on the bed, he asks, "May I undress you?"

Ez nods faintly, her movements slow, automatic. He slips his hands to her shoulders, his fingers brushing the edge of the bloodied fabric. His hand hovers mid-reach, fingers curling inward as if unsure whether to continue or retreat.

They're married, but they're still strangers in so many ways. Yet as his fingers unbutton her dress, guiding the fabric down her arms, something between them shifts. The sullied linen clings to her body, and when he peels it away, it falls to her waist, then lower, pooling around her hips before sliding to the floor.

For a moment, while guiding the damp towel down her back, Ulysses forgets himself. The soft curves of her body, the swell of her breasts, the gentle dip of her waist, the long, smooth line of her legs all hold him captive.

She is breathtaking.

Under his touch, he doesn't miss the way her breathing quickens, the faint flush dappling across her collarbone. She feels it too, the spark between them, alive even now when everything else is anarchy.

His pulse hammers in his ears, his throat dry as his scrutiny roams over her. She's bruised in places, and faint shades of purple mar her ribs. If Zeke wasn't already dead, he'd make him regret hurting her this way. But the white towel turns pink with Zeke's blood, and Ulysses takes a small satisfaction from it.

Picking up the yellow dress from the bed, he holds it up for her. "Here."

Slipping the dress over her body, his knuckles brush against the warm skin of her stomach. The soft fabric settles around her frame, loose and light, but hugs the places where the curves of her body demand it.

"There," he says, his voice barely above a whisper. "Better."

His hand finds her waist, thumb grazing the contour of her hip, and he can feel the faint tremor in her breath. Without thinking, he leans in, his lips brushing against hers. Their kiss is soft at first, gauging if she'll pull away. She doesn't. Her hands rise, sliding against his chest, fingers twisting into the fabric of his shirt as she bends to him. The kiss deepens, a crash of need and comfort, muting the frenzy outside, making it distant.

His fingers trail up her back, finding her nape, holding her to him like the precious gift she is. The panic he felt being dragged away from her, the worry of what would happen to her melt away, her heartbeat a comforting rhythm.

He wants to stay here. Just the two of them, lost in each other, untouched by anything else. But then a shout pierces the air from outside and the spell breaks.

With a soft, reluctant exhale, he pulls back, his forehead resting against hers. Breath uneven, his hands still entwined around her waist. "We need to go."

The sounds of men's warnings blare as Ulysses and Ez step out of the trailer hand in hand. The Main House ablaze, a black smudge against the harsh afternoon light. The air bites at their throats, and the heat brushes against them in waves.

They stand outside as the Order's firefighters surround the house with hoses, the weak streams of water barely reaching the edges of the roaring flames. A mist of water catches the light, glittering uselessly in the air, a feeble attempt to extinguish the blaze. Even as their home burns, the men of the Order would rather struggle alone than call for competent help, stubbornly holding to their self-reliance like a drowning man clinging to a sinking ship.

Families from the homestead gather in groups, zeroed in on the destruction. Nearby, a group of kids from the Youth Quarters dance in the grass. A lanky boy sashays and shimmies, while the others beatbox with exuberant abandon as the Order burns.

"Hey," Ulysses shouts. The boys freeze at the boom of his voice as Ulysses closes the distance between them. He directs his attention to the older ones, his voice softening but firm. "I know you hate it here, and I don't blame you, but there are good people here who just lost their home. People could have died. Try to show a little compassion."

A few glance at him. "Sorry, Steward," a boy no older than

fifteen says, then retreats away from the group, helping a younger child settle in the shade of a tree.

In the distance, Brother Thomas emerges through the haze, his stride faltering at first when he notices them, then quickening toward them. "Can't find the Deacon," Thomas says, shaking his head. "What are we going to do now?"

It's a question that strikes Ulysses as worrisome, asked aloud by a leader among his vulnerable congregants, then the reality hits Ulysses like a blow to the head.

Nobody's in charge.

The Order has taken a major hit. It's an idea that would have filled a younger Ulysses with glee. If someone had told him back then that one day the Order would weaken, that all the rules he resented and the subjugation he'd been forced to tolerate would go up in flames, and he'd be there to watch it happen, he would be dancing right along with those kids. But back then, he thought only of himself. He was powerless over the influence of Thorne and terrified that rising up would get him killed.

Looking around, he sees people who wanted to live a simple existence, who'd been won over by promises of service to community, to God. Though Ulysses ended up here for the wrong reasons, and he's not even sure what he believes—certainly not the cocka-mamie stories the Order had once taught him—what he does know is every sermon he'd sat through since he arrived was about human connection, purpose and gratitude. Maybe that was the front Lang put up, a means to a deceptive end, but to Ulysses, it was the only thing that made this place even remotely worthwhile.

What would happen to these people now?

Mary rushes up to them. "All have been accounted for...except for the Deacon," she says, her eyes holding on Ulysses. Mary is a sharp woman, and from the looks of it, she's already pieced together Zeke's absence isn't a coincidence and that he won't be coming back.

"Thank you, Mary."

She nods quietly. To Uly, it's a gesture of assurance.

It's another day before the ash settles, leaving nothing but the aftermath. Zeke's remains are swept and shoveled into bags, the last traces of him carried out from the house with the rest of the debris. As far as the members of the Order will know, he died in the fire.

The charred skeleton of the Main House casts jagged shadows across the grass as the sun sinks lower. Congregants gather in the yard, their faces taut with grief and uncertainty, their stoicism heavy with the consequence of the day's disasters. In the distance, Erma sits alone on the chapel steps, staring off into the distance, seeming detached from reality.

Ulysses glances at Mary. "Are you sure you want to stay?"

"This is my home, Uly," she says as if the answer is obvious. "How could I leave? Especially now."

He lets her words settle, offering her a slight bow of his head in acknowledgement. "Come with me," he says, marching toward the dining table. It's a place where meals were shared, prayers were spoken, and decisions were made, now resting under the shade of a gnarled oak amid a pile of salvaged furniture.

He places a hand on the bench, hesitating for just a moment, then climbs up. The wood creaks under his boots, and one by one, heads lift, eyes focus. Their attention settles over him and for a second he thinks he might lose his nerve, but he shoves the doubt aside.

"Listen up!" Ulysses calls, his voice cast out across the homestead like a net. A few people shift, their gazes flicking from him to one another. "I'm not going to lie to you. This is bad. We've lost too much. The Main House is gone, and more than that, we've lost people. Lang, Whitlock, Zeke—dead. And not just dead, but violently taken. I know you're scared. And you should be. What happened..."

He pauses, his throat tightening. Sweeping over the crowd, he sees it all. Wide, frightened eyes, faces drawn with grief. He recognizes it. He's seen it before, back when the Order's original founder set a chain of events into motion that changed the course of his entire life.

Back then, it was easier for the church leaders to sweep the

Order's ugliness into the vestry, out of sight, ignoring the horrors in exchange for the illusion of stability. But after years of swallowing down the darkness, of numbing it, digging graves to bury it, he knows now that you're only as sick as your secrets. He's not going to bury this and move on like nothing happened. He needs to face it. They all do.

"What happened is something none of us will forget. Not ever. Blood was spilled in a place where we're supposed to feel safe. Where we're supposed to heal. And now…" He glances toward the blackened ruins of the Main House. He lets the silence stretch, lets them feel the weight of it. "This place feels broken. I know it does. And maybe some of you are thinking it's too broken to fix. Maybe you're thinking about leaving. About giving up." His jaw tightens, and he shakes his head. "But hear me when I say this, we are not broken. Not as long as we have each other."

"Here's what's going to happen. If you have room in your home, open your doors to those who've lost theirs. If you have extra bedding, take it to the chapel. We'll gather whatever supplies we have and make do—for now. But we're not just scraping by anymore. There's money in the coffers, and we're going to use it. Anyone who can work, you'll help rebuild. We'll start again, but this time, we do it right."

He pauses, letting his words sink in. The crowd stirs with mumblings of confusion, a few voices rising in disbelief. "I know some of you are looking at me because of this Steward title," he says, gesturing to himself. "But the truth is, I'm not the one who should lead you through this. I haven't been here long enough. I don't know this community the way you do." He waits a beat, scanning their faces. "But I do know someone who can help."

He turns to Mary, and the crowd follows. She stands near the pile beside a stack of wood chairs, her arms crossed, her face unreadable. For the first time, she looks surprised, caught off guard by the attention.

"Mary's been here longer than most of you," Ulysses says, his voice steady. "She knows this place better than I ever could. She's strong, she's smart, and when things got hard today, she didn't fall apart. She's the kind of person who steps up when it matters, and I know she'll keep stepping up for all of you.

"I'm not walking away," Ulysses adds quickly. "Not yet. I'll stay and help get things organized. I'll make sure you have access to the resources you need to get through this. But Mary's the one who should be leading this place. And if you trust her, if you give her a chance, I know she'll do right by you."

A woman steps forward from the crowd, a toddler at her skirt. "What about food? The food stores were in the Main House."

"I know," Ulysses says. The Order's members didn't know about the staggering fortune the Church has accumulated, but maybe now they'd finally benefit from it. "We'll make a list of what we need and replenish our supplies. Don't worry. I'll make as many trips as we need to stock up, but no one's going hungry."

As the crowd's energy vibrates with anxiety, a wiry man comes forward. "What about the well?" he asks. "The pump's tied to the Main House. No power, no water. How are we supposed to keep going if we can't even drink?"

Ulysses pauses, drawing a blank. He looks to Mary, who seems to recognize the cluelessness on his face. She steps forward and raises a hand to signal calm, bringing the worried murmurs of the congregation to silence.

She looks at the man who raised the question about the well. "The pump's powered by the solar grid over by the barn. That didn't burn. I'll bet the wiring just needs a once-over." She turns her head. "Martin, you're good with that kind of thing, can you check it out?"

An older gentleman in overalls, presumably Martin, nods.

"Great," Mary says, giving him a small nod of encouragement before moving on. "Now, the main kitchen's gone, but we've still got a fine smoker and the fire pit. We'll need help fetching any pots and pans we can save. Who's ready to pitch in?"

Chapter Twenty-Nine

ULYSSES HAS NO CLEAR PLAN. He knows what he wants—turn the Path to Purpose program into something that actually helps kids instead of grooming them for the Order, but the *how* still escapes him.

For weeks, he has been overhauling the program, trying to rework it into something real. Something good. As the only surviving member of the Order's leadership with firsthand knowledge of its inner workings, he knows he has to act. But how do you take something built as a funnel for cash, designed to convert impressionable teenagers into loyal cult members, and turn it into a program that truly helps them?

Dr. Okafor might have the answer.

Now, sitting in Ulysses's office after touring the facility, Okafor taps his fingers against the armrest of his chair. The late afternoon light filters through the blinds, casting striped shadows across the desk. His navy slacks ride up slightly, revealing bright blue socks patterned with tacos. The unexpected detail is almost funny and Ulysses might've laughed on any other day, but today, all he can do is focus on what Okafor might say next.

Okafor finally breaks the silence. "If we move forward with this, we need to handle the transition carefully. We don't want the kids to feel like they're being abandoned. They need to understand they're stepping into something better."

Encouraged by his interest, Ulysses straightens. "Until the sale is complete and the new facilities are ready, we'll continue housing them. We want this program to succeed, even if we're not the ones to run it anymore."

When they spoke on the phone earlier that week, Dr. Okafor seemed intrigued by the opportunity to expand Palms Waterside's focus on youth rehabilitation, not just from substance abuse but from the deeper wounds of trauma, neglect, and mental health struggles that so often lead them there. Ulysses hopes their on-site meeting will be the final push he needs to commit.

Dr. Okafor leans forward slightly, considering. "I'll need to see the numbers and review the legalities with my team."

"Of course."

He studies Ulysses for a moment. "And you? What are your plans once this is done?"

Ulysses blinks, thinking about his wife waiting for him back home. There is still so much she longs to do, so much world she hasn't experienced.

He lets out a quiet chuckle. "We're still figuring that out."

* * *

THE TRANSPORT VAN rumbles past the blackened remains of the Main House, now little more than a collapsed heap of ash and charred beams. The embers have long since smoldered their last wisps of smoke, leaving only the stark reminder of what once stood. Ulysses waits on the chapel steps, his hands tucked into his pockets, watching as the van grinds to a halt.

The door creaks open, and the teens climb out one by one, their faces blank and wary. Jax exits first, tall and wiry, his backpack hanging low over one shoulder. Behind him are Eloise and Claire, their matching beige sweatshirts and pants wrinkled. They stick close together, their eyes scanning the scene with a mix of confusion and unease.

Ulysses rises to his feet, offering them a warm smile. "Welcome."

Jax snorts, glancing at the ruins before turning to Ulysses with a raised brow. "Where the fuck are we?"

The girls burst into laughter, their tension breaking for a moment, though it's unclear if it's from nerves or genuine amusement.

Ulysses chuckles softly, shaking his head. "Come on, man," he says, his voice gentle but firm. "We talked about the language. You can't do that here. Look, I know it's not what you expected. We're in a bit of a transition period, as you've probably noticed." He gestures toward the path leading away from the ruins. "But the Youth Quarters are still standing. I'll show you around. I promise it's in one piece."

Ez and Mary were putting the final touches on the updated rooms. Until the sale of Path to Purpose to Palms Waterside became a reality, the Order's new leaders knew they had to do something to improve the youth's living conditions. They had worked tirelessly to unify the youth programs. No more Chosen Daughters relegated to domestic work, denied the right to read or write. The portable units, once isolated at the edge of the compound, had been moved closer to the center of the community.

Ez and Mary spearheaded the effort to make the spaces more livable: new, thicker mattresses replaced the old bunks, and bright, warm bedding added a touch of comfort. They opened up the cramped quarters by installing windows and repainting the walls in soft, inviting colors.

"There's a communal kitchen just over there." He points to the newly expanded building at the center of the yard. "Fully stocked with fresh fruit and vegetables from our garden, but we share our meals together like a big family. Dinner's at six." He turns, pointing toward the sheltered dining space. "We gather over there."

The door to one of the girl's bunks squeals open and Ez appears. "Good morning," she calls with an excited wave.

"This is my wife, Ez."

Jax leans back slightly, not so subtly checking out her figure before landing on her face. "She's your wife?" he asks, a smirk tugging at the corner of his mouth.

"You sound surprised."

Ez smiles at the group. "Eloise, Claire—I'll take you to your room. Okay?"

The girls follow and as Ez turns to leave, Jax watches her go for a second too long. Ulysses nudges him. "Come on, let's get you settled."

As Ulysses leads Jax into the boys' bunk, the door swings open and two of the boys step out, laughing about something. The boys don't linger after a quick greeting, heading off with a jerk of their chins.

Inside is calm and quiet. The soft blue walls catch the sunlight streaming through the windows, and the air smells faintly of fresh linens. Jax enters hesitantly. The neatly made bunks, the small personal shelves above each bed, the single potted plant by the window, are all details Ulysses hopes will make Jax feel at home.

"This one's yours," Ulysses says, motioning to the lower bunk near the far corner. On the bed rests a wicker basket with home-made sugar cookies Ez baked from scratch.

Jax tosses his bag onto the bed, sitting down heavily. He presses his hands against his knees, glancing around the room again. "It's quiet," he mutters, his tone neutral, almost suspicious.

"It's like that here," Ulysses replies

"Beats the fuck out of the other place."

Ulysses raises an eyebrow. "Language."

Jax shrugs, glancing away.

"You good?" Ulysses asks after a moment.

Jax doesn't look up. "Yeah. Just... I dunno. Feels weird."

"Change always does," Ulysses says, crossing the room to sit on the bunk across from him. "Things will work out. You'll see."

Jax shrugs again, but his movements are slower now, less tense. "Yeah but you're leaving. You're like the only normal person I've met since I got caught up in this sh—" He stops himself, his awkward voice dipping as he self-corrects. "Place."

Ulysses leans forward, elbows resting on his knees. "I'll be around. You're not getting rid of me that easily."

"Why not just stay then?"

"Because it's not just about me," Ulysses says gently. "Ez deserves to see more of the world. But that doesn't mean I'm walking away. I'll be here."

Jax doesn't respond immediately, instead looking out the window. "People always say that. It's like they act like they care but then they forget about you."

A heaviness settles in Ulysses's chest. "I know what that's like. But everyone here has worked really hard to make this place better because we care about you and all the kids here. Once this Palms transition is over, we'll pick up our sessions again. But right now, I've got to do what's best for my wife. And I'm going to ask for you to trust me. Have faith that I'm coming back. Okay?"

Jax studies him for a moment. "Okay."

Ulysses stands, clapping him lightly on the shoulder. "Dinner's at six. Don't make me come looking for you."

Returning on the path to his trailer, he finds Domino sunning in the grass. Domino's going to miss this place, that's for sure. The dog lifts his head from where he's sprawled, his black-and-white coat gleaming. Watching Ulysses intently, his tail wags in slow, lazy arcs.

Ulysses crouches down to scratch behind Domino's ears. "Enjoying the sun while you can, huh?" Domino leans into the touch, letting out a contented huff before flopping back down with his tongue lolling out.

Voices cut through the quiet; women arguing in the distance. He can't see where it's coming from, but it grows louder, until he's rushing up the stairs to his trailer, his pulse racing imagining the possibilities of what's going on inside.

"You need to leave," Mary's voice snaps, but not to him. To Sofie.

What is she doing here? Ulysses is stunned to see her.

"Not until I see him," Sofie says, arms crossed.

"What's going on?"

"She's asking about Father," Mary says, clearly at the end of her rope.

Shit.

After all this time, she's back asking to see a dead man. He knows he should be delicate with her, but what the hell is she doing in his trailer? He draws in a deep breath, letting it out slowly. "Lang…" he starts, his jaw tightening before forcing another centering breath. "He…passed away."

"I know he's dead," Sofie snaps, the edge of her tone softened by her southern drawl. "I know what happened. I had to find out from Erma of all people. What'd you do with him?"

Ulysses leans against the doorframe, crossing his arms as he studies her. "What did we do with him?" he repeats slowly. "We buried him. Same as anyone else who—"

"Where?" Sofie cuts him off.

Ulysses straightens, his arms falling to his sides. She knows just as well as he does that the Order handles its own business. "Behind the chapel. Same place as the others."

Sofie closes her eyes for a moment, her fists still clenched, and when she opens them again, there's a glassy sheen that she blinks away quickly.

"You buried him. Just like that," she says, almost to herself. "Like he didn't mean anything."

"Did you expect us to build a shrine?" Mary says, her posture radiating disdain. "Because trust me, nobody here is interested in worshipping him anymore."

"No one even told me. I should have been here for the ceremony," Sofie says.

It turns his blood to lava. "Are you kidding? There was no ceremony. And even if there had been, was I supposed to send you a postcard? How was I supposed to contact you? Where have you even been?"

She slips into the dining booth, making herself too at-home in his place. Resting her elbows on the table, she lets her face fall into her hands, her auburn hair sweeping down like a curtain. "I thought coming back here would make me better."

He wants to tell her it's impossible for anything to make her better because she's a black hole, but he bites his tongue.

"I thought if I came back here and saw how it's changed I could fix the bad memories somehow. That it would fix me. Make me less...I don't know. Scared all the time."

Hearing that she was frightened disarms him. He'd expected her to say she was annoyed by the rules, or tired of being under her father's thumb and realized it wasn't the life she wanted after all. But to know she'd been failing to quell her own trauma makes him wince at just how much he's villainized her.

No. Don't do that, he tells himself, drawing in a breath. Don't let her off that easily. This is what she does, remember? She hurts people, then comes in and makes them feel bad for her. Makes them open up again to give her a warm place to nest.

"A place can't do that, Sofie. Only you can do that. With therapy, with putting in work."

"Why'd you stay?" she asks.

Mary throws up her hands, glaring at him. "You're really entertaining this?"

"I'm not entertaining anything. We're having a conversation."

Mary's eyes flit between them before shaking her head and shoving off the counter with her palms. "Fine," she says, and marches out, shutting the door hard behind her.

He sighs, saunters over to the booth and sits across from her. "I stayed because I gave up my entire life for you, and you abandoned me again without so much as a goodbye."

"I'm sorry."

"I'm sorry doesn't even begin to cover it. You didn't go for a long drive, didn't disappear for a few days," he says, with a tone that suggests the words had been fermenting in his belly. "Months. You were gone for months."

"I thought you'd come home."

"There was no home, that's the point. I left my job, my apartment. I moved to this awful place because you said you needed it. That's how much I loved you. Then you left me...again...knowing I had nothing to return to."

Her eyes brim with tears. "I know you did, and that's why I didn't want to tell you I was wrong after you gave up everything."

"I would have gladly left with you."

She tugs at her sleeves, wiping her damp lashes with the fabric. "I didn't know. I was scared."

"Well, now you do."

They sit quietly together. The dappled light from outside seeping in through the shade of oaks makes wispy shapes on the table.

"I hear you're married," she says with a nonchalance that leads him to believe that's why she's really here.

"Erma told you that too, huh?"

She shrugs, then pulls at the fabric of her sleeve. "I guess I don't have a right to be upset about that."

"You guess?"

"Uly, you belong to me. We belong to each other. Remember?"

"We most certainly do not."

She sits back, her mouth falling open with surprise. "You mean to tell me after all these years together, after everything we've been through, I go through one little episode and you run and marry some brainwashed cult child?"

"She's not a brainwashed cult child. She's a grown woman, and she's a good person. She makes me feel wanted."

"Oh, I bet she does."

"She does."

With an exhausted sigh, she sinks deeper into her seat. "So we're going to play this game again, huh?"

"What game?"

"The game where you run off with some girl to make me jealous so I'll come back."

He laughs. Not because there's any truth to it, but because Sofie's finally recognized her own pattern, a pattern he's eager to break. "I don't care if you're jealous. I'd be happy never to see you again."

She studies his face as if to decipher if he's bluffing, but he doesn't flinch. The corners of her mouth turn up and she wrinkles her nose. "I think you've said that before, haven't you?"

"This is different. Esme's my wife."

"What kind of name is Esme, anyway?" Sofie huffs with a roll of her eyes. "The Order did a little ceremony and Daddy blessed it. That don't make y'all government married."

"Lang doesn't have a death certificate, doesn't make him any less dead."

Her smug look vanishes. "That's not nice."

"Neither is showing up here uninvited. Think it's time you leave."

"Uly," she pleads.

Ulysses pushes away from the table and stands, his hands resting on the edge of the booth as he leans forward.

"No, Sofie. Where do you get the audacity? You don't get to do this. You don't get to roll in here after turning everything upside down again and expect me to be here waiting for you."

The door screeches open and footsteps groan against the trailer stairs. Ez. She doesn't say anything, she just stands there, zeroed in on Sofie with a deadly glower Uly's never seen… though he suspects it might be the last thing Zeke saw before he died.

Chapter Thirty

"WHAT'S SHE DOING HERE?" Ez demands, her pulse hammering.

Mary had come to warn her that Sofie and Uly were alone in their trailer. Apparently, Erma had sent her there. Of course she did. Erma never cared for Ez, but this was a new low.

"She was just leaving," Ulysses says, his tone clipped.

The trailer is cramped, and they're standing much too close for comfort. Sofie's gaze flicks to Ez, and a slow, saccharine smile spreads across her lips.

"You're Esme?" Her voice is as deceptively sweet as poisoned candy.

"What's it to you?"

Sofie lets out a small laugh, brushing invisible lint off her sleeve. "Nothing, I guess. Just trying to figure out what you've got that's so special."

Heat rises in Ez's cheeks, and words fire out, preloaded and primed as she closes in on her. "I'm not a selfish coward who runs away when things get hard."

Sofie's smile falters, eyes narrowing as she steps forward, shoulders square. "You don't know anything about me."

"I know you've got five seconds to get out of our trailer before I knock your teeth out." Ez's hands curl into fists.

"Whoa, hold on." Ulysses positions himself between them and wraps an arm around Ez's waist. He faces Sofie. "You're done here. Go."

Sofie hesitates, gaze flicking between them, and Ez braces for a fight—part of her even hoping for it. But then Sofie's bravado deflates, and she snatches her bag from the table.

"Fine," she mutters, slinging the bag over her shoulder.

As she moves, Ez catches a whiff of her, and her stomach knots. That smell. The one she'd spent days trying to scrub from the curtains, from the fabric of their furniture. The one that clung to their space like a ghost. It's her.

She never left.

Sofie saunters off toward the door, and once she's no longer in swinging distance, she turns back to address Ez. "You think you're the first girl he's used to try to get over me? You're not. He always comes back."

Ez's breath catches, but she doesn't flinch. Ulysses's grasp tightens around her before she can even think about lunging forward. Sofie straightens up and walks out, the screen door slamming behind her.

Once she's gone, the trailer is too quiet. Ulysses loosens his grip on her.

"Ez?"

She stays fixed on the closed door, her chest tight, blood simmering. How does she know she isn't just a life jacket, keeping him afloat until he's rescued? The thought gnaws at her confidence. Maybe this is what he meant that day in the chapel when he asked for her hand.

"You couldn't guarantee it."

"That's not what I meant," Ulysses says quickly, his voice thick with urgency.

She turns to face him. "Did you mean you couldn't guarantee you wouldn't go back to her?"

"No." Panic flashes in his eyes. "No, of course not."

"Then what?" Ez presses. "Couldn't guarantee we'd last?"

"I take it back."

Ez blinks, thrown. "What?"

"I take it back," he repeats, his eyes glassy. "I can guarantee. I love you, Ez. You are it for me. You're it."

His voice cracks on the last word, and Ez sees the raw, unguarded vulnerability in his eyes. His hands tremble as he reaches for hers. "You're my wife. You're my future."

Ez stares at him, seeing the depth of his fear, his desperation to make her understand, and it shakes her.

"Please," Ulysses begs. "Don't let her ruin this. Don't let her get in your head and take away the best thing that's ever happened to me."

His voice breaks, and Ez's resolve shatters. Before she can think, she's wrapping her arms around him, pulling him close. Ulysses holds her tightly, his arms wrapped around her like he's afraid she'll slip away.

Ez tilts her face up to his, her lips claiming his in a kiss. It deepens slowly, dismantling her fears, piece by piece. It shows her that need is more than just survival. People need food and water, shelter. But she's never known what it could mean to need a person. Not this way. But now, she needs him like she needs her next breath.

Reaching for his belt, she wants nothing but him—his warmth, his weight, the feel of his skin brushing hers, covering her, fitting together with her.

With a ragged breath, he fumbles with the button at her nape, and Ez gasps as the fabric slips down, exposing her breasts to the cool air. The sensation lasts for the span of a flash of light before they're in his hands, his mouth. A sweet ache pulses through her, building in intensity until it bursts, flooding her senses, and she finds herself pushing him into bed.

He attacks the job of loosening his belt and dropping his pants in a frenzy, his hands a blur of movement until he's unencumbered. Gathering her dress around her waist, she slips out of the panties he bought her and kicks them onto the floor.

Before another thought forms, she sinks onto him, drawing a

ragged sigh from his lips as his head falls back. His arms tighten around her, pulling her flush against him, their lips brushing—not a kiss, just the barest whisper of touch—as she rises and falls onto him. Time slips away unnoticed until he shudders, fingertips pressing into her hips. Her body arches into him, pleasure cresting, breaking, as they go over the edge together.

Chapter Thirty-One

One Month Later

THE PAINTING LOOKS LIKE A DREAM, beautiful but unsettling. Ez and Ulysses stand hand in hand staring at *The Hallucinogenic Toreador*. Ghostly *Venus de Milos* repeat and blend together, forming the face of a bullfighter.

Ulysses leans in close, his breath warm against her ear. "Venus represents the feminine," he says, softly, "and the bullfighter the masculine."

Ez tilts her head, studying the painting. "It's weird. But nice."

"That's surrealism for you, hon."

It's their first weekend of their new lives together outside the Order. Earlier that morning, Ulysses had announced there was something very important they had to do, but he wouldn't tell her what.

They'd pulled up to a building that reflects the sky in warped blue glass, like molten mercury sliding down concrete. She read the sign aloud. "The Deli museum?"

"The Dali museum, honey. Salvador Dali. He's an artist."

"Oh my God, really?" she said, laughing at the thought of a sandwich museum. His explanation made more sense.

Ulysses snorted, shaking his head. "You're killing me, Smalls. Come on." He tugged her hand, leading her toward the entrance. Inside, they'd climbed a helical staircase that seemed to twist forever, leading them higher into the museum's galleries.

Now, in a dimly lit room, sunlight streams through skylights catching dust flecks in the air and illuminating the vibrant colors of the paintings. Ulysses pulls her toward a massive canvas that towers over them, at least ten feet tall. *The Santiago el Grande.*

A white horse rears in the center of the painting, its rider gripping the reins as if guiding it into another world. The sky behind them blurs into a storm of blues, swirling together.

"It looks like he's riding into heaven," Ez says, her voice low, awed. She takes a step closer, her eyes fixed on the horse. "It's incredible. It feels like it's full of energy, like it's about to—"

Before she can finish, Ulysses's hand touches the back of her neck, and his lips press against hers. The kiss is tender but electric, and she melts into it, the heat of his body pulling her in. For a moment, the museum falls away. There's no art, no visitors, just the taste of him, the feel of his hand securing her, the vibration of his quiet hum against her lips.

When they finally part, Ez blinks up at him, dazed. "What was that for?"

"Couldn't help it," Ulysses says, brushing a thumb against her cheek. "You're just so cute."

She rolls her eyes, shoving him playfully, though his sturdy body seems immovable. "I am not."

His grin widens. "You really are."

Since they left the Order, Ulysses has been endlessly entertained by her sense of wonder. At first, Ez found it sweet. But now it's starting to feel like he sees her as a kitten chasing a laser pointer.

"You like to tease me."

"I do not," he says, though the grin tugging at his mouth gives him away.

"Oh, please," she says. "It's the same as when we got the apartment."

"That was different."

"It was not different," she says. "Every time I got excited, you looked at me like I was a puppy in a teacup."

They'd rented an apartment close to Ulysses's job at the rehab center. When Ez first saw the sparkling pool and private balcony, she couldn't help herself. She broke into a happy little wiggle, imagining herself lying out in the sun in an actual bikini when the weather warmed up, instead of that turn-of-the-century bathing costume the Order made her wear on the rare occasion she was allowed to swim in the spring.

Ulysses had leaned against the doorframe of the sliding glass door, arms crossed, watching her with a lopsided grin. "You don't even know how adorable you are," he'd said. Then he leaned down, brushing his lips against her forehead before stepping back. "Okay, now do the wiggle again."

She'd nudged him, laughing, and he'd pulled her into a kiss. They'd only had the keys for an hour, no furniture to speak of in the space, but they couldn't stop themselves. Ulysses laid her down on the hardwood floor, the sunlight pouring through the windows and streaking warmth across her skin. Their clothes were scattered, forming a careless pile beneath her. The floor was hard and uncomfortable, but she didn't care. Not when he nipped her jaw with his teeth, completely unraveling her. All she could focus on was him.

Thinking about it now in the museum makes a flush rise to her face.

"I'm not teasing you," he says, pulling her gently into his arms. His hands find her waist, and she can feel the warmth of his palms through her shirt. "I love it. I love *you*."

By the time they leave the museum, the sunlight has softened into gold. They walk hand in hand toward the parking lot, her other hand trailing along the cool concrete wall beside her. "Now what?" she asks.

"You'll see."

As she rests her head against the passenger window, bay waters glitter. Mansions and their fancy docked boats edge the waterside. They park in a hotel lot where pedestrians, broiled bright pink from sunburns, loiter around elevators with beach chairs and towels, their faces shiny with sunscreen. The breeze smells of chlorine and brine, brushing her skin, cool and soft.

They're seated outside on a patio overlooking the water. The sun is a ball of fire touching the distant horizon. It paints the sky pink while a gentle tide rolls in against the shore. The sight of it, the grandness of it all, draws the air from her lungs and a sting rises to her eyes.

It was everything he'd promised.

The server arrives to take their orders. As interesting as Ulysses's stories are and as delicious as the food is, she can't steer her attention away from the sunset. Ez's thoughts drift, slipping in and out like the tide. She thinks about the Order, about her mother, about Kia. Sitting here with the gulf stretching out before her and Ulysses across from her feels almost surreal. Like something she might have dreamed about once in another life. The kind of dream where the edges blur, where you don't trust that it will last because it's too perfect. She wonders if Ulysses feels the same.

She glances at him, watching as he leans back in his chair, his gaze on the water too. There's something detached about him, as if he's here but not quite. Ez thinks of the painting, of the *Venus de Milos* and the bullfighter, repeating and blending into each other. Unsettling and mesmerizing all at once. A perfect, surreal balance of opposites.

That's how this feels. A dream. Perfection teetering on a pin. An uneasy feeling settles in her belly at the thought of waking up.

Chapter Thirty-Two

THREE DAYS back at Palms Waterside, and it's like Ulysses never left. The familiar eucalyptus-and-lemon scent of the lobby welcomes him each morning. Laura, the admissions coordinator, pitches gym and spa services to prospective clients, her voice echoing down the hall. Meanwhile, the new receptionist nervously fumbles with an iPad as she checks in patients.

With the Path to Purpose program now under Palms Waterside, his schedule is set—two days a week just outside Whispering Hope with the Order's teens, three days a week in Tampa. Other than that, nothing has changed.

Dr. Okafor's door is open, and the man himself is perched on the edge of his desk, pulling absently at his woolly beard as he reads something in his hand. He looks up, his thick glasses catching the light.

"Uly!" The deep, familiar baritone fills the space, and Ulysses shoulders loosen. "Back for more?" the doctor asks.

"Oh, you're stuck with me now," Ulysses jokes, not breaking his stride on the way to his office.

By midmorning, Ulysses is in his rhythm—leading group therapy, guiding art workshops, and navigating one-on-one sessions with patients. But he's eager to return home to Ez.

Adjusting to life outside the Order hasn't been easy for either of them, but Ez's struggles are harder to ignore. The world is foreign to her in ways that surprise Ulysses daily.

There were the endearing moments: the way she practically shoved him out of the way to be the one to lay the plastic divider at the grocery store, carefully arranging each item on the belt. Or how she spent an hour and a half in the shower their first night, luxuriating under the hot water until the bathroom turned into a cloud of steam, and he had to knock on the door just to make sure she hadn't passed out.

But then there were the missteps: locking herself out of the apartment because the keypad confused her. Forgetting to leash Domino on walks, letting him dart across the complex until Ulysses lured him back with deli ham. Overdrawing his bank account while stocking up for the apartment, unaware of how fast prices add up. He expected hiccups, just not this many.

After work, he rests with Ez on the couch, enjoying the quiet until she perks up suddenly, hopping up bright with excitement, "Want to see what I did today?"

Before he can answer, she dashes to the bedroom and returns with her wallet, a small card pinched between her thumb and forefinger.

"I'm official," she announces, holding out a shiny new Florida ID.

Ulysses takes it, relaxing as he looks at her picture—her beautiful smile, her pride. "That's awesome, hon. Now we can go on trips together."

"I know! I can't wait to fly on an airplane," she says, sitting beside him again. "But they said I need to bring our marriage certificate to change my last name. Do you know where it is?"

The warmth of the moment fades, a sinking feeling settling into his stomach. He sets the ID carefully on the coffee table, his shoulders stiffening. "We don't have one."

She frowns, her excitement dimming. "What do you mean?"

Ulysses rubs his palm over his face. He'd known this conversation was inevitable, but he'd hoped for a little more time. "The Order. Their ceremonies were symbolic, not legal."

Her brows knit together, the full weight of his words still hovering out of reach. "So, what does that mean? Are we not married?"

"Not in the legal sense."

Ez blinks, focus darting between him and the ID on the table. "Well what other sense is there?"

"The ceremony. That meant something to us, and that's what matters, even if, legally…" His voice trails off, knowing the explanation won't land the way he hopes.

She stares at him, mouth agape, her dark eyes wide and gleaming with hurt. "Why didn't you tell me?"

"I didn't think it would matter," he says, the words ringing hollow even to him. "I wanted you to have a choice. This is all new for you, Ez, and I didn't want to lock you into something that might not be right for you in the long run."

Her lips part, then close again, as if she's working through his words one by one. "You say you want me to have a choice, but then I choose, and you tell me I don't know what I want?"

Sometimes with the silly things she does and the mind boggling questions she asks, he makes the mistake of underestimating her. But her insightful question hits him like a gut punch. There's nothing he can say. She's right. Why hadn't he told her? Is it truly some kind of a protective instinct or is there something more?

Ez shakes her head. "I trusted you. And now you're telling me it's a lie."

"It's not a lie," he says. "I love you. That's real."

"But that's not what you promised me. You said I was your wife."

For a moment, all he can do is look at her, the woman who's thrown herself headlong into a world she barely understands, all because she believed in him.

Ulysses draws nearer, his hand outstretched. "Ez, if you want to make it legal, then let's make it legal."

"How?"

"We'll go to the courthouse tomorrow," he says, the split-second decision surprising even him. "Sign the official papers. I don't care about the law, but I care about you, and if this matters to you, then it matters to me."

She studies him, her eyes searching his face for any sign of hesitation, any fracture in his commitment. Finally, she exhales. A shaky breath, but the worry in her eyes fades. "Okay," she says. "Tomorrow."

The weight of his promise bores down on him as he lies awake in the dark, tracing the faint outline of the still ceiling fan. What will happen when she finally realizes the man he was in the Order isn't the man he is out here? Out here, he has no fancy title, no status to prop him up. He's just another broke, working-class nobody, recognized now and then as *that guy with the missing sister*.

The thoughts are relentless, and a familiar pang settles deep in his gut. He turns his head, watching Ez's peaceful silhouette, the curve of her body outlined by the dim glow of the moonlight filtered through the curtain. She's patient and kind, beautiful and strong. Perfect in every way that matters to him, and she deserves better than this. Better than him.

He sits up slowly, careful not to wake her, and swings his legs over the side of the bed. He rubs his face with both hands, elbows resting on his knees.

The phone on the nightstand catches his eye, the screen lighting up briefly before dimming again. He reaches for it without thinking, the motion automatic. The messages are still there, blinking like a warning light.

> Hey. Just checking in.
>
> You okay?
>
> I'm here if you need me.
>
> I miss you.

Sofie. Always Sofie.

He glances at Ez again, sleeping soundly. She thinks he's steady, dependable, safe. She's never seen him at his worst.

Ulysses stands, unable to stay still any longer. He pulls up his jeans and stealthily wrestles his hoodie over his head before tiptoeing out of their bedroom. Domino stirs from his spot on the couch, watching with sleepy curiosity as Ulysses grabs his keys and slips out the door.

The air outside is cold, biting against his skin, but he doesn't feel it. His thoughts are too loud, drowning out everything else as he starts walking, focusing on the rhythm of his steps, the crunch of the gritty sidewalk underfoot, the distant whir of traffic. He could disappear into the night, lose himself for a while. Just one drink, just one phone call to forget the weight of trying to be this person he doesn't know how to be out here.

He stops at the edge of a quiet park, his breath visible in the chilly air, the phone burning in his pocket. He pulls it out, staring at the screen, Sofie's messages stacked like cinderblocks.

He could call her. Let her pull him back to the place where nothing mattered, where he didn't have to try so hard. He can feel the pull of it, the seductive simplicity of giving up.

His thumb hovers over the screen. She'd understand. She'd tell him it's okay, he's a fuckup and she knows it, she expected it. The thought sits heavy on his shoulders.

Fuck.

Ez flashes in his mind—her dazzling smile when she showed him her ID, her eagerness as she planned their future, her unshakable confidence in him. The thought hits him like a wave, almost knocking the air out of him.

He doesn't miss Sofie. Maybe he did, once. But not since Ez. Sofie isn't a person to him anymore, she's a symbol, something comfortable but corrosive, like a childhood bedroom coated in lead paint. Warm and familiar, but it poisoned him, seeped into his blood and left behind something he couldn't entirely purge.

His grip on the phone tightens, and for a moment, he considers chucking it into the retention pond. Instead, he swipes the screen, deleting Sofie's messages with sharp, decisive movements. Blocks her phone number. Deletes her contact.

Staring at the screen, he waits to feel something.

Nothing.

Hmm. He doesn't feel better, not really. The weight is still there, the doubts threatening to crush him. Not the dopamine hit he'd hoped for.

Move. Just get your heart rate up.

One step, then another, Ulysses hikes through the empty streets.

There's a bar nearby, a place with neon signs he'd pretended not to notice when they searched for their new place together. It's a short walk, a thought that registered and then got promptly filed away into the back of his mind. Addiction has a way of keeping tabs on details he'd rather forget.

Just one drink.

You did the right thing. You deleted Sofie's number. That's practically proof that you're cured. You earned a drink.

His feet carry him closer to the bar. It's late enough that the place isn't rowdy, but the faint sound of music filters through the cracked door. A laugh, a clink of glasses. The kind of noise that used to make his pulse quicken, his mouth water.

The familiar promise of ignorant bliss pulls at him like a riptide. He hesitates outside, hands shoved deep into his hoodie pocket, feet poised on the edge of surrender. One drink to repel down from the mountain he'd climbed, each promise taking him higher, each guarantee hoisting him to an impossible height.

And at the peak? Inevitable failure. A fall neither of them would survive.

He closes his eyes. Ez's face flashes again, her smile, her trust. The way she looks at him like he's steady, like he's whole. His hand moves toward the door, almost without thinking, but he catches himself, staring at his reflection in the glass. His face looks older, wearier, the hollows of his eyes deeper than he remembers. A face that should know better than to repeat the same mistakes of a much younger version of himself.

He tries to imagine what Ez would say if she saw him like this—standing outside a bar, contemplating throwing everything away because he's afraid he's not good enough for her.

He hears her sweet voice in his head, the one that quavered slightly when asking him if he ordered a margarita. If the pizza had alcohol in it. He chuckles to himself, at her innocence, at her attentiveness to him, and a sting rises to his eyes.

He exhales sharply, turning away from the door, as shaken as if he'd climbed down to safety from the railing of a bridge. His body is heavy, every step back to the apartment an act of defiance against the call of the void.

When he reaches his apartment door, he pauses, his hand hovering over the knob. Inside, Ez will still be there, warm in their bed, trusting him, believing in him. For tonight, at least, he'll keep pretending he deserves it.

Chapter Thirty-Three

ON THIS WEDDING DAY, Ez wears a simple white cotton dress. Gathering her long hair into a bun, the dull hum of an electric razor carries from the bathroom down the hall as Ulysses trims his beard. The door is open and he's shirtless, hunched over the sink, the muscles in his back flexing with his small movements. Leaning close, he tilts his head to one side, the sharp line of his jaw catching in the lightly fogged mirror. The air is heavy with steam mixed with the scent of his cologne, warm and masculine.

Ez watches from the bedroom doorway, her breath hitching slightly as her admiration lingers. He's always been handsome to her, but there's something about these intimate moments that makes her heart want to burst.

She wants this more than anything, to be his in every sense. Not just as a symbol, but completely. But he's quiet, and every time she looks at him, there's a tension just under the surface, an almost imperceptible vibration in his body.

Once she finishes her makeup, something she learned to do once she finally got her hands on a computer and discovered YouTube tutorials, she finds Ulysses in the living room, pacing. Noticing her, he stops, his eyebrows perking up against his otherwise taut expression. "Ready?"

"Ready."

He hesitates a moment, a slight sigh escaping him as he snatches his car keys from the entryway table. "Alright, then. Come on. Let's go."

Against her instincts, she puts one foot in front of the other, following him outside. Her body numbs. This is supposed to be a special day. A happy occasion. But he has all the enthusiasm of a man going to take his car in for an oil change.

She gets into his Jeep, clicking her seatbelt into place. He turns on the car, music plays and he hits the road. They make it to the interstate toward downtown before she breaks.

"Uly, I don't want to do this if your heart's not in it."

His jaw tightens and he blinks hard. "This snowbird in front of us is trying to get us killed," he says. His foot is heavy on the gas as he swerves around a too-slow Toyota with an Ontario license plate.

She forces past his attempt to change the subject. "You said you wanted to do this just as much as I do."

"I do."

"Then why are you being like this?" she says, hoping if she's persistent she'll finally coax something out of him.

"Like what?" he says, a stitch forming in his brow. "I didn't even say anything."

"Exactly. You don't say anything. You just get all moody and pissy and you don't say anything."

"I'm not moody or pissy, I'm just…a little anxious, that's all."

"Okay," she says, finally getting somewhere. "What's got you anxious?"

"It's not important."

She could scream. "It is to me. Just spit it out already."

His eyes flutter and he draws in a deep breath, the forced serenity that usually follows absent. This time his eyes glass over. "Ez, I meant it when I said I love you. I do. And I want this, but…" His throat bobs as he swallows hard, seemingly losing the fight to control his emotions.

"But what?"

His hands flex on the wheel and he sinks back into his seat. The words hang between them, the low hum of the music the only sound in the car.

"I don't want to let you down," he finally says, his voice breaking, shoulders sagging, as if the pressure of the words had been too much to hold back. He rubs his forehead, elbow resting on his door panel. "You see something in me that I don't. You always have. And I'm terrified that one day you're going to realize I'm nobody special. Out here I'm just a guy."

Ez's heart aches at the rawness in his voice, at the way he seems to shrink before her, so unlike the steady presence she's come to rely on.

She reaches over, rubbing his thigh. "You're special to me."

"I almost gave up," he says, as if to prove it to her. "Last night, I almost stopped at a bar."

The words land, stunning her. Not that he'd struggle, but that he'd conceal it. That he could be fighting a battle alone right in front of her and she didn't know it.

Ulysses looks away, shame darkening his face. "I didn't. But I thought about it. I walked right up to the door, Ez. I told myself I'd earned it, that one drink wouldn't undo everything. That maybe I'm not built for all this—for us, for being the man you think I am."

"But you didn't. You didn't give up."

"Not this time. But what about next time? What if one day I can't stop? You deserve someone who doesn't have to fight this hard just to stay steady. I'm afraid I'll fuck this up just like everything else."

"You won't," she says. "Because you're not doing this alone. That's what marriage is. I'm not afraid of you failing. I'm afraid of you shutting me out. I'm not perfect either. I've been messing up nonstop, and I know you're frustrated with me—"

He gives her a look like she's being ridiculous, throwing on his turn signal to change lanes, cutting her off. "I'm not. Not with you."

"I see that look," she says, pulling a face, an impression of the one he does.

Ulysses exhales sharply. "I'm not frustrated with you, I'm frustrated *for* you. That you have to struggle because of what the Order took from you. But I don't fault you for it."

She drops her hands in her lap. "See? And I worried myself sick over it."

"You didn't tell me you were worried about that. If you had, I would have told you."

"That's why we have to talk about stuff, Uly. We can't keep holding it all in and hoping the other person guesses right." She tilts her head, undeterred. "I love you, flaws and all. I don't expect you to be perfect, and I don't care if you have some title, but I need to know when you're struggling because I want to be here to fight with you. You said we were married in your heart. You said whatever happens from now on, happens together."

They pull toward an exit, the towering buildings of downtown surrounding them. Stopped at a light, he turns to her. "I meant that," he says softly. "I did."

"Then trust me. Give me your burdens. Let me carry them with you."

"They're heavy."

"I'm stronger than I look."

The light changes and he turns, navigating around traffic and pedestrians in their fancy career clothes. "You say that now," he says. "I pray you never have to see me at my lowest, never have to see the side of me that falls apart."

"I see the good in you, and I know how hard you're trying. You might fall apart sometimes, that's part of being human. But I'm not quitting on you. I'm not running away."

His hand tightens over hers where it rests on his thigh. They turn into a parking structure and the daylight goes dim. A sign reads **Courthouse Parking**. Once they finally pull into a spot, he shifts the gear forward and his eyes meet hers, glistening.

"Uly, I mean it," she says. "I know it's hard to trust someone because you've been hurt before. But I'm not Sofie, I'm not your mom. And you're not my dad. I know in my heart you are a man of your word. The way you looked after me, protected me. The way you protected those kids even though you didn't have to. You're a good man, Uly, and I trust you. What do I have to do to prove you can trust me too?"

"I do trust you."

"Then let me in."

For a long moment, he simply looks at her, as if searching for some hint of doubt or hesitation.

She goes back to the words he said to her on their first wedding night. "Uly, I'll never abandon you. As long as I'm breathing, I'll honor and respect you."

Slowly, his shoulders relax as if surrendering to her vows. His chest rises and falls unevenly as he tries to suppress the feelings bubbling to the surface but eventually he lets his armor fall. He rubs the corner of his eye with his knuckles, swiping moisture across his cheek.

Turning sideways on his seat, knee bent against the console, his arms wrap around her, securing her against him. His body quakes with staggered breath as he holds her tight, clutching her like a buoy. Her head rests just beneath his chin, his hands rubbing circles against her back. "I believe you."

They sit in silence, wrapped in each other's embrace, the noise of the city beyond them forgotten. She's not sure how much time passes before he asks, the steadiness returned to his voice, "Are you ready to go inside?"

"You sure? We don't have to. We can just be symbol-married if you're not ready."

"I'm sure."

Epilogue

"OH SHOOT, THAT WAS IT." Ez squints at the GPS screen, her nose scrunching just as they speed past the exit. The GPS chimes in, its calm, almost smug tone: *In five hundred feet, make a U-turn.*

Ulysses huffs, merging into the left lane. But the intersection ahead tells a different story—a bold red circle with a diagonal slash cutting through the plan. He shakes his head. "Where am I supposed to make a U-turn?"

The journey had been smooth up until now. Tampa to Mobile, then New Orleans, Houston, Dallas. Mile after mile of easy highway. But just outside Albuquerque, as they neared the last leg of their long trek to Leggett, California, things were starting to fray.

Leggett is more of a starting point than a destination. It's where Highway 1 starts. The Pacific Highway. Breathtaking cliffs. Cerulean waters. It's the trip of a lifetime, and Ulysses wants to give it to Ez, to see her face light up when the coastline unfurls, glittering on the horizon like diamonds.

Dr. Okafor's generosity had made it possible. His boss had handed over the keys to his Mercedes Sprinter RV as a wedding gift. To borrow. A little slice of luxury for their honeymoon road trip.

Just the two of them, the open road, and the promise of adventure Ez had always dreamed of.

He glances at her now, perched in the passenger seat. She's so pretty. Her dark, glossy hair loose around her face as she fiddles with her phone. The corner of his mouth twitches into a smile.

Their first detour, Biloxi to New Orleans, had been his idea. He'd insisted they stretch their legs in the French Quarter, grab coffee and beignets at Café du Monde, and snap a photo in front of St. Louis Cathedral. He remembers the way Ez had stood in front of the towering place of worship, her face tilted skyward, her eyes sparkling as the sound of jazz floated through the air from a brass band nearby.

"Wow," she'd whispered, awestruck. "It's so beautiful."

Ulysses hadn't looked at the cathedral. He'd watched her instead, the tug of adoration pulling at his heartstrings. *She's so beautiful*, he'd thought. *Life with her is beautiful.*

Something strange happened in the courthouse that day. After stumbling and nearly falling over his self-doubt, holding her hand and exchanging vows again, he let himself appreciate where they were and how far they'd come together even in a short time.

She'd asked him to trust her, and he did. When he stopped focusing on the inevitability of failure, he realized he was a man standing at a skyscraper window, terrified of falling no matter how assured he was that the glass he stood in front of was fortified and tested. Taking a deep breath, he'd decided to tell himself it was strong enough and let himself believe it. To have faith.

Even after cult politics, a fire, and the struggle of rebuilding something better, it was outside St. Louis Cathedral that he felt the satisfaction of delivering one sliver of the life Ez deserved. She always looked at him like he was her hero. For once, he'd let himself believe it too.

It wasn't just the cathedral that had stayed with him. It was the way she'd turned to him later, bouncing on her toes with excitement as she rattled off plans for what she wanted to do once they returned home: finishing her GED, maybe taking art classes, looking for a part-time job.

She'd practically radiated determination, her energy contagious. Ulysses, who had spent years studying psychology and addiction, saw something in her that stopped him cold. Despite the scars left by the Order, she moved forward with a resolve that he hadn't even known was possible. She wasn't shackled by the past.

It struck him how effortlessly she refused to let the Order define her. Her strength wasn't in forgetting, it was in choosing not to carry it. He realized, with a pang of humility, that for all his professional understanding of trauma, he had never questioned how he'd carried the darkness of his past with him like a lead backpack, dragging its burden through every decision he'd made, every corner of his life.

And then there was Ez, standing before him, a living, breathing example of what it looked like to set it all down. To turn and walk away from it.

All these years, Ulysses had carried the weight of the Order, of Calliope's case, of guilt and regret so ingrained he didn't even recognize how deeply it ran. But Ez had shown him it was possible to let go. Not of the past itself, but of the power it had over him.

He couldn't undo the past. He couldn't erase what had been done to Calliope, or to him, or to Ez. But something shifted in him as he watched her. She'd sloughed off the lies they'd been told, the lies he'd told himself. And for the first time, Ulysses felt something he hadn't dared to hope for in years.

Peace.

At the light, turn left.

"Turn left," Ez echoes as she stretches in her seat, propping her feet on the dash. One sandal dangles lazily from her toes.

"I heard it," Ulysses replies. His gaze catches on her legs, the sunlight brushing her bronze skin, and he lingers there a moment longer before redirecting his focus back to the highway.

Ez shifts, her foot moving back and forth idly, the sandal clinging precariously. The hem of her dress flutters against her thigh, teasingly close to sliding higher.

"You know," he says, his grip tightening on the wheel, "putting your feet on the dash is dangerous."

"Dangerous how?" she asks, not bothering to look up from her phone.

"If the airbag goes off, your knees are going straight into your pretty face," he replies matter-of-factly. But his eyes betray him, sliding back to her thigh, where the fabric brushes against her skin. A flood of heat rises up his body.

"Then you better drive carefully," she teases, wiggling her toes at him.

"It's distracting," he mutters as he shifts in his seat, his voice a touch tighter.

Ez tilts her head, smirking. She trails a finger lazily along the hem of her sundress. "Distracting?" she repeats, feigning innocence. Then, with a deliberate motion, she slides the fabric up her thigh an inch, her supple flesh catching the golden light.

"Ez," Ulysses warns, his voice low.

"What?" she asks with wide-eyed mock innocence, though the sly curve of her lips gives her away.

He hauls his eyes back to the traffic ahead of them, gripping the wheel. The RV hums steadily beneath him, but his focus is unraveling fast. Out of the corner of his eye, he sees her stretch again, her toes curling as her dress shifts higher.

He exhales sharply through his nose, his jaw tightening as he fights the smirk threatening to surface. "Do you want me to take you to Albuquerque," he asks, "or do you want me to pull over, put those pretty legs on my shoulders, and take you to Pound Town?"

Ez bursts into laughter, her head falling back as the sound fills the RV. Bright and unrestrained, it hits him square in the chest, warming something inside him even as it drives him crazy.

"You're terrible," she says, her eyes wide with mock scandal. She pulls her feet off the dash and smooths down her dress.

"You're still laughing," Ulysses says, a smirk tugging at his lips.

"Because it's funny," she admits, then quickly shakes it off, her good humor morphing to mock authority. "No distractions," she announces, pointing ahead. "You promised me the Pacific Ocean."

"And I'll deliver. I found an RV park with an ocean view."

"Close enough to hear the waves?" she asks.

"Of course. Only the best for my bride."

Ez settles deeper into her seat, admiring the horizon, her cheeks still a little pink from laughing. Ulysses risks another glance at her, his attention lingering. Her hair spills over her shoulder in glossy ribbons, and her smile is soft, peaceful.

God help him, she's a distraction—a living, breathing distraction in the best possible way. It creeps up at odd moments: when she's sitting like this, her feet tucked under her, watching the world pass by. When she laughs without restraint, her joy so full and free it seems like it could fill the entire world. When she looks at him with love so convicted it makes him feel like a man worth building a life with, even on days when he doubts himself.

When Ulysses left the Order all those years ago, he abandoned their ideology. But he never lost his faith in something greater than himself. And yet for years, he struggled to believe in himself. To see himself with the same grace he'd ask his clients to see themselves.

Ez changed that. She helped him see beyond the darkness and doubt. When he looks at her now, he doesn't see fear. He sees something bright. Something pure. She loves the man he is—scars, mistakes, and all. The path wasn't hers to travel for him, but she made the journey lighter, just as he did for her.

Sunlight glints off the highway, and the RV hums steadily beneath him. The road ahead is long, but for the first time, he's ready.

Thank You

Thank you for picking up this book. If you enjoyed it, please consider leaving a review. Your feedback is invaluable and helps other readers discover my work.

Acknowledgments

Thank you to every reader of Mysteries of the Southern Gothic who said "ULYSSES DESERVED BETTER." Without your love for Ulysses, this book would not exist.

To my husband, Jacob—thank you for doing everything I couldn't while I was lost in writing this book. I couldn't have done it without you.

To my sister, Monica—thank you for reading all my books and always letting me know the exact chapter where they *finally* start to get good.

Thanks to my editor, Elizabeth A. White, for her keen eye and invaluable guidance.

A special thanks to my alpha and beta readers for your time, thoughtful feedback, keeping me on the rails, and providing sometimes unhinged commentary. They're romance authors everyone should read:

Allie Oleander, for encouraging more spice and pulling no punches.

Layna James, for inspiring playful banter and helping me decide what colors go best together.

Madison Diaz, for never failing to recognize a beat, keeping me on pace, and helping me through from start to finish.

Poppy Fitzgerald, for your love for Uly and helping me decide he deserved a romance.

Additional thanks for encouragement and support:

Benjamin Twigg
Des DeVivo
Varsha Chitins
& the incredible CWC Authors

And to my readers, supporters, and street team—I appreciate you more than you'll ever know.

Also by Jessica Carrasquillo

The Manchineel, January 2024

Elyse shares nature's beauty and danger with her followers, but behind her smile hides a chilling capacity to kill. When she's introduced to Ben, a married older man and charming Hollywood attorney, an undeniable attraction blooms. As their connection deepens, so do the roots of a deadly plan.

Available on Kindle, Paperback, and Audiobook.

Mysteries of the Southern Gothic, September 2024

Ulysses Katsaros, a troubled counselor, struggles with the disappearance of his sister, Calliope. Partnering with Rosario Martinez, co-host of the Mysteries of the Southern Gothic podcast, they delve into the mystery. As their bond grows, they face law enforcement, old flames, and personal demons. Will their quest for truth bring them together or tear them apart?

Available on Kindle, and Paperback

About the Author

Jessica Carrasquillo is an attorney living in South Florida with her husband and two pugs. Drawing upon her observations of human nature, she crafts stories that explore the intricacies of love, justice, and morality.

Sign-up for updates:
www.jessicacarrasquillo.com

Trigger Warnings

Please be advised this work contains scenes that may depict, mention, or discuss: alcoholism, assault, blood, bullying, cheating, child abuse, cults, death, depression, emotional abuse, fire, gun violence, murder, physical abuse, pregnancy, sexism, sexual assault, sexual harassment, stalking, suicide (implied), violence.

It is important to approach this work with caution if you find these topics particularly distressing. Remember to practice self-care and seek support if needed.

While every effort is made to capture all potential triggers, the above list may be updated after publication. For the most up to date trigger warnings, please visit: www.jessicacarrasquillo.com/triggers

www.ingramcontent.com/pod-product-compliance
Lightning Source LLC
Chambersburg PA
CBHW060307310726
48976CB00007B/2243